DOMENICO

K.I. LYNN

Domenico
Copyright © K.I. Lynn

This book is a work of fiction. Names, characters, places, and incidents either are products of the author's imagination or are used fictitiously. Any resemblance to actual events or locales or persons, living or dead, is entirely coincidental.

Editors:
Marti Lynch
Danielle Leigh
Copy editing by James Gallagher, Evident Ink

Publication Date: May 5, 2020
Genre: FICTION/Romance/Contemporary
ISBN: 978-1-948284-28-8
Copyright © 2020 K.I. Lynn
All rights reserved

DOMENICO

PROLOGUE

Somewhere in Chicago…

The chains chafed my wrists, making me wish I were still in my cage. Though it lacked privacy, the cage at least had a bed, and in there I wasn't restrained with my arms above my head. But I was in Domenico's domain. The small bedroom-like area was created from a previous office. There was a lamp and a mattress with a blanket, but those were the only creature comforts. The rest of the room retained both the look and smell of the rest of the decaying structure.

With no way to tell time, I wasn't sure how long I'd been there. All I knew was that I was tired. Being held against my will caused spikes in my adrenaline, and the subsequent crashes left me drained. The small panic attacks had lessened over the past few weeks, but there was an undercurrent of strife, and I feared what would happen if things got out of control.

I stared at the bed, wishing I were on it. All that did was cause the memories of him inside me to come slamming down.

The absolute owning of my body by him and him alone. The way he made me come undone.

Feelings that I shouldn't have with his touch, but I did.

Feelings I drowned in as he consumed me.

I am Domenico's…for now.

And that was the thought that always sent questions spiraling out of control and a spike of fear to run through me.

I was a caged bird. A pet awaiting a sentence bound to be more grim than any fairy-tale horror.

ONE

Another day, another dollar, and another strip in front of a horde of men. Hopefully more than a few, but working in the shitty, low-income part of town wasn't the most enticing for big spenders. Being a stripper, every dollar I made counted.

When I was a little girl, the reality of taking my clothes off in front of half-drunk men was never even a possibility. Not even as a teenager, but life doesn't always go the way you planned.

"Belle, you're on in five," Al called out.

I caught his eye in the mirror and nodded. Returning to my reflection, I fluffed up my hair and added some lip gloss. I slipped on my six-inch patent-leather platform heels and stood, making a quick adjustment to my blue mini dress, perking my breasts up in the deep V of the collar.

Castle Lounge was a topless strip bar, and it drew in a decent crowd despite the lower-income community that surrounded it. Chances were the crowd would probably grow larger if it was full nudity, but it wasn't like the little thong covered much anyway.

Tips were always good, but that had a lot to do with my looks: bright-blue eyes to lure them in, an hourglass figure to make them salivate, and olive skin they could envision their cum contrasting against with not a blemish in sight.

And all of it, including my name, was a lie.

"Give it up for Belle!" Al's voice boomed, signaling my arrival.

The lights were blinding, but the path to the pole was one I was familiar with. One step with an exaggerated sway of my hips was followed by another as I ran my hands up and down my body. A little twirl, a dip, add in a flip of my hair, and the whistles and catcalls boomed out over the music.

The seats around the stage were crowded as they were every Friday night. A good-sized crowd also occupied the tables filling out the room. There were regulars I recognized as well as new faces.

I let the music flow through me, using it to lure them all in, to hook them. My eyes popped wide, and I gave a look of mock surprise when the top of my dress slipped down, exposing my breasts.

Their eyes raked over me, the lust coming off them intoxicating me, driving me to tease them more. Each undulation of my hips and parting of my lips cast a spell on the men.

The harder they were, the more bills they threw my way. A smile here, a wink there, a dip right in front of their faces.

Shake my hips and flirt with every man who looked at me.

It was all a play for power, and on the stage, I made the rules. I was the queen of the castle, and they bowed before me.

I wrapped my fingers around the pole and gave it a sinuous twist. Then I let my weight drop at my hip and spun around.

On the pole was where I felt free. All my thoughts slipped away as I let go.

Dancing had been an escape when I was younger, but I

never envisioned I'd be doing it on a stripper pole for dollars to make ends meet at a topless bar.

Each rock of my hips against the bar pressed the hard metal against my clit. I bit down against my lip as I did it again and again.

I got off on their lust, on the power over them. They couldn't touch me unless I said—only look and want and fantasize.

I made the rules.

Slow rocks of my hips as I pushed the dress down my torso, a swirl of my hips as the dress stretched over them, and a slow bend at the waist as I pushed it down to my ankles.

I could feel dozens of men staring at me, at the place they all wanted to be. Standing, I kicked the dress to the back of the stage, then grabbed the pole again.

That was when I spotted them from across the room, their eyes glued to my body as I swung around the pole. A jolt of fear pulsed through me and I lost my concentration, landing on the stage wrong. My knees hurt, but I pushed past the pain as I spread them wide for the hungry eyes of an overweight, middle-aged man. My hips jutted out, gyrating as my hands moved up my torso until they cupped my breasts. I gripped them tight, my gaze never leaving theirs, and straightened both my middle fingers.

They could go fuck themselves. I made the rules, and I wasn't going to let them scare me.

They stood out in the crowd of lust-crazed men pining for just a taste of my skin or a bat of my eyelashes in their direction. Fuel for their next masturbation session to ease the growing tightness in their balls. Most barely made it to their cars before their cocks were out and they were stroking them with fervor.

The two I was currently flipping off and glaring at weren't there for the show. Messengers in crisp black suits, their gazes were impassive, though I was certain the dark blond one twitched his lips up into a smirk.

I turned my attention back to the men around me, making sure to pay special attention to each one. Legs in splits, ass in their face, a wide-eyed bite of my bottom lip for that innocent edge, though I was far from innocent. I had long ago learned sex was a way to get what I wanted.

Bills flew upon the stage along with a few business cards and words of pleading. Then there were the offers—marriage, sugar daddy, money for the night—that I ignored. I wasn't looking for any of that.

I didn't know what I wanted, but I knew it was none of them. Leaning down, I gathered up my dress as Jimmy picked up everything my admirers had dropped and cleared the stage for the next girl.

I slipped the blue mini-dress over my head. It barely covered my ass and tits, so it wasn't for any sense of modesty, but I knew the power of clothing and how to use it to tease.

Angel's music cued up and the crowd's attention snapped back to the stage. I could still feel the lingering gazes of a few men, including the two dipshits at the back wall. I refused to let them intimidate me, though inside I wasn't as confident, and I headed up to the bar for a drink.

"Hey, Mac," I said, signaling to my favorite man in the place.

He held up a finger as he finished with a tray of drinks. A blinding smile met me a minute later as he turned his attention to me.

"Water?" he asked, and I nodded. I liked watching his muscles flex as he moved around. We had an attraction and had shared more than a few nights of fun, but neither of us was looking for more. I trusted Mac more than most, and that still amounted to little more than the trust I had for my worst enemy.

"Here you go, sexy," he said with a wink as he set the glass down in front of me.

"Thanks, stud." I gave him a wink in return and a smile. Of all the men who surrounded me daily, Mac was the only one who got a genuine smile from me. Maybe if things had been different, if I were a normal girl from the normal world… The thought wasn't even worth finishing.

A moan escaped me as the cold water slid down my throat. Dancing always left me thirsty.

"Don't be making sounds like that, Ella."

I quirked a brow at him. "Using my name? Tsk-tsk, Mac."

He leaned his forearms onto the bar, giving a quick glance toward Al before licking his lips. "Want to punish me for it later?"

The last time we'd been together, I was the punished one—ass spanking, hair pulling, choking. Mac was an aggressive lover—and exactly what I needed.

I leaned in closer to match his stance. Stress relief sounded like fun, especially after I dealt with the assholes on the far wall. "Punish you? And how would I accomplish that?"

"By keeping me hard all night until I get you back to my place."

My thighs clenched, and I bit down on my lower lip. "And then what?"

He crooked his finger, and I leaned in so he could whisper in my ear. "And then I fuck you until you come so hard on my cock, you'll have trouble teasing me tomorrow with your fuck-hot body because you have trouble walking."

A moan slipped from between my lips. "But won't that just turn you on, knowing you are the reason?"

His tongue peeked out between his lips as he looked at me. "Then I guess I'll have to punish you tomorrow night."

The offer was awfully tempting, especially since the last time I'd had sex with Mac was too many weeks ago. I needed release, and I knew Mac was capable of pulling off just what he promised. "What time do you get off work?"

"Two," he replied.

"I'm off at midnight."

"Why don't I come over after?"

That would give me time to go home and shower. "I suppose we could do that, but you've got to deliver."

"Wear that little blue dress. I've got some ideas," he said with a devilish smirk.

"You're on, stud."

I finished my water and then headed to get ready for my second trip around the pole, but before I could slip into the back, someone grabbed my arm, halting me. One of Al's meaty hands was wrapped around my arm at the elbow.

I prepared myself for some lecture for talking to Mac, but the words that came out were not to reprimand me.

"Belle, those two suits over there paid for an hour."

I didn't have to look at where he was gesturing, and I ground my teeth in agitation. "No."

"You'll do it. Candi is taking your next slot."

"I don't want to."

"I don't care what you want—they paid. What's with you?" His brow was scrunched. I never turned down a private dance for a client. Usually they were the type to tip more than I would make in a night on the stage.

"They just creep me out," I said.

Al looked to them, then nodded in agreement. "Yeah, something's not right with them boys. Go on, I'll keep watch."

With a sigh of resignation, I stomped across the room. I wasn't trying to lure them in or tease them, but the eyes on me said that my shoes had my hips doing just that, regardless of what I wanted.

As I approached, they straightened in their seats. With each step my anxiety grew, because I knew they were from my past life. I didn't recognize them but their attitude said it all, and I wasn't going to be taken back.

I crossed my arms in front of me as I stopped in front of them and glared. I'd never seen them before, but they had the look I was familiar with.

"What do you want?" I ground out, letting them know by my posture I wasn't interested.

They glanced at each other, and the stoic bald man spoke. "You're not safe here."

I tried not to let them see the turmoil brewing inside me. Not because of their words, but that they'd just confirmed they were my father's men. "I'm perfectly fine."

"There have been threats. We need to get you to a secure location," he stressed.

"How many times do I have to say no?"

"I'm sorry, did you say something?" the dark blond asked with a smirk. He was the one I'd seen from the stage. The stoic, even nature of most of my father's employees didn't extend to him.

"Miss, you need to come with us," the other one said, shooting a glare of warning at his partner.

Miss. They always called me *Miss.*

"I am home, and your hour is up."

"It's only been five minutes," the cheeky blond said.

I turned back to him. "That's an hour in my presence. Go back empty-handed and beg forgiveness, because I am not going anywhere with you."

They stood, and I instinctively backed up, my heart slamming. They wouldn't forcefully take me, would they?

The blond held out his hand, a small white card hanging between his first two fingers. "If you need anything, *bella.*"

I drew a brow and stared at him, gaining satisfaction at the grumble of frustration that passed before he let go. The card twirled to the ground between us.

My glare followed them, watching them step through the doors. The white card was stark against the dark floor. My lips turned down in disgust before I picked up my foot and shoved my six-inch heel through the paper stock to the carpet below.

"What was all that about?" Al grabbed my arm, twirling me around to look at him.

"Nothing."

"Ain't nothing. Those guys paid, and you're gonna give me a bad rep with that attitude."

"They weren't here for a show," I spat, my anger still sitting at the surface. I twisted my arm to free it from his grip.

"What were they here for, then?"

Nobody knew my past. I was just another runaway, escaping a life, getting lost in drugs and booze and showing off my body to hungry eyes, only without the drugs and booze. My story started differently. I was just as poor as the other girls, but the Louis Vuitton satchel in my locker wasn't a fake.

Sacrifices were made because everything has a price. Freedom was only free if you took it, so I'd taken mine.

It wasn't the first time my father's henchmen had hunted me down and demanded my return, but it was the first time they'd mentioned anything about my safety.

Something about that was unsettling, but I pushed it down. It was just another tactic to get me to heel, and it wasn't going to work.

"They wanted a whore for some party," I spat, knowing Al would be up in arms. Nothing could get his business shut down faster than the suspicion of prostitution.

"Good girl. They ain't welcome here if that's the case."

That gave me hope that they'd be banned, so if my father sent them again, they wouldn't be allowed in.

TWO

A few hours and a few dances later, I was ready for a shower. I washed the makeup from my face, happy to have the layers and the weight of the false eyelashes gone. I was hooking up with Mac later, and he liked the natural look more than my painted-up face.

I liked it better as well.

I pulled on my jeans and sneakers, along with a tank top and my favorite oversized yellow sweater. Outside of Castle, I'd long ago moved from designer dresses and stiletto heels in favor of something more practical.

Every day I sat on edge, wondering if it was the day to run, and I couldn't run well in heels. Plus, dressing casually helped me to blend in better. No different than anyone else around me.

"Hey, Ella, you heading home?" Angel asked as she entered the dressing room.

As with my past, nobody knew my real name, only the name I'd given them. Many of the girls went by their stage names. Al had named me Belle the first day I came in for a job.

Eight years of ballet had given me skills that came in handy. However, I'd never stripped in front of someone who wasn't a doctor or a lover...or my father.

The memory was a sour one and sat heavily in my stomach.

"Yeah. I'm dying to finish this book, then take a nice long nap before my landlord comes calling for rent." She didn't need to know my actual plans, especially since there were a few girls who wanted to hook up with Mac with no success. Besides, what I told her was an average day for me anyway. Just me and my books.

"Those two suits looked like they'd pay well. What happened?"

She was fishing for Al, ever the little side piece, but I wasn't going to give her what she wanted so she could get another hit while she rode his dick.

"Turns out they were looking for a gang-bang girl." They didn't need to know the reality of the men.

Her eyes were wide, lips parted. "Oh."

I nodded and gave her a thin-lipped smile. "Yup."

Unlike most of the girls at the Castle Lounge, I hadn't grown up on the wrong side of the tracks. No trailer parks or low-income parents. No debt or drugs or any of the other stereotypical reasons girls became topless dancers.

The only stereotype I had was daddy issues. Deep-seated ones.

Tyrants demand loyalty, respect, and that you follow every word as law.

Daddy was a lawyer. High powered in one of Chicago's biggest crime families. I was expected to act and look perfect at all times. To behave and be nothing but a pretty doll to display.

Too bad for him, I had too much rebellion in me.

Things weren't always tense between us. Once upon a time I was very much a daddy's girl, but as I got older his hugs became chains. When my mother took her life, they were no longer free but came with a price I was expected to pay.

His quest for power had become a noose around my mother's neck until there was only one way for her to be free again.

"Don't let him cage your spirit," she'd said. *"You aren't made for bowing before false kings."*

She took her life that night. Over the following months my father's affections became non-existent and though there were spots of the man who once looked at me with adoration and love, his thirst for money and power was stronger.

One day I went to the mall, lost my guards, and walked away. That was three years ago. Three years of scraping by, of dancing for dollars, but I was free.

On my way out, Mac caught my eye and I gave him a wink, making sure to flash him a piece of the blue fabric in my bag from the dress he wanted. I wasn't even out to my car when my phone went off.

I'm coming for that pussy—Mac

A shiver rolled through me, and a smile spread as I bit down on my lower lip. When I'd left home, I'd thought freedom would include sex whenever and with whomever I wanted, but I realized once I was out on my own that my escapades were a form of rebellion. Sex wasn't what I wanted. Freedom was.

In the three years since I left home, I'd had a very few select partners, usually months apart. Mac had been a steady partner for two years.

They were there to scratch an itch. Nothing more.

There was no room in my life for more. The life I'd fled was filled with the death and destruction that accompanied the power-hungry high of men.

Maybe one day I would find a good man to have a normal life with, but the guards who popped in and out of my life made even that idea a difficult one to entertain. It would mean telling someone the truth behind my mask of lies.

My pussy is hungry. Don't stall—Ella

Fuck. Keep up with that shit and I'm going to nut in my pants—Mac

Just trying to keep you wanting—Ella

No need. I've been dying for another taste of you for weeks—Mac

I blinked at the screen. Maybe things weren't as casual for him as they were for me. That could be a problem, but I would come back to that after.

Come and get it—Ella

There was a chill in the late September air, and I was happy to have a heavy cotton sweater on. While it wasn't flattering, it was warm. My car took a few minutes to warm up and sweep away some of the cold.

After midnight there weren't a lot of cars on the road, which was always nice, especially in this part of town. In the rearview mirror were two pinpricks of light keeping even with my speed. At the stoplight, the lights blinded me so I was unable to see anything inside.

When the light changed, I stepped on the gas to get some distance from the van or truck that was behind me. It sat higher, and the more I increased my speed to lessen the blinding lights, the more they kept up.

It was a feeling I'd had before. That itch of suspicion, the tickle of paranoia at the back of my brain.

I told myself it was the paranoia instilled by the guards who'd said it wasn't safe.

Each turn I made, so did they. Every increase of speed they matched.

That feeling wasn't going away. My breaths increased, and my hands tightened on the steering wheel. After a few miles with no other cars on the road, it was no longer paranoia.

There really was a car following me.

My heart slammed in my chest, beating harder with each second.

My foot pressed down on the accelerator, and I blew through a red light.

So did they.

Fear spiked through me, but I kept my focus. *Get away.*

Run.

Fight.

Don't let them get you.

As we approached the bridge, a car swooped out from the back of the car behind me. It flew past me too fast for me to see anything other than that it was a panel van.

Suddenly he was in front of me and laying on the brakes. I was careening into him with nowhere to go.

"Shit!" I swore as I slammed on my own brakes. I didn't want to slow down, but we were in the middle of a two-lane bridge, and there were cars coming in the other direction. To the right was a river, and to the left was a head-on collision.

The car behind me also slammed on his brakes, and I was trapped, almost bumper to bumper, sandwiched between them.

Frantically I moved through my list of options, but before I could come up with any sort of a plan, a motorcycle appeared beside me. My eyes widened at the bat in his hand. He swung back and I leaned over, arms raised to shield myself from the spray of glass as my window shattered.

I stomped my foot on the gas, which only propelled me into the back of the much-larger van in front of me, jerking me to a hard stop. The cars coming from the other direction slowed and a spark of hope lit only to diminish without fully forming as they stopped, and a throng of men jumped from the back of two more vans.

"Fuck!" I reached in my bag for my pepper spray, finding it just as my door opened and a hand grabbed my arm and pulled me from the car.

I didn't even look, only turned and sprayed. He cried out and I thrust my foot into his stomach, sending him to the ground. There were at least ten men descending on me, and I broke off into a run, heading for an opening between two of the cars.

I made it only two steps before hands were on me, but I didn't stop.

The driver of the car that had followed me slid out to block the small opening between the cars I was aiming for.

He was tall with broad shoulders and an imposing aura, but I was too busy struggling against the hands on me to notice anything else.

I managed to spray one of the men touching me as I cried out for help. It was futile, I knew, but I wasn't going to stop.

A slam of my foot into someone's crotch, twisting, refusing to go calmly.

I would not go calmly into the night.

I'd trained my body, strengthened it for that moment, but there were so many of them.

The mouth of the man in front of me twisted into a smirk as he watched.

I'd thrown one man off me when a cloth was pressed over my mouth. My eyes went wide as I tried not to breathe in, still fighting.

The imposing figure stepped forward but with each step, whatever was in the cloth began to pull me under. My arms were locked, held out on each side as another man held me by the waist. One of my knees was kicked out from under me, and I slumped in the arms holding me. My vision turned fuzzy when he got close enough for me to see his face.

His hand wrapped around my neck, forcing me to look up at him. I continued to struggle, but my limbs had become sluggish and I knew they'd won.

The only thing I saw was a deep scar—and silver eyes that stared deep into mine.

"Nighty night, princess," he hissed condescendingly.

The last of my strength left me, and I was unable to fight sleep anymore.

THREE

I was cold. So cold. That was the only thought I had as I began to shake the sleep that had ahold of me. More awareness surfaced and something strange kept me from clenching my teeth—soft, malleable, but solid.

I drew in a sharp breath hindered by what had to be a cloth in my mouth. Panic sent adrenaline surging through me and I sat up, only to fail and flop back to the cold ground.

Something sharp dug into my wrists when I tried to move my arms, which were locked behind me while my legs were bound together at my ankles.

I didn't recognize the building, but it was obvious it hadn't been in use for years, as evident by the layers of debris in my limited view.

The darkness made it difficult to see much, even with the moonlight, and my eyes had trouble adjusting. What little light there was streamed in through cracks from what I assumed to be windows and a large overhead skylight. The air was cool, damp, and so still that it stifled a scream that wanted to erupt from behind my bindings.

There were low murmurs in the darkness and the feeling of being watched, but I couldn't see into the blackness of the shadows.

My heart slammed, breath coming out in harsh pants as I struggled against my bindings.

Cold steel bars surrounded me, no more than a five- or six-inch gap between them. Being tied up was horrible enough, but being caged sent my panic into overdrive.

Every inch of me was shaking. A combination of fear, anxiety, and cold seeped through every layer down to my very cells. Every nightmare or scary thought and every horror movie that involved kidnapping ran through my mind, giving me highlights of what was in store for me.

My breath picked up and it was a struggle to keep from hyperventilating as I fought against my restraints.

"She's awake," a voice said from the dark. A figure stepped out from the black, into the moonbeam, and I stared, wide-eyed, at the man in front of me. His hair was dark, the color of oil, but his eyes shone bright and blue. His features were soft, calming almost, and in high contrast to my surroundings.

I managed to get myself up into a sitting position and I noticed how much my knees ached.

"Shh. Don't worry, everything's going to be okay, I promise. I'm Roman." He had a kind face and strong features that didn't seem to hold an ounce of malice, which confused me. What was he doing there?

I couldn't say anything in response, the gag making it hard to swallow, let alone speak. Even so, I could feel the chattering of my teeth.

With his hand he beckoned me forward. "Come on, it's okay. I just want to help."

With each inch I scooted closer, my body shook even harder, almost vibrating. He slipped his hands through the bars and I flinched, my eyes slamming shut as I froze in anticipation. There was no slap or hit, but rather a tug at the back of my head, then a pull, then relief as the gag was removed.

"Can you swing your legs around?" he asked as he flipped out a knife. The blood in my veins stopped, and I blinked at him. He stared back in confusion when I didn't move, then gestured with the knife. "For the zip ties."

Relief seeped in as I wiggled around, my feet closer to the bars. A quick swipe of the blade across the plastic and my legs relaxed down to the ground. They hurt, but it was a good pain.

He motioned for me to spin and I shuffled around, turning my back toward the bars and pushing my arms toward him. Another tug and there was a rush of pain in my shoulders as I drew my arms back in front of me.

"See? That's better." He smiled at me as he removed his hands.

I opened and closed my mouth, making circular motions with my lower jaw. "Thank you." As soon as the words were out of my mouth, I regretted them. My parents had hammered manners into me, and if anyone ever did anything for you, a thank you was warranted, but I didn't think I was in the situation they'd had in mind.

It felt so good to have the restraints off, even with the pain that came as blood flowed back into restricted areas and muscles and tendons released their stiffness.

He smiled at me. "You're welcome."

I opened my mouth to ask a question, but then closed it. A chill moved down my spine as I felt eyes on me.

"Stop talking to her," a deep, gravelly voice said from the shadows behind Roman. It sent a shiver through me, and even the man before me froze.

In the darkness, a figure rose and stepped forward, the small amount of light illuminating a striking figure. Strong, hard lines made up his face, with full lips and dark eyebrows creating a shadow that made his silver eyes almost glow. The aura surrounding him screamed danger, and I couldn't help but stare, unable to move a muscle.

He was the man from the bridge, the one who'd blocked my path.

Clashing against his handsome features was a long, thick scar that ran from the outside edge of his eye all the way down to the corner of his mouth, then moved back up, splitting his brow before tapering off on his forehead. It didn't mar his beauty, but it did increase how menacing he looked.

My heart slammed in my chest as he continued farther into the light.

Roman backed away as the new man stepped forward.

"You're probably wondering what's going on, Ella," he said.

I couldn't help but nod, because I had no clue why anyone would want Ella Delgado. By calling me that, I realized they didn't know who they really had.

"Please, let me go. I'm a nobody."

He ignored me. "My name is Domenico, and I'm your new god. If I tell you to speak, you speak. If I tell you to suck my cock, you do it. Otherwise there are nasty consequences."

"S-suck what?" I asked as I swallowed. Had I heard him right? I begged myself to wake up, to free myself from this strange dream, but the cold seeping into my bones and the grit digging into my palms told me it was no dream. It was a living nightmare.

He grabbed his crotch and dragged his hand along the visible ridge. His lip tugged up and due to the light, his expression was sinister. It sent a splash of cold through me and sent my mind racing.

What was going on?

"Just wanted to make sure I had your attention. As I was saying, I'm your god. Your master of pain and pleasure. If you want to eat, be a good little princess, but if you're a brat, you'll fucking starve," he sneered.

"Why?" I asked. Though vague, it covered so many questions running through my head. The most prevalent: why me?

He stepped forward and loomed over me as he sneered down at me. "Because we can."

Because we can? What does that even mean?

A snap of his fingers and I heard a shuffle of feet in the dark before he turned and faded away into the black.

Once alone, I took in my surroundings. The cell was small, maybe a six-foot cube, placed at one end of a large open space. The ceiling had to be around twenty feet tall, and the expanse around was impressive. A large opaque skylight ran about thirty feet down the center of the room. The moon sat high in the sky on a cloudless night. The half-exposed surface showered the earth with a sprinkle of light and created a soft glow through the dirt-smudged glass.

In the cell sat a twin-sized mattress that looked like it had come from a dumpster, but at least the blankets looked decent, even if they were basic.

In one corner sat a bucket with a roll of toilet paper next to it. I cringed in realization that it was my toilet for however long I'd be there.

I searched for any weakness outside of my cubed prison, any route of escape should I be able to free myself from the steel that surrounded me, but I would have to wait for the sun. Dust motes swirled in the warm beams of yellow light that shone from streetlamps outside. That meant the area was not remote, but populated. Maybe someone could hear me?

"Help! Somebody help me! Please help!" I yelled, praying someone would hear me. I projected my voice as loud as I could. I clung to the bars, begging for help until my pleas turned into hiccupping sobs.

What was going to happen to me? Were they going to kill me? Rape me?

Why me?

Why Ella?

My screams did nothing. Nobody came, not even my captors. By the time my throat was raw, defeat crawled in and took hold. I slumped back against the bars. While my sobs had subsided, tears still trailed down my cheeks.

My stomach opened up in a pit of uncertainty and nausea rolled through me.

I was all alone. Trapped in darkness and suffocating on the emptiness.

The silence was deafening. Devoid of anything. My heartbeat was a war drum, and I could hear the whooshing of blood pumping through my veins—sounds I'd rarely even noticed were blaring, blatantly obvious.

There was nothing within reach, the space empty with the exception of some pillars and another cage about ten feet away. The stale smell of decay filled my nose—a combination of dust, dankness, and dirt.

There was no real way to tell how much time had passed, but I guessed hours since they had retreated into the darkness. I wasn't even sure if they were still in the building or if they had left entirely. My eyes fluttered, and despite how gross and disgusting the bed looked, I crawled onto it and pulled the thin blanket on top of me. In no time I was asleep, my last thought a prayer that I would wake in my own bed.

FOUR

T he chatter of voices stirred me, and I awoke in my nightmare. The cold robbed me of any more sleep, and I opened my eyes to find that it wasn't all a bad dream after all.

With the sun shining, the large expanse was illuminated, exposing the cobwebs hanging in corners and the paint chipping from the walls. One wall was covered in windows that were shielded with some sort of film or paper that was yellow, either due to its original color or time. Tears in the material let in unfiltered beams of light.

I sat up and finally got a look around. What I'd thought was one more cage turned out to be an entire line of them—which meant they could hold up to six girls at a time.

They all sat empty except for the basic materials my own cell was outfitted with.

How many girls had sat in those cells, frightened and alone? My chest clenched as I felt their fear as my own. I imagined the weaker ones working themselves up into a panic attack, struggling to breathe.

What happened to them all? Where were they now? How many were still alive?

Family and friends devastated by their disappearance, never knowing what happened to them.

Maybe it was a small comfort that nobody would miss me, because I'd disappeared long ago. Did anyone mourn me? I knew people searched for me, and found me, but was my void even noticeable to them?

My eyes widened as realization dawned.

Fuck.

Mac.

He had been headed over last night. What had he thought when I wasn't there? Did he call? Where was my phone now? Did he even know I was missing?

Did anyone from my current life?

The hairs on the back of my neck stood up and I straightened my spine as I searched for the source. Hidden in the shadows of a deep alcove, a figure sat so still I barely noticed him. When our eyes met, his head tilted to the side.

"Do you know who I am?" I asked. It wasn't a question of my fake identity but of my real one.

"Of course," he said as he stood.

A shiver ran through me. He called me Ella, but did he know who I *really* was? Maybe it wasn't some random kidnapping. Maybe they knew exactly who they were abducting. The sudden regret that I didn't take my father's guards seriously rocked through me.

As he emerged from the darkness in a fluid motion, I got my first good look at my captor.

The version in the daylight was just as menacingly beautiful as the one I'd seen the night before—and just as chilling.

"There are some rules we need to go over, princess, and you will follow them. First is that you do what I say without question, or you will not like the punishment for disobedience. Second, don't bother screaming. You can scream as loud as you want, but there's nobody around to hear you. Those few who might won't lift a finger, because I rule this area."

"And just who are you?"

"I am your god, remember? The third rule I told you yesterday—be a good princess and you get food. Be a brat and you'll starve."

"How long will I be here?"

"Until the boss says so."

"I thought you were the boss?"

"I am a god to everyone in here, but even gods have a ruler," he said before leaving me and heading over to a man I hadn't even noticed.

He was the leader of everyone in here, but in the end, he was still a henchman. Whoever he was past that, I didn't know, and he refused to give anything up.

The sound of laughter caught my attention, and I turned to find a group of men sitting against the wall, cups of coffee in their hands as they spoke. Every once in a while a set of eyes would glance my way, but otherwise my presence was ignored.

Near them another member appeared from a staircase. As I looked toward the only door in the room, I understood—we were at least one flight up.

My eyes stung, and there was no way around it. I wiped my fingers as much as I could before pinching my thumb and first finger together and pulled the contacts from my eyes. Once both were out, I blinked and tried to produce some tears to lubricate and clear any debris.

The green contacts used to cover my natural light brown sat in my hand and I sighed. There was no need for them anymore. Another one of the lies used to hide myself.

I settled back down to the bed, pulling the blanket tightly around me. As I lay there, I listened closely to every word I could.

The bare walls created an echo that made it difficult to make some things out.

My whole day was spent that way—gathering information, observing, learning.

More men came, and those who barely noticed my existence were replaced by newbies leering at me. The new group did little to keep their leader's secret.

Domenico was the name that floated on hushed tones that echoed around the grand space.

He was younger than many of the other men. Probably not even thirty, and he didn't dress the part of a capo in their crisp business attire. Some of the men wore suits, but there were others who didn't. Domenico appeared more casual, with jeans, boots, and a leather jacket with a hoodie underneath.

It seemed odd for someone like him to be high up in the rankings. As I looked around, I spotted a few differences in the men. Most were soldiers. Men that had sworn an oath. Men that killed to become made men.

The ones that came and went with more frequency were associates, constantly being sent out under the soldiers' orders. They were the grunts hoping to become part of the family.

Domenico was definitely the capo. The captain of the band of rag-tag men. He directed the soldiers with tasks.

Maybe he was a new capo and the crew was his first.

The day wore on with little to no answers to my question of why me. The sun was high in the sky when Domenico appeared in front of me.

"Eat," he said as he slipped a paper plate through a slit in the bars.

I sat still, unmoving, locked on his silver eyes, which were glaring at me. He let out a sigh and opened his hand.

The plate fell and landed on the ground, food bouncing onto the dirty floor.

"Ew."

"It's the only food you'll get today. If you don't eat it, I'll take it as a personal insult, and what did I say about brats earlier?"

A shiver ran through me, which was visible to him.

"So be a good princess."

I flinched when he called me that. The condescending way he said it didn't raise any alarms that he knew who I really was, but rather it was a degradation highlighting my situation.

I stared down at the sandwich covered in dirt and dust, my stomach roaring in complaint. How long had it been since I'd eaten anything? My snack after my last set? That was well over twelve hours ago, but my last meal was seven hours before that.

With great reluctance under his hawk eye, I picked the sandwich up from the ground. My mouth turned down in disgust as I brushed off flecks of darkness from the pale slice.

"Does it come with a drink?" I asked as I glared up at him.

His lip twitched up. "Roman," he said without breaking his stare.

The man from the night before, the one who'd broken my bonds, stepped forward. He gave me a friendly smile as he drew near.

"Yeah, Dom?"

I caught the flex of Domenico's jaw out of the corner of my eye. "Did you bring the water?" He waited for Roman to give an indication. "Give her a bottle."

In my periphery I watched Roman walk across the large expanse, all while keeping my gaze glued to Domenico. It was only a moment later when Roman slipped a bottle through the bars of my cage.

"Here you go," Roman said with a smile.

"Thank you," I said, once again stunned that I had thanked the man. There was just something about him, a sense of propriety and decency that was out of place.

I drew in a breath as I eyed my point of sandwich entry and took a large bite. It was a move I instantly regretted. The sandwich was as basic as they came—bologna and mayonnaise.

I hated mayo.

Bologna was also not high on my list of edible meats, but my stomach didn't seem to care and became ravenous for its first food in a day.

With every bite I stayed strong, never taking my eyes from Domenico. Even when my mouth turned down when I crunched a piece of grit and I wanted to spit the mouthful out, I refused to break our eye contact.

"You're a defiant one, aren't you?" His lips twitched up into a smirk. "The wild ones are the most fun to break."

There was a cascade of snickers and whispers of agreement.

When I finished, I opened my mouth and stuck out my tongue to show I'd swallowed all of it.

His lip twitched up again, but he said nothing before retreating back into his darkness.

Every hour I took in more of the space, picking up on more of the details: dust and debris from the crumbling walls, chunks of plaster that dropped from the ceiling. The wood plank floors were mostly clear in the areas where they seemed to walk, like someone swept it from time to time.

There was a table on the far wall with a bunch of folding chairs and one well-worn sofa chair. That was where the men who came and went seemed to congregate.

What surprised me most was in all the decay, on a broken-down, beat-up wood table sat a black vase with a single pristine red rose. It was so out of place. Shortly after noticing it, I watched as Domenico walked over to it and pulled a single petal. His fingers opened, and the silky red petal floated to the tabletop.

I stared at the rose, trying to discern the meaning of it. Something about it itched at the back of my mind. The family my father worked for was well known for their use of roses left as calling cards on men they killed.

Was that who had me? I wanted to yell out to him, to ask him, to tell him who I was, but I stopped myself.

No. I wouldn't do it. Not until it was completely necessary. I wasn't even certain it was them, and telling him would be an admission that I needed protection, help, and I wasn't going to go begging, crawling back.

I locked my secret back down and observed.

Just another runaway.

FIVE

I stared up at the ceiling, completely bored and wishing something would happen instead of the nothingness. My stomach was a constant knot as I wondered what they were going to do with me.

For two days it had been nothing but waiting, and it continued to be so. Food was minimal, entertainment even less so.

After that first day, I'd resigned myself to the fact that I was sitting in reality. I had been taken against my will, but that didn't mean I was defeated. Far from it. I kept mostly to myself, not engaging in the cat-calls and egging from the animals around me. I stayed focused, continuing on my quest to keep the fear minimal and my mind busy with the task of finding some weakness that would allow me to escape.

But the awful truth was that there was no way. From the constant guard to the inability to even escape the cage that held me, I was well and truly trapped. There was no way to even *maybe* loosen the bolts on the door, because someone was always watching.

Instead, I cataloged information.

There was almost a constant half-dozen men who came and went. Sometimes there were as many as fifteen, sometimes as few as two. Domenico gave orders, talked about shipments and goods. Guards were assigned, men sent out on shakedowns and errands.

They all showed great respect when Domenico was speaking, never faltering when he gave an order. When Domenico wasn't present, a man named Marco directed the men.

It took me little time to determine that Marco was Domenico's second. Marco was older, more distinguished, and seemed just as ruthless if need be, with salt-and-pepper hair, lightly lined face, and eyes that seemed to see all.

When I wasn't under Domenico's thumb, I was under Marco's. I would have preferred it be Roman. He always gave me a smile when he brought me food, and he spoke in soft, reassuring tones as he tried to get me to eat. Roman was able to sneak me another blanket, despite Marco's scrutiny.

The blanket was a godsend, and thankfully Marco didn't take it from me or reprimand Roman, who was so nice and out of place with the rest of the men.

Roman didn't belong in such a position, and the wheels began to spin, thinking that maybe I could use him to escape.

The meager sandwich really was all the food I got every day, but sometime in the evening of the third day, when darkness descended and my stomach growled for more, an angel came.

"Hey." Roman appeared behind me, a water bottle tapping me on the shoulder.

"Hi."

He glanced up to the shadowed alcove before reaching into his pocket. "Here," Roman said as he slipped a Coke between the bars. "I thought you might like it, so I snuck one in."

"Thank you." I smiled at him as I took the can, then popped

the top. My lips pressed together as I began to salivate. The sweet fizz danced across my tongue and a moan crawled out of my chest. It was the best thing I'd had in days. "So good. Thank you."

He beamed back at me. "You're welcome."

My brow furrowed as I looked over toward the alcove. "You won't get in trouble, will you?"

"Dom isn't here and Marco is busy. I'll just sneak the can back out." He pulled a granola bar from his pocket and handed it over as well.

"Why are you being so nice to me? Are you this nice to the other girls?" I asked, hoping to gain some information.

"I was just assigned to his crew." He hung his head. "I don't like hurting people, but my father said I had to learn."

"That's sad." I reached out and put my hand on his.

He shrugged and opened his mouth to speak when a voice boomed out. "Away from the girl, Roman."

Something flashed in Roman's eyes and his jaw clenched. He forced a smile and slid his hand from the bars. "I'll be back later."

I nodded and took another long pull from the can, gulping down as much as I could before Roman gently took it from me.

Marco stood glaring at Roman, his arms crossed in front of him.

"Just sharing a Coke with a friend," Roman told him, giving him a flash of the can.

"She's a prisoner, not a friend." I didn't like the way Marco said *prisoner*, indicating there was little chance of me getting out. Though I knew the truth—there was no escaping, not without help.

The evenings turned cold, and a few of the guys pulled in two metal barrels. Soon the warm yellow and orange glow of fire danced around the walls and ceiling. Still, the deep shadows where Domenico perched remained.

It was hard to tell sometimes if he was there or not. The beast lurking in the shadows.

The soft glow from his phone sometimes illuminated his features, which remained neutral with the occasional tic of his jaw. I was lost watching him, studying his features, his posture. The scar that tore through his cheek and forehead. What could make such a line? How old was he when he'd gotten it? It was obvious it healed over long ago.

I started, a jolt of adrenaline racing through my system at the sudden lock of predatory eyes on my own. They didn't leave mine when he swung his legs down to the ground and stood. His gaze flicked to the men, lost in some football game on a computer that had been brought in.

Unnoticed, he silently stepped across the dark, dust-covered debris field to the edge of my cage.

My heart jumped in a staccato beat with each step, and I straightened my spine, my muscles waking up and engaging, poised for whatever was about to happen. It was dark, but my eyes had long ago adjusted to the low light, and with the almost full moon beaming in through the large skylight, I was able to see him with muted clarity.

"Nobody is looking for you, princess," he said in a low tone. His voice was deep and smooth, with a hint of gravel. There was something about the way he held himself, the straightness of his posture, the confidence in his gait, which could command a room simply by walking into it.

"Why would they? No family, no friends, just a fucktoy and a job."

He let out a small chuckle, one side of his mouth sliding up. "Which one are you missing most right now?"

"The fucktoy," I replied without a thought. It was a stupid response, one that I for some reason thought would show strength. In actuality, it served as proof that I was worth the money someone would pay for a woman who placed sex above her job.

He nodded and looked back over to the men. "Don't tell anyone else that."

"I'm not ashamed." Again, the wrong choice of defiance. The man in front of me was not my father. No, the consequences here would be much worse if I ticked him off.

"Shame has nothing to do with it, but many will volunteer for the position."

"Yourself included?"

He arched a brow. "Why would I need to volunteer for a position that is already mine? I rule all here, and if I wanted you, you would be mine."

If he wanted me.

I glared up at him. "That's a hard no."

A dark chuckle left him. "You are an interesting creature. Such spirit." Whatever interest drove him to talk to me ended, and he turned back toward the alcove.

"Are you going to tell me how long I'll be here?"

"No."

"Are you going to tell me anything?"

He turned, those silver eyes glowing in the low light. "Why would I?"

My heart thumped hard in my chest. The conversation was odd. It revealed very little to me—and probably more than I wanted to him. In the end, what I was most confused about was why every nerve lit up with each word from his mouth, each caress of his eyes, while at the same time my insides shook in trepidation.

It seemed like a simple conversation, but the way he stared at me as he plucked another petal from the rose sent a shiver down my spine.

SIX

Days had passed, and still no information.

It was a sex-trafficking ring—that much I'd gathered, but why was I the only one? And why was I still there? I listened in to every conversation I could, faking sleep for inside information, but there was nothing.

Marco was in charge. He said little to me, barely even acknowledging my existence. He directed those who were there and fielded a few phone calls.

Domenico showed up late in the afternoon, with what looked like a case of sports drink under one arm and a duffel bag in the other. Marco took the case from him, and he passed by, not even looking at me as he headed to the crowd of men who were playing a game of poker. From what I could tell the one named Joey was winning handily, so much that the others were claiming that he was cheating.

They were right.

I was as invisible as a piece of furniture to them most of the time. While someone was always watching me, the others leered only from time to time, and I watched as Joey dealt himself one card too many and slipped the extra up his sleeve. It was a move so slick I doubted any of them noticed, but from my lower vantage point, I caught the movement.

I followed Domenico around as he talked to some of them, and I caught the small start of a smile once, which was startling. The scar made him so imposing, especially in combination with the scowl that always seemed to be plastered on his face, but talking with them, he was more relaxed.

Angular features, fit body, and striking eyes—I was suddenly aware of how attractive he was.

Odd.

Very odd. Why would I notice that about the man who had me locked away?

There was a scramble as yelling and screaming came from the floor below. All the men went on high alert, getting up, and some even grabbing for their guns. Domenico stepped out of the shadows, and a few men stepped in front of him.

"Shut the fuck up!" someone growled, but the wailing continued.

"It wasn't me! I'm telling you, I didn't do it!"

A man in a crisp dark suit emerged from the floor below, pulling a bound man by the arm. The men relaxed, making it obvious they were familiar with him. The sniveling continued as they awkwardly made their way toward Domenico. I couldn't take my eyes off the man in the suit, his aura similar to Domenico's.

He threw the bound man to the ground, landing him at Domenico's feet.

"I didn't do it, I swear. Please, sir."

"I believe you were looking for this," the man in the suit said.

"Thank you, Javier," Domenico said as he motioned to Marco, who pulled an envelope from a case. "Give my thanks to Malcolm."

"You owe him."

"I know."

At that Javier left, leaving the bound man crying and kneeling before Domenico. He glanced in my direction and paused. There was something about him that was familiar.

"Only one?" Javier asked as he stared at me.

"Inventory is low right now," Marco replied.

Javier stared a beat longer, then was gone.

"I didn't…I didn't…" The sniveling man quivered on the ground.

Domenico's eyes narrowed on the man, his body rigid, muscles coiled tight.

"Oh, but Elio, you did." Without warning, a wave of energy burst through him and his fist connected with Elio's face, sending him down to the ground.

I jumped and pressed back into the bars of my cage. While I'd always felt the alarm of danger in his presence, that he was a beast about to pounce, I hadn't seen it.

The men righted Elio, and Domenico pulled a chair over to sit in front of him, his arms resting on his thighs. "You stole. You lied. You sold. Worst of all, you betrayed the family." Another swing of his fist, another righting of Elio. "The family you swore an oath to. You were a made man." Domenico pulled a gun from behind him, and my eyes widened.

My heart slammed in my chest. I may have had ties to the life, but I'd never been witness to what I knew was about to happen.

Above all, you did not betray the family.

Without thought, I crawled to the other side of the cage, my chest clenching.

"Trusted." Domenico pulled the slide back, loading a round.

"Please, Dom. It wasn't me. I swear."

"Do you think I execute with no evidence?" he sneered. "I

don't take this task lightly, Elio. You were one of my most trusted, but you got greedy." Domenico's eyes seemed to glow as he held the gun in front of him. "And greed is a sin I can't abide."

Three loud booms fired off, and I felt a fine mist on my skin. Elio slumped to the ground, blood spilling from his chest.

A ragged breath left me, and I glanced down to my hands, my breath speeding up at the red droplets that clashed against my skin. My eyes widened, and I turned back to the gruesome scene in front of me and the lifeless body lying not ten feet from me.

"Fuck," Domenico hissed. "Clean this up. I don't want anything left."

"The river?" one of the men asked.

Domenico shook his head. "Leave him on his porch with a rose. Remind his wife what is on the line."

Again with a rose? Knowing what I knew about my father's world… knowing that a rose was the calling card of the family my father worked for, I was sure my suspicions were correct.

"What about the cops?"

"She knows if she wants to live she knows nothing. And I want every trace gone, including every droplet that hit her." He pointed to me. "Scrub everything."

Marco watched the men as he stood at Domenico's side. "I told Javier to bring him here."

"It's fine."

"I know you don't like doing that here."

"Because it makes a fucking mess."

"And it usually riles the girls up." Marco looked at me, but I was still sitting in shock. "She's shaking."

"Send Roman to get her some food."

They spoke as if I wasn't there, as if I wasn't staring at them, but I couldn't look away. I was trapped, locked onto the man who was intimidating every moment he was in the building.

I'd just watched him kill a man with a casual ease. It wasn't his first, nor his second. No, Domenico had long ago made his first kill.

Marco nodded and headed off while Domenico disappeared into the shadows but reappeared a few seconds later. He headed toward me with two bottles in his hand.

"Drink this," he ordered, pushing a bottle of Powerade through the bars.

I stared at him, unable to move, unable to think of anything other than the man he'd shot. It shouldn't have fazed me. I knew the sort of people who held me, but I'd never watched someone be killed before.

He blew out a huff of air in aggravation before pulling keys from his pocket and opening my cell. "Don't even fucking think of trying anything unless you want me to hurt you."

Like I could if I wanted to. Real fear had me in its clutches for the first time. The reality of where I was finally sank in. He stood in front of me, and the shaking kicked up another notch. Another huff with a roll of his eyes and he squatted down in front of me, setting the other bottle down and twisting the top from the Powerade.

"Drink this, or I'll make you drink it."

I stared at the bottle, unable to respond. For some reason I couldn't shake it off. I'd been stupid to think that my fate was so far from Elio's.

Ella Delgado was a nobody who wouldn't be missed if she were killed or sold as a sex slave.

Fire burned my skin, and I drew in a hissing breath of surprise. Domenico's hand rested on my neck, thumb moving across my jaw, tilting my head back.

I was frozen in a completely new way when our eyes met. The eyes that always seemed to glow captured me with their clarity and seemingly never-ending depth.

He gave nothing away.

Cradling my head in his hand, he pulled on my chin with his thumb, parting my lips. I blinked, thinking he was going to pour the liquid into my mouth.

A heartbeat, then another passed as our eyes locked before he took a swig from the bottle and pressed his lips to mine.

A splash of liquid filled my mouth, and his eyes stared deep into mine as his hand moved down my neck, coercing me to swallow. It was strangely erotic. Warmth spread slowly from his touch, like the sun melting ice crystals.

I stretched up toward him, trying to get more of the warmth, but he pulled back.

Those silver eyes swirled with fire.

"How's she look?" Marco asked from the doorway, a plate in his hand.

The fire quickly died, and Domenico took the plate. "She'll be fine. Get her a bath."

Marco nodded and stepped away, leaving us alone again, but the heat from Domenico had faded away, replaced by the cold.

"Eat and drink. Now."

I nodded and brushed away a tear when he slammed the metal bars closed again and turned the lock.

I needed to find a way out.

I needed out.

I need out!

SEVEN

In all my life, I never envisioned I would ever be in the predicament that I found myself in—taking a sponge bath, in an open cell, in an open room, in front of ten men, half of whom were watching.

Still, it felt good to get the blood and grime off me. However, a bucket of warm water wasn't enough, especially when returning to the same clothes I'd been wearing for days. The warmth leached away, the cold air cooling the water quickly. A shiver moved through me, and I pulled my clothes back on, trying not to give them a show. The days of showing off my body were over the moment they cornered me on that bridge.

My eyes locked onto the splatter of blood dried into a deep red and clashing against the yellow of my sweater.

A lackey, some young, thin guy about my age, opened the door to my cage to retrieve the bucket. I blinked, saw nobody in my periphery, and shot up.

I bolted, knocking the guy over and sprinting toward the door. My muscles hadn't been used much for days, causing them to seize, but I pushed through, my goal in sight.

It was a spontaneous, desperate maneuver, and it was working.

Feet from fresh air, a hard body collided with mine. Strong arms wrapped around me, a hand holding on to the back of my head as we tumbled to the ground in a heap.

By the time we stopped rolling, I was flat on my back, the strong scent of spice invading my senses. The warmth of another person soothed me, if only for a moment, and I reveled in the heat.

For a fraction of a second I felt safe—then the rush of cold fear flooded through my system. The tail end of a scar caught my eye, and the warmth left. I was caged in the arms of the monster, the leader of death's disciples. A minute tilt of his head and our eyes met. For a brief heartbeat something sparked inside me. His gaze moved to my lips before a flash of anger enveloped his features.

He mashed his teeth together as he pushed off the ground, and his grip hard on my arm as he tugged me up from the floor. His hand wrapped tightly around my neck as he pulled me close, his lips curled up into a snarl, his glare scaring even Death himself.

"Do you not remember the rules, *princess?*" he sneered.

My nails dug into his arm before swinging up and swiping at his face. A growl erupted from deep in his chest, unfazed by the light trails of blood slowly seeping from the fresh slices on his cheek.

"No food it is." He pushed me away and into the waiting arms of multiple men. "Put her back."

"You shouldn't have done that," Marco grumbled before throwing me in the cage, down to the floor and the dirty surroundings.

"N-no!" I cried out as I scrambled for the door before it latched. Cold eyes glared at me, his chest heaving. He was angry, furious, and I crumbled inside. My chest heaved as a sob rose with the clang of metal on metal. For days I'd kept the fear, the despair, down to a vibration below the surface, but the dam was broken.

"If this continues I can introduce you to my Russian friends, the Volkovs," Domenico growled. "Their favorite thing is breaking a woman until she's nothing but a cock sleeve."

The smallest taste of freedom on my tongue, but I wasn't fast enough or strong enough to get away. The lack of food kept me from having much energy, and the cell left little room to move.

I fell down on the bed, my tears dripping onto the gross mattress as I curled in on myself.

Everything about my situation was wrong. I wasn't supposed to be there. I shouldn't have been there, but I was.

Trapped in a nightmare with a devil king.

I couldn't shake the fear after my near escape. The floodgates opened up, and I couldn't seem to contain the bone-deep uncertainty that infested every thought.

I could still feel the warmth of his arms around me, the buzzing in my veins at his touch. And that was more frightening than my situation. Maybe I was touch deprived—that could be the only explanation why his tackle had felt like so much more.

One thing became clear—I had to keep my strength up. I was losing muscle mass every day, from both the lack of calories and the lack of movement. Perhaps that was their strategy—keep the girls weak so they couldn't fight back.

But I wasn't most girls, and I refused to let the fear and desolation take me.

It didn't mean I wasn't frightened, because I was, but I wasn't going to let that infest every part of me. I still had a card I could play if it came to it, but I prayed I wouldn't have to. Which fate was worse was still up for debate.

I grabbed hold of the bars that made up the ceiling of my cage and pulled my knees up, letting my body hang for a second, stretching out stiff muscles. Once my shoulders released the tension they were holding, I pulled my knees up to my chest, then with my arms hoisted my body up to the bars.

Slowly I released back down, then repeated nine more times. Then I moved to squats and sidekicks. Yoga stretches and poses—anything to help keep my body limber.

They were all exercises I was familiar with, as I did them nearly every day. They were how I kept fit for the pole—and for the need to run, if it arose.

Every movement was a spectacle for my unwanted audience, but I shut them out and focused on my breathing. It wasn't for them—it was for me.

It was all I had to keep me busy, but I often couldn't get through very much before fatigue settled in.

"Why am I here?" I asked, knowing I would receive no answer. It wasn't the first time, and it wasn't likely to be the last.

Men came and went through the space, some sitting at a nearby table playing cards while talking trash. A quick flick of their gaze, a lingering flash of hungry eyes, and more than one man came by the cage to leer at me while grabbing his crotch. There were conspiratorial glances and wayward conversations in hushed tones.

Even with all the movement around me, all the people, I was just a spectacle. I suddenly understood how animals at the zoo felt.

Every breath I took, every movement I made, someone was watching. I avoided going to the bathroom as much as possible because it drew in the truly depraved.

And that brought the panther out from his perch.

That was what Domenico reminded me of. Lithe, strong, and watchful, ready to strike—and strike he did.

The sound of water splashing hit me before the strong smell of urine invaded my nose. A menacing laugh sounded from a slug of a man who took pleasure in my discomfort. He had his dick out and was pissing on the floor next to my bed. He was young, maybe my age or a few years younger, with unkempt dark hair, crooked teeth, and dark eyes.

I had to force down the shiver from the sickening look he was giving me. It was one I'd had aimed at me before, but back then I was on stage and holding all the control. I had no control and no recourse anymore.

Before he finished Domenico emerged, grabbed the slug by the neck, and threw him to the ground.

"Don't try and mark what isn't fucking yours," Domenico growled.

"She ain't yours either," the slug spat as he jumped back up to his feet, glaring at Domenico.

Domenico stepped forward and swung his fist with such speed and force that the slug didn't even have time to process what was happening before he was slammed back to the ground. It was the same swiftness I'd seen with the man he'd executed.

"Who the fuck is this?" he asked to nobody in particular before landing a swift kick square in the slug's ribs.

The slug howled in pain, gasping for breath. None spoke up, but a crowd began to gather.

"You think you can just piss in here like some fucking animal?" Domenico grabbed him by the shirt and hoisted him up, only to slam him into a pillar. The slug turned around, only to be met with Domenico's fist again.

"He is an associate sent from Jax's crew," someone finally spoke up.

"Seems Jax needs to teach his shits some fucking manners and what a fucking toilet is," Domenico said before slamming his other fist into the slug's face.

The crowd watched with rapt attention, their bloodthirsty cheers gaining volume. Many of them thrived on the carnage, while I vibrated with anxiety. An out-of-control mob of men with no fear of the law or much respect for rules was worrisome. Domenico always reined them in, but did he have enough presence to stop them?

When the bloodied mess of a man slumped down to the floor, I had my answer. Cries for blood became cheers of victory. The victor stood in the middle, blood dripping from his fists, and when he moved forward, the crowd parted, giving him a wide berth.

He squatted down beside my cage and scratched at his chin. It was the closest his face had been to mine in both the daylight and when I wasn't frozen in fear, and I saw for the first time the depth of the scar that marked his face. With something that deep, there had to be issues, like nerve damage. I studied his features, the way the right side of his mouth failed to draw out as far as the left of his cruel smile.

"See something you like, princess?"

My gaze narrowed on him. "I see something I'd like to give a nice kick in the junk."

His eyes never left mine. "Marco."

My brow scrunched and Marco stepped forward, picked up his knee, and slammed his foot down hard onto the slug's crotch. There were sympathetic groans of pain along with the high-pitched cries of possible damaged goods.

"That wasn't what I was talking about."

"That's all you're going to get. The closest you'll get to my junk is down on your knees when you're swallowing my cock."

"Fuck you," I spat.

The movement of his hand was so swift that I had no time to pull away before his fingers wrapped around my throat and tugged me to the cold metal of the bars.

"Don't tempt me, princess."

He released me with a shove, and I fell back, my hands reaching out to brace my fall.

"Piece of shit," Domenico called out and waited for a response.

There was none—then Marco's leg swung out and impacted with the slug again. "You answer when the boss is talking, roadkill."

"Fucking shit, man! She's just another bitch to sell."

Domenico froze. I couldn't see his face, but the men backing up from around him told me it wasn't a happy expression.

"Who wants to become a made man?" Domenico asked. His tone was calm, cool, and deep. He held everyone's attention, and many of the men dropped down to one knee in front of him. My brow scrunched as the memory of my father doing that to someone flashed in my mind.

The slug's eyes, one of which was almost swollen shut, popped wide. "No, man. I'm sorry. Please!"

"This shit doesn't even understand who you are," Marco said as he stared down at the slug.

"Let me teach him, sir," a younger man the same age as the slug said as he fumbled to pull a gun from the back of his pants. It was the guy I'd toppled over in my escape attempt.

"Not yet, Tito."

Tito nodded, and his head dipped in respect.

Domenico squatted in front of the slug. "You're a disrespectful piece of shit. How you even made it this far, I don't understand. Who are you that Jax would send you here?"

The slug looked away, to the other men, to the ceiling, anywhere but at the man leaning over him. Domenico gave a huff of annoyance, pulled his gun from his waistband, and pressed it against the slug's chest.

"No-nobody. I'm nobody. I just heard this is where the girls were."

"And you thought, what? You'd taste the goods?" Domenico asked.

"They're here to be sold for sex."

"Damaged goods don't fetch as high of a price. If I were to let every man here fuck every girl, we wouldn't make any money."

Did that mean Domenico's words were simply a scare tactic? A way of keeping girls in line with the threat of being used sexually?

"I'm sorry."

Domenico removed his gun and stuffed it back in his waistband before standing. "Get him cleaned up and back to Jax."

"Be grateful la Bestia granted you mercy," Marco said to the slug.

My brow scrunched at the name—the *Beast*. It was fitting.

Once again, the slug's eyes widened and snapped to Domenico. He immediately turned onto his knees, bowing in front of Domenico, arms outstretched on the floor, his head down.

"Forgive me, sir."

"Clean that shit up," Domenico growled, pointing to the puddle of urine. "When you're done and there is no more piss smell, get the fuck out of here and never come back. If you do, no amount of groveling will save you from my bullet."

The man nodded but stayed down until Domenico walked away.

He didn't go far, stopping and kneeling in front of me again as he reached through the bars. His blood-stained fingers gripped my jaw, and when I tried to yank away, he tightened his grip and pulled me closer.

Our eyes were locked, and I was tempted to turn my head and bite him, but at the same time I'd just watched him beat a man to a bloody pulp. What would he do to me?

"Just because I told him all that doesn't mean it doesn't happen. Keep being defiant, and I will break you." His thumb ran across my bottom lip. "I bet you taste like roses and honey."

I didn't break our stare-down. "Can a prisoner at least get a book? I mean, if you're not going to entertain me in any other way…" It was probably not wise to poke him, but I wasn't some weakling he could bend with a few harsh words and threats.

He stared at me before disappearing into his "office" but surprised me when he came back over with a book in his hand.

He let loose a battered and beaten flutter of pages through the top of the cage. It landed in my lap with a thump. The binding was cracked and the worn pages indicated it was a much-read book. The cover wasn't familiar, but it was also scuffed and torn.

A shudder rolled through me at the book's mistreatment, but by the many dog-eared pages, it was much loved.

"Tolstoy?" I asked as I read the author's name. In my hands was one of Tolstoy's greatest novels, and one I could admit I'd never read—*War and Peace*.

I looked up at him but he was back in his shadow, talking to Marco, though his eyes never left me.

I flipped open the pages, happy to have something to read again, since my unfinished book was somewhere in my bag that they'd done who knows what with. I greatly missed reading and was desperate for anything to help get my head out of my present situation.

It wasn't until I was halfway through the first page that I realized it was all in Italian. I blinked when I got stuck on a word. While I did read Italian, I still got tripped up from time to time. What surprised me more was that the book had come from the backpack he'd brought in. There was definitely more to Domenico than I'd believed.

From the corner of my eye I watched the slug clean up his mess. His gaze flashed to me before quickly returning back to his task.

I was the one in the cage, but somehow I almost felt like I was in a higher position than he was. Perhaps it was the price my body carried versus his lowly position on the totem pole. After all, if he was simply an associate, he held no real value to the organization.

Cannon fodder, frontline thug that could have potential, but at that moment I held more value than he did.

I returned to my reading but not before I glanced toward the alcove. I caught Domenico's eyes as he cleaned the blood from his hands. His brow was scrunched up as he stared at me, at the book he'd given me.

I held it up. "Grazie. Non l'ho mai letto." I thanked him for a book I hadn't read.

Marco's eyes widened, and he snapped back to Domenico, whispering hushed words.

They argued, but the few words I caught were neither English nor Italian. None of the men around seemed to understand, returning to whatever they were doing before all the commotion.

I had revealed critical information, even if it was something as simple as knowing another language. But I'd ruffled feathers.

It was becoming more obvious—I wasn't like the other girls they held.

EIGHT

I was watching Domenico pluck another petal from the rose, trying to remember how many that made. Seven? Ten? I could easily remember at least six and the rose still looked full, but that may have been due to its opening up. The rose was dying but it retained its shape, the head beginning to droop.

While I was transfixed by the odd ritual, Roman stepped into view.

"Your dinner is served," he said with a smile.

"Thank you," I replied, returning his smile, taking the plate and setting it down before relieving his hands of not one but two drinks.

"A little something extra," he whispered, giving me a wink before walking away.

Immediately I downed over half the bottle of water. I'd been constantly parched since about day three. Whatever food and drink I was allotted was always just enough to keep me from starving or dehydrating, but only just.

The sandwiches ranged from the terrible bologna and mayo

to ham, cheese, and mustard and other deli concoctions. Which was why I was pleasantly surprised by the tart strawberry jelly and thick, creamy peanut butter.

A small moan left me, and I dug in for another taste.

With each bite, I stared into the darkness, at Domenico. The soft glow of his phone illuminated his face, and when he looked up, I nearly choked on my bite of sandwich. It wasn't a menacing look nor did it inspire horror like it would with a flashlight, but it illuminated his eyes, and the hitch that moved through me was far from fear.

His eyes tore at me, ripped me apart from the inside out as if he knew me, as if he could see my soul. It was intoxicating. There was no way I should have been the least bit attracted to him, but I was. His confidence and ruthlessness matched up perfectly with his chiseled facade.

Every time he'd touched me there was a spark, and he was touching me more and more.

What if he touched me more? Everywhere?

The way he pulled me from my shock, the warmth of his lips against mine as he forced me to drink. His hand on my neck and the roughness of his touch. It was possibly the most intimate thing to ever happen to me, and I didn't want it to end.

A wave of heat rolled through me with that thought, so I turned my attention back to finishing off my sandwich and gulping down the rest of my bottle of water. Roman had also given me a Powerade and a small bag of crackers, which I eagerly dug into. It was the largest meal I'd had in over a week.

I took my time, savoring each small, crunchy bite, the sting of the salt as it melted on my tongue, and the way a stack of two or three would crack and crumble in my mouth.

When there was no more, I let the tart, fruity taste of the Powerade slide over my tongue.

My skin tingled, the familiarity sparking somewhere in my

mind, which was becoming muddy. Silver eyes stared at me, un-blinking. Watching, waiting to strike.

A shiver moved down my spine, sending heat through my fire-laden limbs. There was something else swirling in their depths that made my body sing. A heat that lit me up.

My mind focused on that. On my captor's long, slender fingers. My own danced across my skin as I wondered how they would feel, pulling from the few memories I had.

If it was anything like his gaze, I shuddered at the hard, ap-preciative, and power-filled feeling.

In the back of my mind I wondered if something was wrong with me. My thoughts weren't right, nor was this tingling and desperate desire that crept through my veins with each beat of my heart.

My nipples tightened and my mouth parted, each breath heightening the sensation across my skin.

His eyes flashed away, and his jaw clenched. Sound filtered in, but I had a hard time focusing on the whispered words.

"Split her open…see what she looks like from the inside."

I couldn't pinpoint where they came from, only the soft clarity of them. There was a dark chuckle.

"Tap that shit until she's airtight."

Airtight? Will whoever she is blow up like a balloon and float away?

If I hold my breath, will that happen to me?

I couldn't seem to focus on anything. Half a sentence, the cool air across my skin, Domenico's eyes.

Domenico's fire-filled eyes that showed the beast within.

I wanted him.

The beast.

Did I?

Why?

I wetted my lips, wishing I had something to drink. *What happened to that bottle Roman gave me?*

I scanned around my cage, lightly touching the blanket beside me, its normally coarse fabric setting off every nerve. A shudder rolled through me, and I rocked, a moan slipping between my lips, my clit pressing against something hard.

What was I looking for?

Oh, the bottle.

It sat on its side on the dirty floor, empty and making my thirst grow. My eyes were heavy when I looked up. Domenico still stared and my fingers flitted across my chest, imagining they were his hands.

It was a thought that should have disgusted me. Domenico was a godlike figure, and his assertive nature, combined with the way he watched me, was oddly appealing.

I was so thirsty. Where did my drink go?

I pulled my sweater over my head, my breath speeding up, and I bit down on my lower lip.

Domenico stared at me, and I watched anger and lust and other emotions cross his face.

The whispers were there, talking about fucking the girl until she broke. Poor girl, whoever she was.

Domenico's expression hardened and he disappeared deep into the darkness.

A minute later a growl erupted from deep in the shadows, and Domenico burst into the low light.

Finally.

With each heavily placed footfall the need for him grew. I leaned back, my eyes never leaving him, pinching my nipple over my shirt between two fingers.

Yes.

There was a cacophony of sounds around me—men talking, some cheering—but all I could hear was the beat of my heart and the clang of the lock turning. I could *feel everything* and wanted only one thing.

Of all the men who came and went, only one had me in his clutches. Hypnotized by his eyes, humbled by his command, and left craving the warmth of his touch.

But the man before me was la Bestia in all his furious glory. Fear pumped through me, and I pulled away when he reached for me.

There was no avoiding him, and I was yanked to my feet and pulled through the door. The concussive wave that pulsed through me upon contact with his chest left my knees weak. I couldn't make sense of where my limbs were.

He spun me in his arms, back to chest, and my head fell against his shoulder. One arm was wrapped around my waist, holding me up, and the other gripped my jaw so that I was looking straight at ten men.

They all had the look in their eyes, the one I'd seen so many times from the stage, the one I'd seen in the eyes of my father's guards, the one that wanted to tear me apart for their own sexual gratification.

"Ella seems to want to give you a show."

His hands. *His hands.*

A moan slipped from my lips when Domenico's fingers slipped between my jeans and my flesh, not stopping until he was cupping my pussy. I shuddered in his arms.

I could hear everything but make nothing of it. Every neuron was focused on his touch.

A loud moan left me when he pinched my clit before sliding down my slit and roughly shoving his fingers inside. My whole body convulsed at the overwhelming sensation. I was so wet for him, so ready to be filled by him.

"This is for your own good," he whispered in my ear. A shudder rolled through me at his gruff voice so close, every nerve lighting up.

My mind whirled, trying to understand. Not just him, but my response. How could this be good for me?

But I wanted it. I wanted *him.*

To take me, to fuck me with all the power that flowed through him.

"If I don't, they will." *If he doesn't, they will what?*

He seemed to answer my unspoken question.

I chanced a glance over to our audience, at their hungry eyes devouring me. They all wished they were him. I knew the world, the way those men thought. They were bottom-feeders, and they destroyed everything thrown at them.

They wanted me, but la Bestia had me.

He walked us over to the table, and each step ignited me further. My eyes threatened to roll back as my breath came out in pants.

A groan of displeasure left me when his fingers retreated.

"No," I whimpered. I needed his touch, his hands, to help with the fire that was spreading through me. Only he could put it out—I just knew it.

He spun me around and picked me up before dumping me on the table. His fingers worked my button and zipper, then yanked my jeans from me, throwing them on the ground.

I never stopped watching him. I heard the others, felt their eyes, but none of it could take me from him.

A growl left him as he fisted my panties and pulled. The force lifted me before the fabric tore. He grabbed my leg and dragged me to the end of the table. Each unintended swipe across my skin only charged me more, my mind completely consumed.

I barely noticed him pressing in when my whole body exploded. My eyes were wide, back arched as he thrust into me without mercy. I was coming hard around him. The ruthlessness of his possession only drew it out into a never-ending spiral.

The situation was all wrong. The man above me was wrong, but every millimeter that our skin touched sent my whole body reeling with pleasure.

I choked on a sob, my body rocking with each thrust of his hips. He felt so good.

He bunched up my tank top and yanked it off. One hand gripped my breast hard.

The minions cheered him on in the background. I could hear them egging on their leader to hurt me more, to fuck me hard. To break me.

And I did break. If just for that moment, I did. Every touch was an explosion, every thrust setting off a bomb from the inside.

My mind was overwhelmed, consumed by the desire for him to never stop. I was coming again and again. There was nothing left of my mind. Just a sack of flesh and bones lost in a sea of never-ending lust.

His hand moved up and gripped my neck. Our eyes met, and I couldn't look away, mesmerized by the fire that burned back at me.

He let out a roar, his teeth bared as his hips slammed against mine a final time. My skin still tingled, but I couldn't move, completely spent.

After a moment or two he pulled out. A whimper left me, desperate to have him touch me again.

"She's mine," Domenico yelled out to the room. The sound reverberated off the blank walls, deep and sharp at the same time, and it made many of the men jump. "Nobody touches her but me. If you don't understand or you forget, I will remind you."

My head lolled to the side. There were smiles and cheers, but there were also frowns. In the back, bright-blue eyes I knew so well morphed into pure hatred, in total contrast to the rest of the group.

I blinked, slowly, then again.

Roman was gone.

The cold began to seep in, my skin slick with sweat as exhaustion blanketed me. My eyes drifted closed just before Domenico's strong arms slipped under me and carried me away.

NINE

ighting the sleep in my eyes was hard. My mind was foggy, weighed down. Something said it was better to sleep, but something else nagged at me.

As I surfaced, the nagging began to slowly become apparent. From the pounding that turned into a thumping in my head, to the nerves firing off around my body and the cold that was seeping into my skin, it all paled to the ache between my legs.

The putrid smell of decay filled my senses as I roused, ever the reminder that I was nothing more than a caged animal.

As my senses awakened, cold seeped down to the bone. Cracking an eye open, I found that I was lying naked atop the grimy mattress. The blanket was haphazardly lying across my body. It shielded little and warmed almost nothing.

When my eyes were able to focus, there was only one thing in my view. His silver eyes stared at me, and their shiny surface gave nothing away.

The memories were sluggish and fuzzy, but two things were

obvious in the light of day: I'd been drugged at some point—just before my captor had had sex with me.

I'd used ecstasy once before and understood what I'd been given. Understood the sex that I'd had with Domenico had been chemically heightened. I could deny the truth all I wanted, but it didn't change the fact that sex with him was the best I'd ever had—chemically induced or not.

Still, questions whirled through my mind, and I wondered if it was a mercy. Why had he drugged me? So that I wouldn't remember? But then he should have just given me ketamine or one of the other multiple date-rape concoctions out there if he was going to drug me. Did he want my struggles as much as my surrender? He wanted me desperate for his touch, but why? To feed his own ego, to make what was happening easier on me, or simply to entertain the men watching?

He took me. Held my thighs open.

And I wanted it.

I was practically begging him.

To scratch the itch that consumed me, all because I'd been drugged.

I sat up, a groan leaving me, and pulled the blanket tighter around me.

Where were my clothes?

I looked around and located my jeans, sweater, tank top, and bra—and then the memory of Domenico ripping my thong from me answered where that was.

"Grab your clothes," Domenico said from the door.

I scrambled to pick them up, making sure my blanket was secure around my body. Not that everyone in the room hadn't already seen me naked, but it was also cold. The second I was at the door, his fingers were wrapped around my arm.

"Don't try anything," he warned.

"Or what?"

He didn't answer me. Instead, he pulled me away from the cage toward a door I'd seen him go into from time to time in the opposite corner of his beloved dark alcove.

My bare feet stung with each unprotected step.

The room was large, barren, but held as much trepidation as the main room. Shackles hung, bolted to the wall. A mattress lay in the center. It was at least covered in clean sheets.

A stool and a lamp were all that remained, except for a large steel tub that sat near the small window.

"What's this?"

"A shower." He took my clothes, then ripped the blanket from me.

I expected him to peruse my body, but that cold detachment I'd so often seen was at the forefront. What he was doing was simply another task.

"Get in," he commanded.

I stepped forward, my eyes surveying the tub and everything connected to it—a hose at the bottom for drainage and a second hose that connected to a pipe with a pull chain and a showerhead.

An ice bath was very much not wanted, and I hesitated to pull the chain. There was a spritz of cold that made me jump before it quickly changed over to warm. The water burned my cool skin, and a loud gasp left me. I didn't know how they were heating it, but there was only one temperature level, and it was hot.

I let it soak in before picking up the tiny bit of soap that he handed me.

"Am I leaving now?" I asked as I spread the small sliver of soap around my body.

"Why would you ask that?"

"Because this is better than a sponge bath." I let the water rain down again, loving the scorching burn. "You tasted the goods, so I figured that was it."

"You're staying right where you are." His presence was

imposing, and I flinched when he stepped to stand in front of me. "Clean pussy is more enjoyable." His hand slipped between my legs, and my eyes went wide as I slapped and pushed against him.

"What the hell do you—"

His fingers pressed deeper, and I drew in a hard breath. My fingers clenched against his chest, and I drew in a ragged breath, hating myself each second that I didn't hate his touch.

"Make sure you clean out here real good." He leaned down, his lips inches from mine. "I came hard and deep. Wouldn't want you to get fucked up with my kid, huh?"

I shook my head, my eyes never leaving his. "Wouldn't happen."

"Why not?"

"IUD." Before I'd left my father's, I'd gotten a birth control implant. I didn't want to take the risk of getting pregnant.

"Smart stripper."

I narrowed my eyes at him. "You know nothing."

"Mi sorprendi."

I'd surprised him? "What?"

"Non molte puttane sono bilingui."

My eyes widened, and I wanted to reach out and slap him. *Not many whores are bilingual.*

"If you think that's impressive, you should see the three others I know. My home library is filled with them."

"You mean your stacks of books that lie strewn about that shithole you call an apartment?"

My stomach sank. He'd been to my home, violated my one and only sanctuary. "It's a roof over my head that I pay for."

"Scoprirò I tuoi segreti."

He wanted my secrets. I'd given too much away.

"Quali segreti?" I pulled on the chain again and he stepped back to avoid the spray, his eyes never leaving mine.

There wasn't a lot of water, and it wasn't as good as the

shower in my apartment, but it was much better than the limited sponge bath. With only Domenico in the room, there was another level of privacy in the room than in my cage.

He handed me a towel, and I twisted my hair to wring out as much water as I could. The warmth had already been zapped away by the cold air.

Sadly, my newly cleaned skin went right back into my grimy clothes. Still, it was better than the alternative.

At least I knew I wasn't going anywhere yet.

Domenico stepped in front of me and reached out. I flinched, stepping back, but it wasn't enough to be out of his reach. However, it wasn't my arm he was grabbing for. My brow furrowed in confusion as I stared at him. His thumb rested on my jaw and his fingers wrapped around the back of my neck.

His touch did what it always did and sent heat spiraling through me. The drugs were out of my system, so I couldn't blame the feelings on them.

He pulled me forward, our mouths inches apart, bodies pressed together, and I watched the ice melt in his eyes. His nostrils flared with each hard breath.

Every muscle was frozen, eyes wide as I tried to figure out what he was doing. A split second and his lips were pressed to mine. My lips parted to gasp as the feeling of lightning shot through me. A low growl rumbled in his chest, and his kiss moved from soft to demanding. His thumb parted my jaw more, his tongue brushing against mine.

I was caught between melting into it and kicking him in the balls. So, I compromised. I relished the softness of his lips, the tingling sensation his tongue created, but then I took his bottom lip between my teeth and bit down. Hard.

"Fuck," he cursed as he stepped back. The fire that burned in his eyes after that was no longer desire, but anger. "Not the best idea, princess."

I hated when he called me that, a sneer on his lips when he did.

I didn't back down from his glare. His hand shot out again, but he didn't take hold of my neck. His fingers dug into my upper arm as he pulled me out of the room and practically tossed me back into the cage.

After slamming the door and locking it, he moved to the rose and pulled another petal. I let out a sigh as I once again tried to comprehend the meaning behind it. Asking its significance would do no good, as there was no way he would ever tell me.

A plate of food awaited me, and I stared at it warily. My gaze moved to Domenico, but he wasn't looking.

Was that how I'd been drugged? Would it happen again?

I found my socks and slipped them on, then wrapped my blankets completely around me in an attempt to push the chill from my bones.

I ignored the food and sat there, trying to forget the night before. How I behaved, how much I wanted him. Trying to forget the feel of his lips on mine.

I didn't want that. He took me without my consent. It may have seemed like I wanted it, but that wasn't me—that was the drugs.

"…ella, get in here," my father's voice boomed out, echoing around the walls.

I slammed the door shut and stomped my four-inch heels toward my father's office. The foyer was two stories tall, and when I made it to the foot of the stairs, his guards, his underlings, gathered and parted to let him through.

"What?"

He looked at me, his lips curling up into a snarl. "Where do you think you're going dressed like that?"

"A party." I turned to leave but was stopped by a hand clasped around my wrist. My father held me tight as his guards circled around us. I glared at each one of them. They weren't going to stop me. I'd flirted with most of them, teased them, to get my way in the past, and I would do it again.

"You want to act like a whore?" my father asked, anger emanating from him.

"How dare you!" I spat back.

His arm swung out and I spun, nearly falling down. Pain radiated from my cheek, and tears filled my eyes. Two of the guards caught me and got me standing again.

"Have you fucked them all yet? Teased them with your body?" my father sneered. He stepped forward, his fists clenching onto the fabric of my dress. The sound of the fabric giving way, ripping apart in his hands, echoed around the walls.

My breasts were exposed, but he kept going all the way through the hem. Even that wasn't enough. He pulled the fragments of fabric from my shoulders, leaving me in only my thong.

I covered my chest with my arms, but he swatted them away.

"You wanted to be a whore, to show your body off. Let them look. That's what you want, isn't it?"

I clenched my teeth, trying not to show him that he affected me. "I'm not a whore."

"Your behavior is not acceptable. You will stop this defiance, or you won't like the consequences."

"You can't control me. I will fuck whomever I want, and you can't stop me."

Fire rolled in his eyes, and his arm swung out again. I stumbled to the ground a second time but wasn't there long when he fisted my hair and pulled me up. I reached back, a cry leaving me as I tried to get him to release me.

"*You will fall into line,*" he hissed before fisting my thong and ripping that from me.

A scream left me, and he slapped my breast before squeezing it. I cried out in pain.

His nostrils were flared, eyes wide, drunk off his power over me. I'd never seen him so angry, and I knew I'd pushed him to the brink.

"*I will fucking break you if you keep this up.*"

"*I'd like to see you try,*" I spat back. What I expected was another blow to the face, maybe being thrown to the floor.

His hand between my thighs, fingers shoved inside me, was never a path I foresaw.

"*How many dicks have you had up here? More than you can count? Should I just give you to the men and let them keep you? Nothing more than a toy to play with.*"

"*Let me go!*"

He removed his hand and released me, glaring at me with such contempt. "*Don't you ever disrespect me in this manner again, Daughter. If you're not good, I'll sell you. Now go get ready in something respectable, and maybe I'll forgive you.*" He stormed out of the entry.

I stood there, trembling, shielding my private areas with my hands as tears streamed down my face.

My eyes snapped open and my heart slammed in my chest. A couple of blinks and my vision cleared. Darkness surrounded me.

I sat up, searching for the usual group of men, but there were only a couple I could find asleep in chairs. Fire still burned in one of the barrels, and there was a light on at the other end of the space, creating a soft glow.

I drew in a sharp breath and snapped my head to the side. Everything was quiet, but I could still feel someone watching me. Deep in the black, I knew silver eyes were trained on me. Watching. Plotting.

But what did they want? Why was I still trapped in my iron cell? It had been days since he touched me, days since my shower.

The dream was the memory of the moment that changed the course of my life. It was humiliating and made my first time on stage, stripping my clothes off in front of Al, easy. Having my clothes ripped from me when I was on my way out to a party while my father called me a whore, that was worse. Not a single employee stepped in to help me. Instead, they all watched.

My father had violated me. Touched me in a way no father should, all for a show of power. In that moment, I knew I had to get out. In that moment, I realized I had nothing to offer but the way my body moved.

I had a taste of freedom, even though I knew I would never be free of them. A normal life could never be mine. No boring nine-to-five job because I had no real papers for my fake name, no skills or much education past high school. I graduated and finished almost a full year of college, that was all.

No husband, kids, and a white picket fence for me.

The dream only showed me the parallel of my current situation.

I was a spoiled brat who used my sexuality as a way to get what I wanted. It was stupid and just me acting out. It was the only outlet I had, the crushing weight of my father's control leaving me no other way.

I was trapped, held captive in a palace built from death. A gilded cage.

Tears welled in my eyes, and I blinked them back.

I lay back down to try to get back to sleep, praying I wouldn't have another dream.

A shrill scream echoed off the walls as I stared up at the ceiling. I sat straight up, taking a second to make sure the sound wasn't coming from me.

TEN

High-pitched wails, sounds of begging and pleading, rang around the empty walls, and the few men were suddenly on high alert. All except Domenico.

My chest hurt at the sound because I knew, I just knew. There was about to be one less empty cage.

Another girl abducted from the streets.

One associate was carrying a lantern, lighting the path as Roman and two other men carried the struggling girl up the stairs. I hadn't seen Roman since he'd given me dinner that night, the night Domenico claimed me. His eyes locked with mine before quickly looking away.

I swallowed hard. Was he ashamed of what I'd done? How I had reacted to Domenico? I remembered the anger in his eyes.

"Shut her up!" Domenico yelled from the darkness.

My hands were white-knuckled on the bars as I watched them throw her into a cage a few down from my own. Her eyes were wide, tears streaming as she begged to be let go.

"No! No! Please!" Hiccupping sobs rang out as she drew in

ragged breaths, her words heavily accented. "Help! Somebody help!"

The group who dragged her in washed their hands of her once she was in the cage. I noticed Roman's gaze locked on her. Doing this wasn't something he was equipped for. I could only imagine that her screams were tearing him up.

After a few minutes her cries had yet to subside, and Domenico was forced from his lair. He stomped past me, his jaw locked tight. Every man he passed shrank back, even the strong ones. Nobody wanted to be in la Bestia's path when he was on a rampage.

Feet before her cage, he pulled the gun from his waistband and pulled the slide before aiming it at her.

"Shut the fuck up!" he growled. "Or I will fucking shut you up."

The girl cowered and her sobs became strangled gasps as she began to hyperventilate. I had sobbed for hours after I'd woken, screamed and screamed, but nobody had threatened me or told me to shut up. I hadn't even been sure anyone was there, but she'd only been going off for a short period of time when Domenico lost his composure.

"Yesli ty ne uspokoish'sya, ya pozvolyu im iznasilovat' tebya."

My eyes widened as I translated his Russian. *If you don't quiet, I will let them rape you.* Another scare tactic?

Looking around the room, I saw many of the men had scrunched foreheads as they whispered between them. All except Roman.

None of the men knew Russian.

The girl continued to cry, begging.

"Ya pokazhu tebe," he said before he stomped back over to my cage.

He wanted her to see, and as he turned the key in the lock, I knew he was going to use me to show her.

"Get out here," he growled.

I blinked at him.

"Don't make me fucking come in there to get you."

His hand wrapped around my wrist, and I hated the warmth that spread.

"Ty sobirayesh'sya nasilovat' menya seychas?"

Are you going to rape me now?

His nostrils flared.

"Ya budu trakhat' tvoi sekrety ot tebya," he spit through clenched teeth.

I will fuck your secrets from you.

I heard the girl gasp in horror, understanding every word. "Nyet!" she cried out.

He pulled me out and walked me to the table. It was closer to her, and he wanted to make a point, to assert his threats as truth. He pushed on my back, pinning me to the table as he ripped my jeans down my hips. Heat rushed through me, unbidden.

I struggled against him to prove I wasn't just going to give up, that he hadn't broken anything in me. I wanted to kick him, to hit him.

But maybe he had broken something inside me, because my pulse had picked up, and that fire coursed through me and settled between my thighs, desperate for more.

The head of his cock pressed against me and then he thrust in. I cried out, revealing at the very least that no matter how much I wanted to protest, I was also desperate to feel more of his brand of savagery. After all, I was already wet, ready for him from only a heated gaze and a few verbal volleys. With just a few strokes he was slamming all the way in, and my eyes were rolling back.

A growl erupted as he gripped my ass before slapping his hand across the flesh there.

His hand slid up and gripped the back of my neck as he leaned over, his lips close to my ear.

"Vashe telo pokazyvayet slishkom mnogo."

Your body reveals too much.

I turned to glare at him, my teeth bared. "Idi trakhni sebya."

Go fuck yourself.

His grip moved around my neck to the front, and he pulled, bending me back as his hips pummeled my ass. I was lost in each hit to my G-spot, crying out in pleasure.

The girl was crying, pleading with him to stop. My chest clenched at her worry for me, but I was more worried about her.

She was the first girl to arrive in all the time I'd been there, and I honestly didn't know if they would touch her or not. With the hungry looks in their eyes, the way they circled her like a pack of wolves closing in on their prey, I feared for her.

"Vy khotite eto, nuzhno eto."

"Nyet," I lied, my body betraying me. I did want him, need him, just as he said.

His fingers tightened and my eyes rolled back as a shudder moved through me.

"Ty moy."

You're mine.

A shudder moved through me. I tried to play off my hatred for the control he had over me, but I couldn't lie to myself. And what was worse…

He knew.

As much as I said I hated it, as much as I said I didn't want it, he was right—ty moy. I was his.

Only he had claim of me. My life was his. My body was his.

For now.

The girl finally quieted down, her sobs becoming muted whimpers, and Domenico pulled out.

"Back to fucking work," he growled, then grabbed my arm. His cock was still out, still hard, and he threw me over his shoulder. He headed to the room with the bed, his fingers slipping into my pussy before he slapped my ass and gripped the flesh.

We passed the threshold, and he threw me onto the bed. He reached down and tugged my jeans the rest of the way off, then his shirt.

My eyes widened at the ink that covered his skin. Red. Black. Blood and death. Skull, lion, rose—symbols of who he was.

He pressed my thighs down to the side against the mattress.

Our eyes were locked, and I couldn't hide it anymore, couldn't lie, because he saw right through me. Each time he slammed in I cried out, my body tensing. He picked up the pace, a relentless, unforgiving thrust that took my breath away. The force of his thrusts sent goose bumps across every inch of my skin and rocked my body with the magnitude of an earthquake.

I couldn't stop it, couldn't slow it down. There were no drugs in my system to blame it on. He could feel it, too, the way I tightened around him.

His teeth nipped at my bottom lip before pressing his lips to mine. A small moan I tried to hold in crawled out. He moved to rest his head in the crook of my neck. I didn't even notice I'd wrapped my arms around him until he held me so tight I could barely breathe.

I felt a light scrape of his teeth just below my ear. I cried out, my whole body tensing as his teeth sank in. Not hard enough to break skin, but enough that every muscle snapped, and I convulsed in his arms as I came.

"Fuck," he hissed as his hips pinned me to the bed.

Every twitch could be felt, every groan drawing out my orgasm. He kissed and licked the spot where he'd marked me as he regained his breath. When he pulled back, I expected to see a sated man, relaxed and happy, but that wasn't what I got.

Domenico's eyes were on fire, and with each second his relaxed muscles began to tense again. His expression was unreadable—he never gave away more than he wanted to.

I held back a moan when he pulled back and slipped out, suddenly missing that connection. It was the only thing that gave me any good feelings in this shit of an existence I was living.

"Don't trust Roman," Domenico said as he pulled up his pants, his fingers deftly buttoning them.

I swung my legs over the edge of the bed and shifted my shirt back over my breasts, pulling the stretched-out collar up my shoulder. The floor held my jeans, twisted and torn. If it wasn't for the fact they were the only thing I had to wear, I wouldn't put them back on. Domenico had shredded my underwear, leaving me with no choice but to slide the grimy denim up my legs.

"Why?" I asked as I wiped up the mess he'd made with the sheet.

"He's not what you think he is."

I turned and stared at him, those silver eyes so intense it caused a hitch in my breath.

"He doesn't violate women."

Domenico's eyes widened, his jaw tensing.

"Trust me, princess, I'm not doing this for the pleasure," he hissed, his eyes darting around.

We were alone, the others having retreated when he'd dragged me in the room—an invisible barrier that kept them out—their entertainment over.

I pulled my jeans up, noticing how loose they'd become. "What does that mean?"

Voices trickled in, getting closer. He grabbed my arm and pulled me to the wall, where he closed the shackles around my wrists.

I stared at them, then at him. It threw me, and I didn't have time to react until I was trapped.

"Stay," he said.

My jaw clenched, and I glared at his back as he disappeared through the doorway. The cold began to soak in with nothing extra to help insulate.

Raised voices drew my attention back to the door. My whole body jolted at the bang of a gun firing, followed by screams of agony.

Domenico appeared, his jaw locked tight, eyes alight in anger, his gun at his side.

"Did you just shoot someone?" I asked.

He didn't look at me, but he did set his gun down on the dust-covered table.

"Cosa mi stai facendo?" It was barely a whisper, but I heard it.

What are you doing to me?

Days passed and I spent half the time chained up, and the other half in the cage. The time that Domenico was gone shrank day by day, especially after the arrival of the Russian girl. She quieted down after Domenico's threat and subsequent fucking of me.

Still, I heard the whispers, the plans.

Domenico's possession of my body became daily, and I hated that I came every single time. He was aggressive and dominating, and every thrust of his hips was a shot of pleasure through me. Each press of his teeth into my neck had me convulsing around him. He knew just what to do to get me off, and he was merciless about it. But, in the quiet of my mind, I couldn't deny he was right—he was my god and he'd masterfully taken control of my body.

It was the most powerful fucking I'd ever had. I hated to even admit to myself how I got wet just looking at him.

The temperature dropped to the point that even the men were complaining. Gas-powered space heaters were brought in. A small one was set up near my cage, and I reveled in the warmth. It was much like sitting in front of a fire. Part of my body remained cold, but overall it was the warmest I'd been in weeks.

And it had been weeks. The pile of petals at the base of the rose amounted to more than were left on the drying flower.

The new girl didn't have a rose, which I found odd, but not as odd as when I awoke to find her gone.

"Where is she?" I asked. I expected to receive the usual silence, but someone spoke up.

"Sold," Tito replied, earning a glare from Marco.

Sold. She had no rose and had been sold off in days.

My own holding became more and more mysterious. There was something else at work, something different about my capture.

Did they know who I was? Was it all a power play, a way to break me? No. Domenico had claimed me, which afforded me security because nobody would cross him.

Roman's eyes were dark when he delivered my food, and he seemed angry.

"Thank you," I said, as I always did.

His hand shot through the bars and wrapped around my wrist. "You're not special."

My heart sped up and my brow furrowed. It was a move I wasn't used to with him, aggressive with none of his usual gentleness. "What?"

His expression faltered, losing the edge. "To him."

I opened my mouth to ask what he meant when suddenly he cried out, his hand releasing me.

Domenico stood next to him, hand around Roman's bicep, digging in.

"You don't touch what's mine, Roman. *Ever.*"

A chill rolled through me as they glared at each other. Roman was being defiant, unwilling to back down. It was a characteristic I had never seen in him before, and I began to heed Domenico's warning.

ELEVEN

I wasn't sure how many petals a rose held, but I guessed somewhere between thirty and fifty. More than half the petals were gone, and I began to wonder what would happen when the last petal fell.

A pit formed in my stomach as I looked at the number of men. Something had shifted and Domenico's crew had either surged in membership, or they were all converging on that building.

Most of them were familiar faces that I'd at least seen before, but out of the more than twenty men around, there were one or two I didn't recognize.

All day I'd watched, listened, and waited. Even Marco seemed on edge as he sent men out on different jobs. Domenico had been gone for almost the whole day, and I vibrated without him near.

The increase of testosterone had led to a few scuffles, and my anxiety increased as the day progressed. There was a safety I'd begun to feel with Domenico, but when he wasn't around I felt a darkness stirring.

He arrived late in the afternoon, but if it wasn't for the scar,

I wasn't sure I would have immediately recognized him. Gone were the jeans and leather jacket. In their stead was a perfectly fitted gray three-piece suit.

A suit that looked deliciously good on him, and I couldn't help but stare.

He didn't look happy, and he glared at me as he pulled at his tie. I blinked back, trying to figure out why, and a sinking feeling settled. A glance over to the rose showed the decimated remnants of a once vivid and bright flower.

I wasn't imagining the shift. It wasn't an overexaggeration of paranoid thoughts.

Marco tried talking to Domenico, but he seemed to only half listen, his attention focused on me.

A few minutes later he was still in his suit as he pulled me from my cage. "Come on."

I didn't pause, didn't take my time. I was desperate for the security I felt for some reason in his arms. For him to soothe the anxiety that surged through my veins and replace it with the fire only he could.

"Get to fucking work!" he yelled out before dragging me toward the corner room.

I looked back to the group of men. Some dispersed, but just before I lost sight of them, blue eyes locked onto mine.

A shiver rolled down my spine as Roman stared at me, one side of his mouth twisted up.

What was that about?

I bit down on my finger, head back as high-pitched moans slipped from my lips.

The world disappeared. The room long gone. All that was

left was the man slamming into me and the pleasure he filled me with. A keening sound left me from the pleasure that spiked from his teeth digging into my shoulder. Another mark to add to the others that peppered my skin.

He gripped my jaw and pulled my mouth to his. His kisses were always soft yet demanding and soul devouring as he took the breath from me.

Loud bangs and yells pulled me from the trance he always put me in. I watched as clarity returned to his eyes, a grumble of anger audible as he glanced over his shoulder.

"Fuck," he hissed before abruptly pulling out and standing.

I began to admire his mostly naked form when the sounds of fist on flesh filtered in.

He quickly stepped into jeans he pulled from his bag. "Stand," he commanded as he slipped a shirt on. There was no time to dress myself as he tugged on my arm and pulled me to the wall. My eyes widened when he picked up the shackles that were anchored into the wall and wrapped one around my wrist, then the other. I was left standing there with only a short lead of a few feet.

"Stay," he said in a low growl before gripping my chin again for a harsh kiss.

It wasn't my first time in the shackles, but it was my first time naked in them.

The commotion ebbed and flowed, the noise level crescendoing up again, and the anger rose in Domenico. He tossed a pillow my way and pulled on his shirt as he walked out.

"What the *fuck* is going on out here?" he yelled.

The noise stopped before erupting again.

The testosterone level was dangerously high, and my heart thumped in anxiety. At least they couldn't see me where I was.

I couldn't hear much from the other room except the occasional string of words from Domenico when his anger showed through. But the pit formed in my stomach again.

While standing felt good, the lack of movement wasn't comfortable. Being that it was bound to be a while before he returned, I grabbed the pillow with my toes and brought it closer before sitting on it. The position left my arms hanging in the air and my body exposed.

A chill moved through me, and I hissed when my skin hit the cold plaster.

I couldn't tell how much time had passed, but my fingers were going numb from the combination of cold and them hanging in the air. Another shiver moved through me, and my teeth began to chatter when Domenico's voice came from right outside the open doorway.

"Then give them a task. Send them on searches. Half the reason she is the only one is because nobody is doing their damn job. They are sitting there, fucking around, eye-fucking her and not doing shit. There are three times as many people hanging around here, which is gaining attention. Cut down on the crew and send the rest to guard the incoming shipment. Just get them the fuck out of here."

"How many?" Marco asked.

"Seventy-five percent."

"That's a lot, Dom."

Their voices lowered, and I missed some of what they were saying before I heard a voice that was clearly Marco's.

"I'll get it done," Marco assured.

"Good."

A shuffle of feet and Domenico appeared in front of me, alone. I watched as the anger rippled through him, transforming into a brutal lust as he stared at me. My heartbeat picked up with each step he took, a combination of turned on and frightened. He tugged at the button and zipper on his jeans, his still-hard cock slipping free, a hiss leaving him.

I moved to stand, but his hand on my shoulder kept me

down. His cock jumped, the tip brushing against my lips, leaving a swipe of precum on my lips.

His nostrils flared, jaw tight, his touch gentle as he caressed my cheek before moving down my jaw. The tip of his thumb hooked onto my chin, and I let my mouth drop open.

In all the times he'd fucked me, he'd never had me suck him like he'd threatened that first night. By the look in his eyes he was beyond reason or care, desperate to release the mounting tension inside him.

I slipped my tongue out and brushed it against the deep-red tip before closing my lips around it, getting my first taste of his cum. A low groan left him, growing and morphing with each inch down I moved.

Halfway was all he could take. Too slow, too teasing, and no release.

The move took me by surprise, my eyes popping wide, gagging as he pushed my head down. I wasn't ready, and he gave me little respite. I pulled at the chains in an attempt to move back just a little, but he held my head in place as he pulled his cock from my mouth, then plunged it back in. When I made it down to the base he held me there, his breath harsh.

I drew in one lungful of air before he plunged back in, thrusting as if it would cure the madness that drove him. Using me as he always did.

All the way, forcing his way down my throat, he held himself there for a beat, a roar leaving him as his cock jumped, firing off straight down into my stomach. He convulsed above me before retreating, drops continuing to leak onto my tongue as I drew in much-needed air.

He stared down at me, both of us breathing hard, but said nothing.

I was curious about what had happened, but I knew he wouldn't tell me anything. The rare snippets of secrets he told me continued to be obscure and riddle-like.

He tucked himself back away, then released my arms. The muscles burned when released, and I cringed in pain.

Silver eyes never left me as I slowly stood and walked over to where my clothes, or the remnants of my clothes, had fallen when he pulled them from me. I knew the drill. Back in the cage.

Maybe I'd become adjusted to this semi-life, or maybe I just understood the rules better. Escaping was a dream that I was losing faith in ever happening. I thought maybe I could get help from Roman, but Domenico's warning rang out whenever Roman did anything for me. Then there was the look he gave me. Just the memory of it sent a shiver down my spine.

It could have been Domenico's words or me opening my eyes to the charismatic man who seemed to have a growing loyalty within the crew, but I had a feeling Roman was the source of the strife brewing.

TWELVE

I n the days that followed, I spent more time out of my cage and chained up close to Domenico. The atmosphere held more tension than usual, even with fewer men.

The rumble beneath the surface was obviously unusual, especially because I'd seen both the fear and reverence for la Bestia. The atmosphere created a buzzing in my veins, an anxiety of what would happen when it came to a head.

Domenico entered the room carrying a box. It was evident by the flex of his muscles that it had some heft. It clanged when he dropped it to the ground near me.

"What's that?" I asked, but as usual I received no response.

A groan left me when he released my arms from the shackles, but when I stood, he pulled me to a stool and sat me down. He handed me a sandwich and drink that were sitting on top of the box, then stepped to the doorway. It was just a blink that he wasn't watching, a blink that I was fractionally free, but with a small window and no level of real strength, there was no use even thinking about escape.

Instead, I tried to enjoy my sandwich. At least it was a fruit punch Powerade, my favorite. I savored each sip of sweetness.

He stepped back in, but he wasn't alone. A man littered with tattoos was in step behind him, a large case in his hand.

I looked between the two men in confusion, watching as the man silently opened the case and began pulling items out. The last was in pieces, but I recognized it immediately.

It was a tattoo machine.

My heart began to pound as he set up a light and plugged it and the machine into the extension cord that the only other light was plugged into.

"What are you doing?" I asked as alarm crept in.

Had the day finally come? Was I getting a number or some other identifying marker? After so long, I'd almost forgotten that I was simply goods to be sold to the highest bidder, no matter Domenico's claim.

Domenico stepped behind me and pulled back the stretched-out collar of my sweater, exposing my collarbone. He kept his hand on my shoulder, holding the fabric back.

"There?" the man asked for verification.

"Yes."

The man nodded, then slipped on some gloves. He splashed some liquid—maybe rubbing alcohol or just water or something else, I didn't know—on my skin, cleaning the spot.

The buzzing of the machine made me jump, and I pulled back, but Domenico stopped me. He wrapped his arm under my chin and held me tight against his chest, my head unable to move.

The man's eyes met mine, then looked to Domenico, but he said nothing. Instead, he dipped the tip in ink and leaned forward.

He met my eyes again. "Don't move. Please."

My hands were in white-knuckled fists on my thighs. I was trying to regulate my breathing when the buzz of the machine sounded just below my ear.

The sting of the shallow area was low, but each swipe of dry paper towel was like sandpaper across the newly punctured skin. He used no stencil, free-handing. I tried to focus on the movement, to figure out what he was doing and blot out the pain, but it was more fluid than the harsh lines of numbers I'd anticipated.

It didn't take long for him to finish, and with a final swipe he cleared any overflow of ink. That towel was wet and felt so good as it moved across my aggravated flesh.

"You're mine now," Domenico growled against my ear.

My brow scrunched, and then the man who'd tattooed me held up a mirror. My appearance shocked me. Weeks of poor nutrition had thinned out my face and my body. My hair was a rat's nest of tangles, greasy and knotted (despite my limited efforts), with some of the natural shine missing. Dark circles sat under my eyes, and a light layer of dirt was smudged all over my skin. No matter how hard I tried to bathe, a bucket sponge bath was no substitute for a shower. Even with the makeshift shower I was occasionally allowed, it simply wasn't enough.

The only clean patch of skin was where he'd cleaned off my right clavicle. The skin there was red from irritation, and in the center, in black cursive lettering, sat one word—*Domenico*.

I'd been branded with his name. *His* name.

I was caught between fear and elation and confusion. What did it really mean? What was the real reason behind the new ink embedded into my skin?

Oddly, it gave me back a small spark of the hope that had almost completely left me. If he, the leader, had marked me, maybe I wouldn't be sold, maybe I wouldn't have to use the one and only card I had up my sleeve. The only thing I knew that could save me was the same thing I refused to use.

But maybe I'd been handed a new way of survival...at Domenico's side.

Every day since Domenico had ordered Marco to reduce the amount of crew, the loiterers had decreased. Only the trusted few circulated, and I noticed Roman was not one of them.

The sad-looking rose was a ghost of its former self. The amount of petals that remained was small, and I couldn't help the hard thump of my heart when I again wondered what would happen when there were no petals left.

Domenico had marked me, but would that save me from whatever fate was only days away? I'd managed to survive weeks. A couple of the guys were watching the news on a laptop and I overheard how Halloween was fast approaching, only fourteen days away.

I'd been in my cell, surviving, beating the odds and keeping my secrets locked tight, for over three weeks. Yes, I'd been violated in many ways, the worst being my dignity over the corruption of my body. I didn't like what was done to me, but he somehow made up for it. None of it was enough to break me, but it was enough to weaken me.

More than once I almost slipped, the words sitting on the tip of my tongue.

Domenico seemed more on edge since the explosion of testosterone and subsequent culling of men. The fewer there were, the more alert he became, almost like he was waiting for an attack.

Everything was about to change. I could feel it deep in my gut. The only problem was that I didn't know what that meant for me.

"Ella?" someone called, rousing me.

My eyes tried to focus, but there was no strength in me.

"Ella!" the voice hissed.

In my haze, I heard the door to my cage rattle and groan before creaking open, clanging when it slammed against the wall.

"Come on, we don't have much time."

I didn't move. I couldn't. Sleep had me, and my weakened state made it harder to comply.

"Get the fuck up!" he growled.

It wasn't enough.

He stomped forward and gripped my arm tight, rolling me onto my back. Lazily my eyes found his and the sharpness of his gaze forced a shot of adrenaline through me, waking up my tired limbs.

"If you want out of this shithole, get the fuck up," Domenico hissed.

THIRTEEN

I stared up at him, my brain trying to process his words. My gaze bounced between his eyes, confusion flooding me. What was he talking about?

I had less than two seconds to decide what my response was. Go or stay? And which was the right answer?

Did I trust him enough to leave? Or was he simply dragging me to another level of hell?

The silence made up my mind. There was nobody around, not even Marco. We were alone.

He slipped my shoes on as I sat up, then pulled me to my feet.

His hand sat in the space between us. I looked from it to his eyes and made my decision—I slipped my hand in his.

"Why are you helping me?" I asked as we raced across the open space to the door leading to the fire escape.

"Because I'm your knight in fucking black armor, princess. Now let's go before they notice your cage is empty."

My muscles were still, and his arm wrapped around my waist to help hold me up while we descended the stairs.

There were a couple of beat-up cars in the gravel lot, including my familiar sedan. He popped the trunk, and I noted the bags upon bags before he pulled out my duffel and my Louis Vuitton bag.

They had cleared out my apartment. Domenico had packed me a bag in anticipation.

"Did you grab the photo of my mother?" I asked, my chest clenching.

"We didn't grab any pictures, just some of your clothes to make it look like you bailed."

I grabbed hold of his arm. "It's the only thing I have of her. Please."

His jaw clenched and he growled, "We have two minutes." He turned toward an older car, one I recognized, and who wouldn't? It was a black sixties-era Ford Mustang. "Get in."

He threw my bags into the trunk, and in seconds we were off. The Mustang's engine roared as he pressed the gas pedal, rocketing us down the street, kicking up gravel in its wake.

"When are you going to tell me what's going on?" I asked when we were a couple of blocks away.

His eyes scanned the mirrors to make sure we were in the clear. "When we get somewhere safe."

Somewhere safe. My pulse sped up as a new rock settled in my stomach. Whatever safety being Domenico's had provided was abolished by his act of freeing me.

I wasn't safe anymore, if I ever was in any measure.

What unnerved me the most was my calmness. Domenico had freed me. He had stolen me away. The leader.

La Bestia.

And I was oddly fine with it.

Was it shock, or the simple knowledge that I was his and I went where he went?

I didn't even tell him how to get to my apartment, but after a while the scenery became more familiar. Was there anything left? Were my few prized possessions still there?

My rent was paid up, even with my disappearing for three weeks. His men had emptied a lot of my stuff out. Would they have left the two items I desperately needed? Or were they stuffed in one of the bags still in my trunk?

He pulled into the small parking lot of my building and quickly headed up. The shitty metal steps clanged beneath us with each step up to the second floor. When we got to my apartment, I realized there was a fatal flaw in this plan.

"I don't have my keys."

Domenico pushed past me and pulled a set of keys from his pocket. I recognized the yellow leather rose key chain—he had my keys.

Once the door was open, he held it for me while his eyes swept the parking lot one last time.

My apartment was trashed. Books were strewn everywhere, furniture flipped, and my tiny kitchen had dishes everywhere. It felt like a violation worse than what Domenico had done.

I ran in and immediately located a plastic bag on the floor and tossed in a few of my books that were littered around. In the bathroom I grabbed a few missed items and tossed them into an empty makeup bag.

Maybe after over three weeks I could finally have a hot shower. The thought alone felt like heaven, especially after my sponge baths in front of hungry eyes in a dirt-filled cage.

"One minute," Domenico called from the door.

At my dresser, I pulled out a few more missed pieces of clothing. On top lay my jewelry box, but there was only one item that I was desperate for.

I heaved a sigh as I pulled the gold chain from the box. For my sixteenth birthday, days before she killed herself, my mother had given me a locket. I slipped that on, then grabbed the photo of her that sat beside it.

I didn't *need* anything else, but I took one last look around for anything I wanted. Domenico called it, and I walked out the door.

We made it down the steps, but a few feet from the base my legs gave way. All the strength I had was gone. Domenico caught me and once again wrapped his arm around me and helped me to the car.

Weeks of barely enough calories to survive had zapped my body of energy. I'd grown weak, my muscles unused to so much activity, a level that was much more than I had become used to.

As we drove, I wondered if we were heading out of the city, but he didn't get onto the interstate, instead taking city streets deep into the South Side. With each mile, I watched the buildings and surroundings become more and more run down.

We drove deeper into the overcrowded streets until he turned into the parking lot of an old motel.

"Come on," he said once the car was parked, the engine off.

I looked around, my mind whirling with a dozen questions. I stared at the open space, to the street and the buildings across the way. If I ran, could I get away?

The slam of the trunk pulled me from my thoughts, and I climbed from the car.

It was a stupid thought at that point, and I needed more information and more strength before I tried to pull off a maneuver such as that.

"Ella, come on."

"Ari," I corrected as I shut the door. It was a gamble, but I knew Domenico was a smart man. There was more going on than either of us knew.

"What?"

"I like Ari."

He furrowed his brow before he gave a stiff nod and led the way. We entered the small motel room, and he shut and locked the door before throwing the bags down on the bed and turning to me.

"What the fuck just happened?" I asked.

He shook his head. "First, you will still follow my rules."

I tilted my head to the side. "Why should I?"

"Because by now they've noticed you're missing and so am I. The penalty if they capture you will be hell compared to the last few weeks—and death for me."

My gaze flickered between his eyes to dig for the deeper meaning. Unbeknownst to me, my lead captor was my savior, taking unseen steps to make my capture more bearable without being noticed. What he did wasn't good or decent, but it was a show of dominance over the other men, marking me, keeping me from their torment.

"Why me?" It was a question I'd asked for weeks, and I thought I knew the answer, but now I wasn't so sure.

"You're payment."

"Payment for what?"

He shook his head. "I don't know. For the Ferrante, I'm a faithful servant in charge of many men."

Ferrante.

Shit.

I knew it.

In all the weeks, I'd never heard anyone utter the name of the family they worked for. They'd always said the family or the organization, but my every suspicion had been confirmed.

"Yet you just threw that all away," I said, knowing what his betrayal would mean.

His eyes were hard, jaw clenched tight. "Everything was going sideways, and all I know is that *you* are the answer."

"Why me?" I asked again. He was as observant as I'd suspected.

He shook his head. "Before we picked you up, Ferrante's

consigliere called me in. He gave me your information, told me to hold you, and asked me to keep you safe."

My heart slammed in my chest. The consigliere was an advisor, a trusted confidant, and third highest ranking member.

The Ferrante consigliere was also my father.

I wasn't random.

"So you're my protector?"

"My job was to keep you safe, no matter what."

"And yet they will still kill you. You traded your life for mine?" I crossed my arms in front of me. "I don't believe it."

"You can believe what you want," he said, refusing, as always, to give away any information. But we weren't in his headquarters, if you could even call it that. It was just him and me, and I was going to figure out what was going on.

He drugged me and took me, to keep me safe? "After what you did to me?"

His gaze stayed locked on mine. "There was no other way."

"No other way?" I quirked a brow at him. "You fucking say that like forcing your dick in me was a favor?"

"It was," he growled.

I shook my head. "What you did to me could *never* be a favor."

His eyes narrowed. "Trust me, it wasn't something I wanted to do."

"Your dick seemed to like it just fine," I bit back.

"Jesus, Ella, you don't fucking get it. If I didn't, they were going to, and it would have been much worse," he ground out.

We were standing face-to-face, on even ground for the first time and I wasn't going to back down, but his confession stopped me. "What?" Words he'd said floated back to the surface and nagged at me.

Trust me, princess, I'm not doing this for the pleasure.

He ran his hand through his hair, another tic of his jaw

visible. "You get me hard just by being in the same room, make no mistake, but those guys? They revel in that shit. Seeing how far they can break a girl, and I'm not just talking about mentally."

I shook my head. "They wouldn't have hurt me." My father would have had their heads. That was why he'd told Domenico to keep me safe. Right?

A loud, cynical laugh made me jump. "The only arrangement was that you were to be kept alive. There was nothing saying what condition you would be in."

I blanched at that. Oh, so safe simply meant *not dead*. That shouldn't have surprised me, but it did.

"I listened to the ways they were going to violate you. Their plan was to pass you around. By claiming you and keeping you by my side, I kept you from being raped by a line of thirty guys day and fucking night."

I tried to sink down to the bed but my knees gave out, landing me on the carpet. My brain was unable to handle the information.

"The drugs were heavy in your system, and your attention was locked on me. You either couldn't hear or couldn't process their whispered words," he revealed as he stood over me.

It sounded sick and twisted and wrong—he'd violated me to save me.

In doing so, he'd kept me from becoming a sex slave, nothing more than a pussy to ruin.

But at the same time, he did ruin me. Domenico was hard, dominant. It excited me as much as frightened me. The way he touched me set my skin on fire. He owned my body like no other man ever had or ever could.

My body ached to have him again, and that scared me even more because it wasn't what I was supposed to want. Not from him. Never from him.

But I did.

"You always seemed angry," I whispered.

"I was. I may be a monster, but I don't do that, Ella. I was angry. I *am* angry. Forcing myself on you was not what I wanted."

"So you drugged me so that when you took me, it wouldn't traumatize me," I said as the puzzle pieces clicked together. When he didn't agree, I looked up.

Domenico was silent, his teeth clenched. "You have it backwards. I took you *because* you were drugged."

My blood ran cold, and I stared up at him. "Wait, you didn't drug me?"

Everything I believed shifted.

His hard eyes locked with mine. "He forced my hand. If I didn't do it, they would have eaten you alive, some physically and not just metaphorically."

I was frozen in disbelief. "Who?"

"Roman."

Roman? Roman, who always seemed too fragile and out of place? It didn't make sense.

But Roman was the one who fed me that day. Before then, Domenico was all words and harsh grips, enforcing his dominance and superiority, but nothing more. And then there was the way he looked at me the last time I saw him.

"He rapes women, and when I saw the way you were acting, I knew what he'd done. He's not above using any and all means to get what he wants."

It was hard to process, to understand. Roman, the man who'd brought me blankets and sneaked me extra food. Who was always so kind and fragile but was really two-faced.

I felt violated in a totally new way, one that hit to the core. I trusted him. If Domenico hadn't claimed me, what would Roman have done? "Did you want to…do that to me?"

He squatted down in front of me, his fingers knotted in my hair, and pulled back, making me hiss. "I already told you no. I may be harsh, rough. I fuck hard. Doing that to you? No. I want you willing to do anything for my cock. Begging for me to fuck you until you can't walk. I want to ruin you for any other man, not ruin you for life." His teeth dug into my bottom lip and pulled. "I did what I had to do to keep you safe. But make no mistake—I've claimed you as mine."

"What if I don't want to be yours?" I spat, even though my body reacted to his, my blood heating up at his closeness as it always did.

His fingers splayed out across my neck, eyes dark. "If that were true, why are you breathing hard and begging me to fuck you with your eyes?" His hand trailed down, squeezing my breast. "First, there were whispers—split her open, see what she looks like from the inside, tap that shit until she's airtight—remember?" I shook my head. "Roman doesn't think much of me, so he doesn't always notice when I'm around."

"Why doesn't he think much of you?" I asked, trying not to seem as desperate for his touch as I was.

Domenico was the leader, and every man in that space gave him respect and didn't question any order he gave. The way he interacted with Roman, their shaded words and tense atmosphere. There was history there.

"Because he is the son of Giovanni and Renata Ferrante, and he believes that makes him above everyone else. Like I said, I heard the whispers, the plans they had for you. I wasn't going to touch you, but as they were talking, you began to change."

"What did I do?" I asked, still in disbelief that Roman, quiet, *sweet* Roman, was really like that.

"Your lips were parted, and you shed your sweater so that you could touch your skin." His fingers slipped around my nipple and pinched. "Your nipples were hard." He moved his hand down to my waist and tugged on the waistband. The seam pressed against my clit, and I drew in a sharp breath. "And you kept pulling at your jeans, just like that. Little moans slipped out, and I watched you become more and more aroused while they devised a plan to share you. You don't remember, but afterward I threatened anyone who touched you and shot the vilest one in the leg."

I didn't remember anything after he made me come and come again.

"You asserted your dominance."

He nodded. "I was forced to. Roman doesn't like that he has to follow my command."

"Why is that?"

"Because he is a Ferrante, and above everyone in the organization who isn't a Ferrante."

There was more. A secret, but he wasn't going to willingly give it up.

"What's your last name?" I asked. I knew him only as Domenico or la Bestia.

"Mancini."

"So you're not a Ferrante, but he has to follow your commands?" Something didn't quite add up. There was animosity between them—I'd felt it before.

We both had secrets, and I wasn't sure if they would destroy us or set us free.

"He does." He stood. "Go take a shower. I'm going to order some food."

At the mention of food, my stomach rumbled. "I've been on the edge of starving for weeks."

His jaw clenched again as he handed me my bag. I could barely lift it as I dragged it to the bathroom.

A shower. A real tub with real plumbing and temperature control. I didn't care that we were in a shithole. It was an upgrade from no heat and no real shower.

I stripped off my clothes, happy to burn them the first chance I got, and stepped into the shower. The warm water rolled over my body, relaxing my muscles, bringing blood flow back to parts of my body that were cold to the bone.

And then I scrubbed. Weeks of dirt and grime were scoured from my skin, washed down the drain. Again and again, every inch I could reach until I was satisfied I was actually clean before doing the same with my hair. Then I shaved everything.

I was in heaven. I couldn't remember a time when a shower felt so good. After three weeks of sponge baths and hillbilly half showers, nothing could beat it. Even better was the knowledge I would have clean clothes to put on when I got out.

Clean. Clothes.

Something so innocuous and simple—and so desperately missed.

When I got out, my reflection was a pale version of myself. I barely recognized the woman who stared back. Weeks of near starvation had adverse reactions. I'd lost a fair amount of weight, leaving me in an almost skeletal state, every rib showing.

Every part of me was too thin, including my face. Lack of proper nutrition had left my skin an off pallor. My eyes held a dull edge, as did my hair.

Sifting through the bag, I found clothes to put on, opting for a pair of yoga pants and a tank top—both of which were too big. After brushing through the rat's nest that was my hair, I twisted it up into a bun, then gave my mouth the same kind of scouring I had my body.

"I look like death," I said when I came out of the bathroom. While I looked terrible and was malnourished, at least on the outside I felt refreshed.

He clenched his jaw as he looked me over. "It's to keep the girls alive, but weak."

I nodded as I placed my bag on the bed. I needed something on my arms and some socks. "I just can't believe the difference a few weeks makes."

He stepped forward, his fingers lightly tracing the ink on my back.

"I saw these," he said as he traced the gauzy-looking wings that draped over my shoulder blades. "But I could never get a good look at them."

"Is that why you tattooed me? Because you knew I could take it?" The tattoo of his name was still healing, and I knew it would take some getting used to seeing it in my reflection.

"It didn't matter if you could take it. It was another way. They all had to be reminded. Everyone needed to know that you were mine." His touch was softer than I was used to. "Why wings?"

I returned to sifting through the bag, looking for a long-sleeve shirt to wear. "Because I freed myself. I grew wings and flew away. Freedom."

There was a knock on the door, and I froze.

"Food," he said as he stepped toward the door. He opened it just enough to get the boxes in and hand over some cash.

Cash. Crap.

I had a stash of cash I forgot to grab. It wasn't much, but a couple hundred dollars that was probably confiscated when they trashed my apartment.

The only things I had to my name were in the few bags sitting on the floor. I was about to check the contents of my Louis Vuitton when the scent of pizza hit my senses and I began to salivate.

I almost jumped him for the cardboard boxes in his hand, but he held me at bay with a look.

"Drink this first," he said, holding out a bottle of Coke.

I didn't ask why. Instead, I chugged the soda, moaning at the sweetness that bubbled on my tongue.

"Oh, sweet heaven." Once it was half empty, he handed me a slice of pizza.

"Eat slowly. Don't just devour it."

"Why?" I asked. Every part of me said to take the entire thing in one bite.

"So that you don't throw it up. You haven't had much. You need to take it slowly to get your body used to food again."

I blinked at him. "Why are you being so…caring?" There had been instances over the last weeks, ones laced with his dominance, but it didn't feel the same.

"Eat."

Apparently the time for revelations was over.

As much as it pained me, I took small bites, and when I'd eaten a whole slice, he had me finish the Coke before handing me a second slice. I got only halfway through it, despite my body begging to inhale the entire pie.

"Fuck, this is good," I said as I took one last bite before surrendering.

"Try for more in an hour," he said, moving the boxes to the dresser.

I finally took the time to look around. It was unlike any hotel I'd ever stayed in by less than a few stars. Everything was dated, dirty, and stained, but it was a big step up from my cage.

I fell back onto the mattress, a moan crawling out of me. The mattress was old and lacked a pillow top, but it was clean, as was I.

The bed dipped beside me and I turned to find Domenico propped up against the headboard, his long legs extended.

"I haven't decided if I should thank you or not," I said.

A deep chuckle, something I wasn't used to, rumbled from him. "All those times you said that to Roman and you never saw through that friendly facade. I free you, and you have to think about it."

I shrugged. "Different reactions. A smile goes a long way."

"To making people believe you're something you're not."

"It's politeness as well," I pointed out.

His eyes met mine. "So if I fucked you with a smile, would I fall into that category?"

"Hmm, I suppose not."

I turned back to stare at the opposite wall. "It was all his act."

"You've never been anyone that you weren't." It was a statement. La Bestia was who he was through and through.

"No reason to be. I am who I am."

I rolled onto my side and scooted closer, drawn to the warmth of his body. "I wish I was that confident in my own self-image."

"Is that why you dance?" he asked.

My brow scrunched. "What do you mean?"

"Why do you dance? Why choose to do that?"

The hairs on the back of my neck prickled. While not lies, secrets sat just below the water, ready to bubble up and be exposed. "Why not?"

"There are other ways to make money."

"Maybe," I said, not mentioning the need for proper identification, which I didn't have. I'd bought my car in cash, Al had registered it for me, and I'd made damn sure to drive by the rules. Al had also paid me under the table. I wasn't the only runaway, and at times I thought he felt like a surrogate father and helped how he could.

At nineteen, I had a crash course in life and he helped to guide me.

I sat up and faced him. "But they're just another cage. Dancing is freedom. Dancing is power and control. What I do, the way I move, entices. I control the game—I control what is done. I control how turned on a man is. And I control whether or not he touches me."

He straightened at my last words. "That's it, isn't it? Someone touched you."

His perceptiveness was spot on again. "Someone forced me to stand naked in a room full of men after ripping the clothes from my body and calling me a whore. Someone who was stronger and more powerful than me touched me to show his dominance and to put me in line."

I blinked away the wetness filling my eyes. After over three years I still feared him. His home was not my home. It held no comfort or sense of family. No, he had killed it all until it was a temple, a testament to his power.

"Then I touched you."

I blinked at him. He had. Again and again. It didn't matter if I wanted it—he'd taken me. And I had to admit one of my deepest shames—I did want it. Every single time. In his grip, a possessive passion set me aflame.

He'd never hurt me. He'd grabbed me and dominated me but never truly hurt me.

I crawled up the bed to him and straddled his hips. I tore at his belt. The button of his jeans and his fly were next. Then my hand was inside his jeans. His dick was limp but began to fill as I pulled it out.

A groan rumbled from deep in his chest. I fisted his growing cock, running my hand up and down.

His hands landed on my hips, fingers digging in. My arms stretched as he pushed me back.

"Ella," he growled as he tried to pry me off, but I could see the lust darkening his eyes, taking over. "I won't hurt you."

"Then don't. And it's Ari," I reminded him.

I wanted this, wanted him. It was a desperation inside me. A need crawling in my veins, expanding like a virus. I needed to know the difference between the man making a show and his true desires.

Still dominant, but different, reverent.

I stood and pulled my yoga pants and thong down. They were

just past my knees when Domenico leaned forward and ran his tongue against my slit, giving my clit a little flick at the end. My knees went weak and I fell forward. He caught me and settled me right over his face.

I drew in a ragged breath, my fingers tightening on his hair, fisting it as he devoured my pussy. I was practically seeing stars, and I couldn't stop sharp little moans from slipping past my lips. His eyes were hooded as he stared up at me, watching me.

My legs shook and he gave one last long lick before pulling my leg from my pants and moving me down to where the head of his cock kissed my opening. His hands left me, arms spreading open.

His eyes never left me. "Take it."

I stared at him, trying to understand. I lifted my hips, thinking he would grab my waist and plunge into me, but he didn't move.

Take it.

Take the power back.

I cradled his face in my hands and pressed my lips to his before reaching between us and repositioning him.

I sank down on him, my lips parting as he filled me. Euphoria, fireworks, and every other wondrous feeling collided the deeper he went.

Still his hands didn't move. A groan left him as I lifted off.

"Kiss me," I whispered. "Kiss me like it's the last."

His arms finally moved, and his fingers gently cupped my face as he drew me closer. "Never the last."

Plush lips pressed to mine. Then our lips parted. Each swipe of his tongue against mine drove me to ride him harder, faster. I dug my nails into his chest before wrapping my hands around his neck, holding him close.

His stubble was rough against my skin, lips burning as he moved up my neck, tongue soothing. "This is what I've been fucking dreaming of."

"What?"

"You wanting me."

"Domenico," I whimpered. My legs began to shake, and he understood.

He gripped my waist, pushing and pulling me along his length to meet his thrusts.

"Make me come," I said against his lips.

He changed the angle slightly and began drilling up into me. My mouth opened in a silent scream as every muscle froze—a stuttered breath, a tightening grip, then his teeth digging into my neck.

I snapped and began rocking in his grip, a keening sound ripping out of my chest. My pussy pulsed around him, and a low groan vibrated against my skin. His hips thrusted up as his hands slammed my hips down, his muscles jumping with each twitch of his cock.

After cleaning up, I fell asleep draped over Domenico, feeling oddly safe for the first time in weeks.

Feeling cared about for the first time in years.

FOURTEEN

The next day I was feeling better. While not the healthiest, pizza was definitely higher in nutrition than my sandwiches. By noon I had managed to eat three slices. I also drank and drank and drank. Dehydration was part of my issues, it turned out.

The more food and water I was able to get in me, the better.

Domenico was different. Still dominant and grating, but now his touch set me on fire. I knew more, understood why.

He was not a sadist. He was my savior.

"He told me to do whatever it took to keep you safe."

Whatever to keep me safe included how he had to hurt me, because the alternative was far worse.

"How long are we going to be here?" I asked, nibbling on the crust of the last piece I'd gotten down. Even full, I felt a surge of energy that I hadn't felt in weeks.

His lips formed a thin line. "I'm still working out a plan."

"You planned out the whole escape, didn't you?"

He nodded. "But there wasn't time to plan past this point.

There are those loyal to me who informed me of a plot to kill me, and there were only a few hours' notice."

I stared at him. "Kill you?" It was unfathomable. I'd seen firsthand the way those men worshipped him.

"Marco sent everyone out right before a shift change, then went to dinner."

"Did you tell him…you did all that to take me with you? Why didn't you just leave? Form some other plan."

His gaze bored into mine. "I couldn't leave you to be taken by Roman."

"Why?" My constant question. Why would he risk so much for me?

Domenico's phone went off, and I jumped at the sudden sound. His jaw clenched as he glanced at it.

"Can't they trace us with that?" I asked, my eyes wide as I looked toward the door.

He shook his head. "Not mine."

He pressed his finger to his screen, and a voice floated through the speakers. "You know what this means. Return with the girl and you won't be killed."

My brow scrunched. "Know what this means?" He turned the screen toward me. The man speaking wasn't in the frame. Instead there was a single red rose sitting in a black vase. "I don't understand."

Domenico stopped the video. "If I don't return by the time he takes the last petal out, he'll kill me."

The last petal… "You already knew that would happen when you freed me."

He shook his head. "This is to show me there is leniency. That death is not the end if I return you."

"What would happen to you?" I asked. Concern crawled in, and I began to feel on edge. Would he return me if there was a chance he could go back to his life?

"Sometimes death is better."

The significance wasn't lost on me. The rose, just like mine. "How long until all the petals are gone?"

"At least three weeks. He'll pull one petal a day."

Memories of Domenico gently plucking the rose each day ran through my mind. It wasn't without purpose. "Just like you did," I whispered.

Did that mean I'd been days away from being killed? That thought didn't sit right with me, and I knew I was going to have to come clean.

He nodded. "Your petals were running out."

"And then you were going to kill me?" I asked.

He took my face in his hands. "I will never do that to you. You're mine, and I will do anything to keep you alive."

"And if you didn't want me?" I asked, my breath hitching. The conviction in which he said I was his made my chest clench. There was more than just ownership, something deeper that stirred.

"Then you would have been sold off as a sex slave to the highest bidder or given to the men."

The reality was staggering, and I would have faltered, using my one lifeline.

"What do we do? We can't just stay in this motel forever." Was there anywhere to go? He said my father wanted him to keep me safe, but going back to him still seemed to fall under crawling back to him, under his rule in exchange for sanctuary.

"Roman is coming for us."

"How do you know?" I asked.

He was looking off in the distance, not focused on anything in particular. "Besides the plan he already made, I gave him the perfect excuse to kill me."

"Why?"

His eyes locked on mine. "He wants to finish what he never could get close to doing, and he'll use you."

Finish? My brow scrunched before it hit me.

"He did this, didn't he?" My finger lightly traced the large scar on his face. I could only imagine the pain he'd been in. From his scalp to the corner of his mouth, then swooping up across his cheek, barely missing his eye, and through his brow, stopping halfway up his forehead.

"What happened?"

His gaze met mine, and he took a moment to answer. "I told you, don't trust Roman."

"Why would you trust him?" I asked. I wanted more. I was craving more of Domenico, of the man he was.

He shook his head. "I never did. I grew up with Roman. From the time he could walk, he looked down at me. As we grew, he would do things like punch me and then go crying to his mother that I hit him. He was a devious little shit that got whatever he wanted."

"Were you punished?" I asked.

He shook his head. "Not often. My mother believed him the first time, but after she caught him punching one of the maids because she put him in the wrong sweater, she knew. He was a tiny tyrant. After that, my mother would pretend that she was going to take me to be reprimanded, and instead she iced where he hit me, gave me a kiss, and made me cookies."

"Why didn't she do anything?" I asked. Placating him after the fact did nothing to stop the treatment. It was a loving gesture but didn't stop the aggressor.

"She couldn't," he said faintly.

"She should have! You were being hurt, and she could have done something to stop it."

Domenico shook his head. "She did all that she could."

"What about your father?" I asked. Didn't someone stand up for him?

His jaw twitched. "He sided with Roman and told me to

toughen up. So I did. Roman wasn't the only one to pick on me. All of the Ferrante children, including their mother, did."

My eyes widened. Why did he grow up in such an environment? Why was he subjected to that?

"Their mother? She hurt you?" I'd once seen the matriarch of the Ferrante family, and she seemed as slippery as a viper, and just as quick to strike. It didn't surprise me that she would attack a child who wasn't one of her own.

He nodded. "She hated me, and her children followed suit. Throughout school, with each fight, I grew tougher, stronger. By high school Roman was no match for me on his own, so he roped in some friends to help."

"My God." I straddled his hips and pulled his shirt up and over his head. Littered across his skin were scars, including a healed bullet wound. Some were hidden under the black and red tattoos that covered his skin. I'd never gotten to make such an inspection of him before, up close like that. To see the battle scars and war paint that littered his tanned complexion. "So much pain," I whispered and leaned down to press my lips against his skin.

"Carne di lupo, zanne di cane," he whispered.

You must meet roughness with roughness. It wasn't just a saying, but a mantra, evident by the story shown on his skin.

"Senior year Roman and his friends won as many fights as I did, to the point that nobody wanted to fight me. I sent more than a few of them to the hospital."

"I'm surprised you're not in jail." From what I'd cobbled together, they'd gone to school together, meaning probably a private school, maybe even the same one I went to. The school wouldn't have allowed such behavior, so why were there no consequences?

He shook his head. "Giovanni wouldn't allow it. He saw promise and offered me a job, one that led to right here and right now."

"Where you gave it all away for me. Why?" It was a favorite question of mine—why? One that never received an answer. *Why me?*

His gaze was locked on my lips and he reached up and cupped my chin, his thumb swiping across my bottom lip. His breath sped up while his teeth mashed together.

"I've aided in the sale of many women in the past. There is money in people, and I know what happens to those that I transfer. Killing people? I've killed more than I can count, but the thought of sending you to either of those fates was something I couldn't handle."

"*Why me?*" I was desperate for the answer, to know why I mattered.

I drew in a breath as his hand snaked up my back, and the roughness of his palm sent a ripple of fire down to my core. A hard tug and we were chest to chest, his eyes locked onto mine, our lips a few short inches from touching. "You're mine."

A shudder rolled through me. "As much as this is exciting me, you're not answering me."

"But I did. You. Are. Mine." His lips ghosted my neck, his teeth sinking in, nipping as he went. "No man but me will ever touch you."

He was distracting me, and I was so close to letting him. "How is this different than being sold to the highest bidder?"

"Because the only thing you have to fear from me is the intensity of my need for you."

My chest clenched again. He wanted me, needed me. *Me.* "Tell me why."

"Why are you wrapped all around me after what I did to you?" he asked.

I pulled back and blinked at him. "W-what?"

"I've answered your why with the basest explanation I can. Now it's your turn."

My gaze bounced between his eyes. "Because maybe, just maybe, you aren't the monster I believed you were."

"I am a monster."

I shook my head. "Not to me."

There was a hum deep in his chest. "Oh, but I am."

"How so?"

He rocketed forward, tipping me down to the bed as he caged me beneath him. "I want to devour every inch of you."

I drew in a sharp breath as his touch filled me with warmth.

"Because you are the heaven I'll never reach."

"Anche in paradiso non è bello essere soli. I go where you go." *There is no greater torment than to be alone in paradise.*

His eyes met mine. "You *are* my paradise. With you, I am not alone."

FIFTEEN

S ex was so much better after I admitted how much I wanted him. After he told me how much he needed me.

For three days we'd remained locked in the hotel room. There were many hours that he kept watch out the window while I read one of the books I'd picked up from my apartment. I'd finished Domenico's *War and Peace* while still in my cage and I was ravenous to read more.

Oh, how I'd missed reading. I was elated to read again.

"Isn't your car conspicuous?" I asked as he stared out the window.

"It's not there."

I blinked and turned to him. I knew it was a bad neighborhood, but wow. "Someone stole it?"

He gave a small shake of his head. "The motel owner has it in a storage garage in the back."

"Do you trust him?"

"Not particularly, but a grand in hand and no questions were asked."

Based on his car and his status, money didn't seem to be much of an issue for him. He was paid well. "So your little gang… what does it do for Ferrante?"

His brow furrowed. "Why do you ask?"

"From what I remember of Ferrante's men, they were always well dressed in three-piece suits, but you are usually…casual." I fed him a morsel, and I waited to see if he'd take the bait, but it seemed his attention was too focused outside.

"Men in suits that aren't Ferrante are guards and brown-nosers. Assassins whose only purpose is to kill. I am the task master, the collector, the informant. The enforcer. I carry out what Ferrante needs me to. I have a crew that is a mix of soldiers and associates."

"What types of things does your crew do?"

"Whatever is required."

His half answers were starting to grate on me. "Are you going to keep up this whole secrecy act now?"

His jaw twitched and he turned to me. "Do you want me to tell you that you're the only girl I've plucked from the street? Because you're not. The market for girls is bigger than you think."

"That's what the Ferrante do?" I asked. My father's threats came back to me. Maybe this was all a ruse to sell me.

"It's a lucrative piece of a larger puzzle. You should know by now that the Mafia makes the world go round. Influence by any means—money, blackmail, and force. Secrets are worth more than money, and the Ferrante are better at secrets than any other."

He wasn't wrong there. "Any other what?"

"Family. Organization."

"What other families are around?" I asked. It was me throwing out a lure, to see if he really didn't know who I was.

"Our number one enemy is Vitale."

I tried not to react to the name, especially when *enemy* was thrown in front of it. "I've heard that name before."

He nodded. "They are well known. I'm sure you heard it on the news. Their leader, Laureano Vitale, is old school."

My spine straightened, and I froze. Laureano? My heart hammered as I realized that Domenico *really* didn't know who I was. At all. "I thought the leader's name was something like Thomas."

"Tommaso," he corrected. "He died a few years ago and his brother Laureano took over."

I stared at him as tears welled in my eyes.

"What's wrong?" Domenico asked as he moved to sit beside me. His finger tipped my chin up.

"Do you like what you do? Finding girls and selling them?" I asked, pulling the conversation away from me.

Domenico's expression darkened. "No. Like I said, it's very lucrative, but it isn't something I particularly like doing. It's my job, and I do it. I carry out the tasks assigned to me by Ferrante and I keep everyone in line."

"Out of fear?"

"Fear is a great motivator. Was fear what you saw while in your cage?" he asked.

I tilted my head. "A little, but it was mostly respect."

"I am the fourth-highest-ranking member of the organization."

I froze at that. "The fourth?" By his dress, I would never have thought he was so close to the top of the family hierarchy.

He nodded. "Even capos have ranking."

But he wasn't a Ferrante. "Wouldn't Ferrante's sons, like Roman, be higher than you?"

He shook his head. "They have status, but not ranking."

"What's the difference?" I asked.

"Being a Ferrante demands a level of respect from everyone who is in the organization. They are untouchable, but they still have to earn ranking."

That explained a lot, like why Roman had to take orders from Domenico, despite his family standing.

"Like Tommaso and Laureano, right? If Laureano took over, he had to rank, right? Tommaso was the older brother, and Laureano was second in charge. If Tommaso had sons, they would have been next, right? Instead, he had a daughter who was killed at a young age."

Domenico stared at me, lips parting, eyes widening as I spoke. Everything I'd led him to believe, my lack of knowledge of the world, was crashing down around him. I'd let slip my knowledge of multiple languages brought about by my private schooling. Quite possibly the same private school he went to.

"How do you know all that?" he asked, a wary edge to his tone.

I swallowed hard and fidgeted with the sheet. "Because someone lied to you. Or, rather, omitted some information."

He reached out and grabbed my arm. "What information?"

Domenico knew I was full of secrets, that there was something different about me. He knew I wasn't just some girl from the streets. I knew he'd picked up that much.

I blew out a breath. "My name."

He froze as he stared at me, waiting for the other shoe to drop. I knew he could tell my next words would change everything. Every suspicion that I was important was about to be confirmed.

"Ella Delgado is the name I gave myself when I ran away from the life, but the *family* never lets you go."

He dragged his hand across his mouth. "Who are you?"

"Arabella Santoro, daughter of Maurizio Santoro." Ferrante's consigliere.

His eyes widened and his hand went lax. "Fuck."

I bit down on my lower lip. "It makes sense now, huh? Why he wouldn't want me ruined."

"Why didn't you say anything earlier?" he asked with a hiss.

I shrugged. "What would that accomplish?"

"Better accommodations than a fucking cold, dirty cell," he boomed out, clearly angry.

I shook my head. "Then you're not getting it. Everything my father does is moves and countermoves. He wanted me to break. To come to heel. To use his name in exchange for better treatment."

Fire burned in his eyes, and his jaw clenched tightly. "And you should have."

"No, I shouldn't have," I argued. "Doing that would mean relenting, willingly going home. I didn't tell you because you were told to get me, to hold me, to keep me safe."

"You didn't know that." He jumped up and began pacing.

I shook my head. "No, and that scared me. I would have used it, if the time had come."

He turned toward me, teeth bared. "The time came when I held your thighs open!" he growled.

"You were still protecting me."

"You didn't know that." His voice grew louder each time he spoke as anger rolled off him.

"And you know why I didn't, why I couldn't. I wasn't in my right mind." All my body had wanted was his body, and my mind had been a fog of confusion and lust.

He shook his head as he tried to calm himself. "There were only days left on the rose."

"At that point, he would swoop in to the rescue, and I would be under his control again."

It started to click. "And you would lose all freedom."

I nodded. "But then you tattooed your name on my skin, and it gave me hope again that my situation was temporary. That I was yours."

"You are mine. This changes nothing." He paced again, the

explosive energy eventually draining away, and he sat down on the bed, facing me. "Why did you leave?"

Because I was buried alive, clawing my way out, desperate to breathe fresh air. Desperate to live.

"After my mother died, that house became suffocating and he became overbearing. I was dying there. I wanted to live, and that's what I've done for the last three years."

His hand moved up my chest to my neck, his fingers gripping before pulling me forward. "I am even more suffocating. I will consume every bit of you." His jaw tightened and his lip curled up into a snarl. "Your body and soul are mine. All of you is mine, and I'm not giving you up."

"Who said you had to?" I asked as I bowed into him.

"You might not like how possessive my love is."

My heart skipped and I drew in a ragged breath. "Do you love me?"

He bit down on my jaw before grabbing my hips with his other arm, yanking me to him, my thighs spreading to accommodate his.

"I've marked you in nearly every way, and I *will* mark you in all ways." His thumb brushed against my lower abdomen while his lips swept across my own. "Nobody will take you from me."

Tears filled my eyes as my chest clenched.

All I ever wanted was the freedom to be my own person, but that was changing. I wanted to be with him and never leave him. He made me feel alive in a way I never could on my own. I was still me, but I could see how strong we could be together.

Us against the world.

SIXTEEN

The weight of Domenico's arm around my waist along with his chest pressed against my back gave me the best night sleep I'd had in a long time. The bed was shitty and hard, but the safety I felt lulled me into a deep sleep.

I stared at the drab walls with the dirty, peeling wallpaper and waited, snug in his embrace, for him to wake up.

His arm flexed, pulling me tighter to him.

For days we'd been holed up in that small motel room.

My strength had greatly improved with the increase in calories and fluid. My skin no longer looked like a corpse. My eyes were no longer encircled by darkness. Even my weight had begun to bounce back a little.

After five days, the biggest secret had been revealed. We were both part of the same family organization, only I was a deserter. That was why my treatment was different.

Later in the day, I was reading when a question that nagged at me sprang forth. "That Russian girl was only there a few days. Why was I given a rose and she wasn't?"

He looked at me, his thumb making small circles on my ankle. "The rose was your father's doing. I didn't understand why, obviously, but it's now apparent it was a way to make you stand out. However, it only made you stand out as valuable."

"That girl had value," I argued. I hated not knowing what happened to her, remembering how terrified she'd been.

"Yes, she did, just like all others before her. Hers was monetary. Yours…I haven't figured out yet."

There were only two reasons—to get rid of me or to use me. Both terrible options. "Once upon a time he was a loving family man, but the deeper he got into bed with the Ferrante, the more he changed. Slowly at first, but by the time I was twelve, his quest for money and power were the only things he loved. That was the first time I saw him hit my mother. She protected me from him for years after that until she couldn't take it anymore."

"What happened?"

I twirled the locket in my fingers. Talking about my mother's death was difficult because I was never allowed to talk about it before. It was one of those forbidden topics—and also the reason my father slapped me for the first time.

I stared down at the locket, tempted to open it up and look at her picture. "She killed herself after making me promise to get out. I think she hoped my father would grieve and it would give me a chance to escape, but it didn't work. He became a tyrant, and I was guarded every minute of the day."

"How did you get away?" he asked.

Not without help and careful planning. It was the hardest thing I'd ever done. Months of prepping. "I went to the mall, slipped my guards by telling a store attendant while in the dressing room that they were stalking me. While security questioned them, she snuck me out the back. I left my phone in the dressing room and my wallet, along with a bracelet my father insisted I always wear. I could never confirm it, but I think it had a tracking device in it."

He nodded. "It probably did. Then what?"

I closed my book and sat up to face him. "I hitched a ride with some guy out smoking. Holed up in a hotel for a few days. I was out but constantly on edge that they were going to find me, so I moved to the South Side, and that is where I met Al. He hired me and helped me find a temporary place to live, and the rest is history."

"That's all you've done? Strip?"

I shrugged. "There weren't many other options. I lived for myself for the first time in my life. I made my own money, paid my own bills, and looked out for myself. Yes, I was always looking over my shoulder, but even that lessened. At least until a year ago when two guards showed up trying to tow me home."

His brow scrunched. "Are you sure they were sent by your father?"

"Who else?"

He shook his head. "I'm not sure, but when we spoke he made it sound like he'd just found you. There was little time given, just two days, to get you into that cell. He was practically frantic about it, which was only one reason you were different."

Frantic. The only reason he would be frantic was to have me under his control again. I was worth something to him, but I had a feeling love had nothing to do with it. "I have no idea what he wants and why he can't just let me go."

"Because…you belong to the family."

I shook my head. "No, I don't."

"You did then, and you especially do now," he said as he reached out to lightly caress the letters that lined my collarbone.

"Even if we're on the run from them?" I asked.

"I have a few ideas brewing."

Ideas. For days, that was all he would tell me. He kept his

phone charged and close, occasionally typing something on the screen.

I just wished he would fill me in, tell me something.

"Let's do some exercises," he said as he swung his legs off the bed.

We began working out together once I had energy again, because I needed to build my muscles and range of motion back up. I think it was more for me than him. A therapy of sorts after weeks of neglect.

It was amazing the kind of workouts you could come up with lacking any type of equipment, like him bench-pressing me. Pushups, sit-ups, yoga, burpees—we did them.

Whatever we could to get some physical exercise in, including lots of sex, which was where most workouts led.

By day nine, we were both a little stir crazy. While I was happy for temperature control and showers and clean clothes, the room had become another cage.

I'd finished all the books I'd managed to grab, and I was ready for something, anything, to end our purgatory. Because that was what we were in. Trapped between the life we ran from and the next phase, whatever that was.

"What about the diner across the street?" I asked as I packed my bag. Domenico wanted all bags ready to go just in case, which was a wise idea.

"What about it?"

I was desperate to get out, to walk more than the path I'd created around the room.

"It's close and would get us out of here for a few minutes. Breathe some fresh air."

"I think we need to move. We've been here too long." It was the first time he talked about our next step, but there still didn't seem to be a plan.

"Where are we going now?" I asked. As crazy as it seemed, I would follow him anywhere. My feelings for him grew deeper every day, but I knew there were still secrets we were both carrying.

I'd given up one secret that changed everything he understood about me, and the other one was just as bad. His? In my gut, I knew his secret was just as powerful as mine. Everything about him screamed power, but there was also the softer side. Dark and turbulent to everyone, he was nothing but intense and caring with me.

Which was just another reason I was falling hard for him.

"Out of this city for now."

"They'll never stop looking for us, will they?" I asked. I knew from experience.

He shook his head. "And I stand out too much."

Between his scar and the red and black that covered his left arm, not to mention all the other ink that covered his skin, he was very recognizable.

"Why are we biding our time?" I asked. It seemed odd that we'd been just sitting on our hands for over a week.

"I've got Marco working on something. I'm just waiting for word."

I pursed my lips. After everything, he still had trouble opening up. In reality, I knew what it meant—he didn't fully trust me. That was something we would both have until all the secrets came spilling out. Until the truth that weighed us both down was revealed.

"Are you going to tell me?"

His brow furrowed. "I'm not sure it's an idea you'd like, and still not one I'm sure we'd survive."

I patted my bags. "Well, I'm ready, but I'm also hungry. Why don't you get the car out, and I'll grab some food."

He stared at me for a few beats but said nothing. I stepped forward and fisted his shirt. "I'm not going anywhere," I assured him. "You're stuck with me. I've just been eyeing the stupid chicken sandwich on that flyer for a week." I pointed to one of the flyers he'd found tucked in a drawer. He'd ordered from a few places but not from there because they didn't deliver.

"I don't like the idea of you going out there without me."

"You just admitted you're conspicuous. I can slide in there, blend in. Think about it this way—I've spent the last three years avoiding Ferrante's men."

After a minute, he finally growled before pulling me flush to him and slamming his lips to mine. "Fine, but let me get the car out first."

I jumped up and wrapped my arms around his neck, pulling him down to press my lips to his. "Thank you," I whispered.

He pulled me tighter, his lips running up the column of my neck. "I'll go get the car, and keep it in the back lot."

He released me and threw on his hoodie, flipping the hood up to obstruct the view of his scars before slipping on his jacket. He grabbed the bags and took one last look out the window. "I'll be right back."

I nodded and watched him leave. When the door latched, I felt a pang in my chest. After everything, I didn't like being separated from him.

While he was gone, I threw my hair up into a messy bun and slipped on my jacket, which had thankfully been packed. I searched the room for anything else and noticed his phone charger still plugged in. I pulled it and spun it up before stuffing it in my pocket.

Peeking out the window, I could see the diner was still fairly empty, which was good. I'd hopefully be able to get in and out in a few minutes.

The door opened, and Domenico immediately searched me out. His arms wrapped around me, and he pulled me close. I melted into his embrace, astonished how much my anxiety had risen while he was gone. By the way he held me, I had a feeling it was the same for him.

It amazed me that someone like him could be so affectionate. It was like he was starving for a loving touch, and I had no problem giving it to him.

"Be careful," he said as he pulled back. The tic of his jaw told me how much he didn't like this plan.

"I'll be right back," I reassured him, rubbing my hand around his chest.

He nodded. "The car is in the back lot, but I'll be in the front watching."

I nodded. "Red meat or white?" His brow quirked as he stared down at me. "For your sandwich."

His lips twitched up into that half smirk, the right side never lifting as far. "Red. Always red."

I nodded and twisted the door handle, giving him one last look as I stepped out.

My first steps past the threshold were the first I'd taken on my own in a month. There had always been someone pulling me along, or Domenico right beside me. It was freedom I didn't realize I missed.

And each step was frightening on a level I wasn't expecting. For so long my adrenaline had been in the forefront, but in the last few days it had receded. The gap that grew between us had it spiking to unfathomable levels.

I was stepping out of the safety of his reach.

I crossed the street with no fanfare but jumped when a bell chimed when I opened the door. Thankfully nobody seemed to pay attention, and I grabbed a seat at the counter.

"Evening, hun," a friendly waitress said as she handed me a menu. "Can I get you a drink?"

"I'm going to order to-go, so can I get a Coke in a to-go cup?"

She gave me a smile. "Sure, sweetie. I'll go grab that, and you take a look at the menu."

It felt so good to be out and around people again. People whose smiles were genuine.

Erica, as her name tag read, set a cup down in front of me a minute later, drawing my attention from the menu. "Ready?"

I nodded. "Can I get the buffalo chicken sandwich with blue cheese and extra buffalo sauce, with fries?"

"Sure can. Anything else?"

I scanned the menu. "Can I also get the steak sandwich, fries as well, please?"

"Can do. That it?"

I nodded. "Yeah, I think that's it." My last-minute perusal landed me at the bottom in the desserts section. When was the last time I had anything sweet that wasn't a drink?

The memory of the peanut butter and jelly sandwich entered my mind, but I shook it off.

She let out a small chuckle. "You're eyeing that cake, aren't you?"

I smiled and nodded, a bit embarrassed. "Can I get one of those as well?"

"No problem. Should be ten to fifteen minutes."

"Perfect," I said with a smile.

The news was playing on an old TV in the corner, which served only to remind me how much time had passed. It didn't really matter to me, but I did wonder if anyone had reported me missing. I searched through my Louis Vuitton but my phone wasn't there. Another thing that didn't matter. It was a cheap pay-as-you-go phone that had served its purpose.

There were no photos on it and only a small handful of numbers. Just another reminder of how, while free, I was isolated. Nobody could know who I was. Nothing could link to who I really was. I had no social media. No photos were allowed in the club.

Once, I'd let Mac take my picture, but my hands were covering my face.

"Why don't you want your picture taken?"

"Because they can figure out where I am."

His brow scrunched. "Who?"

"The men in suits."

He quirked a brow at me. "Are they white suits? Do they have a jacket with really long sleeves they want you to wear?"

I smacked his chest. "I just don't like it, you ass."

"Speaking of ass," he said with a wicked grin before picking me up and tossing me onto the bed. I giggled when he jumped on me.

Mac didn't think it was real. He thought I was playing around.

In the end, it didn't matter because they found me anyway.

Which led me to another thought—would I have met Domenico if I'd stayed? I was fairly certain we'd gone to the same private school, but it was obvious he was older than my twenty-two.

In a few short weeks, I'd completely fallen for him. The last week alone was the best week I'd had in years. We'd gotten to know each other more, and the attraction was insane. He was comfort and strength and everything I needed. The surge of emotions that filled me was unlike anything I'd ever encountered.

The bell rang and I froze, suddenly realizing my error—my back was to the door.

Rowdy voices filled the quiet hum of the restaurant. I didn't turn, keeping my eyes forward, but I noticed the shake begin in my hands.

The voices were familiar, and I swallowed hard. My heart hammered. Thankfully there was a man sitting two stools down, mostly blocking me from their view.

They'd found us. Fuck. They'd found us.

I wanted to bolt, to leave, but that would only cause a commotion and draw attention to me. I sat still, quietly sipping on my Coke as I listened in.

"We gotta be close," one man said.

"That driver said he delivered to that motel a week ago." The blood froze in my veins. That voice I knew. That voice that I'd believe belonged to a caring man, but I was freed of that delusion. I knew the truth—Roman wasn't good or decent. He was vile and evil.

"Would he really stay in the same place that long?" one of them asked. "I don't see his car."

"He may have ditched the car," another voice said.

"His Mustang? He loves that car."

They were all voices I recognized, though I couldn't put names to them. Leering eyes were another thing.

My breath was coming out in stuttered chatters, and I jumped when Erica set a bag down in front of me.

"That'll be twenty-two eighty-one," she said.

I nodded, wide eyed as I set the two twenties down. "Keep the change," I said quietly.

She blinked at me. "You sure?"

I nodded and gave her a strained smile as I picked up the bags. "Thank you."

"No, thank you, hun." She grinned.

I made sure to turn away from the group and that my steps were even and slow. I cast a side-eye glance at the table as I passed through the door, I then quickly bolted back toward the motel.

Domenico sat in the motel parking lot, resting against the brick exterior, and I ran full out toward him. He straightened and ran to meet me as soon as I crossed the street.

When he reached me, his arm swung out, sweeping me behind him and sending the bags of food to the ground.

I knew then it was too late. Roman had seen me. Even more, I realized it was probably because I'd said "Thank you" to Erica. If I hadn't, I might not have caught his attention.

He pulled his gun out. "Get to the car," he hissed.

I was frozen to the spot and unable to move.

"Ah, there you are, Domenico," Roman called from across the street.

"Roman," Domenico growled.

Looking around Domenico's shoulder at Roman, I no longer saw the gentle face and kind soul he portrayed. His boyish features had a devilish hue, his smile a grim foreboding. The twinkle in his eyes had morphed from friendly to fiendish.

"You ran away with our toy."

"Your toy?" Domenico shook his head. "No, my toy. Even has my name on it."

Roman shrugged. "You ran off with my father's—the boss's—property. She's worth more than you know."

Worst of all—by that wicked gleam in Roman's eye, he knew.

Roman knew all my secrets, and he was taunting Domenico with that knowledge.

"Ari is mine."

Roman shook his head. "No, she's mine."

"Over my cold, dead body."

"That's the plan."

Sirens rang out, a flash of blue and red, making everyone stow their guns. Taking it as the opportunity to run, Domenico grabbed my hand and pulled. I spun around in time to watch the cop car speed by and see one of the guys run toward us as the others split up and climbed into two cars.

I still wasn't strong enough or fast enough, and we were almost to the car when a hand wrapped around my arm. A scream burst from me and Domenico spun around, his fist connecting with the man who had hold of me. Two powerful hits, and his grip loosened and he fell to the ground.

The second we were both in the car he had it in gear, and we sped off. I pulled on my seatbelt as we bounced onto the street, barely missing another car.

It wasn't far when he turned into an alley, and I stared into the rearview mirror, watching for anyone following.

A car suddenly appeared from a side street, and I screamed when the back window exploded.

"It's okay!" he yelled as he slammed his foot on the gas, propelling us down the alley.

I wasn't sure where the other car was, but I hoped we'd lost them. Twists and sudden turns rocked me back and forth in the seat. My hold on the door handle was white-knuckled as I held on for dear life, hoping to lose them, to stop the horror.

The Mustang lived up to its reputation, the engine roaring with each press to the gas, propelling us down the road.

More explosions blasted the car, and I shrank into the seat as I glanced at the side mirror. Roman hung out the passenger window, firing off another round of shots, though only a few hit the car.

"Make a hard left," I said as I watched him lean out the window again.

Domenico kept his foot on the gas, then shifted. I slammed against the door at the sudden move, then was shoved back into the seat from the acceleration. The move left the car behind us struggling to follow, and we put some distance between us and them.

We were finally getting away from them when a sudden jolt rocked through me as the whole car jerked to the right.

"Fuck," Domenico hissed as he regained control.

The first car we'd lost reappeared and sideswiped us. My eyes were wide as I stared out the window. I flinched back, drawing in a sharp breath as the glass in front of me shattered but didn't break.

My heart hammered as I realized it would have hit me.

The car was bulletproof. That was why the back window didn't shatter. That was why he said it was okay.

"Hold on," Domenico said between clenched teeth.

I took hold of the armrest and braced against the door. A sudden jerk of the wheel and we slammed into the other car. The force drove them onto the curb, where they slammed into a light post. The car bounced off the pole, the momentum pulling the back end around until it was blocking the lane, then came to a stop.

Seconds later we were flying onto the interstate, and Domenico really opened the engine up.

"I think we lost them," Domenico said as we raced down the interstate doing well over the speed limit.

"What do we do now?" I asked, because we were drawing a lot of attention as we weaved through mid-day traffic. I stared at the bullet hits on the back glass. The windows were still standing, to my shock. Large white circles indicated where each bullet had landed, and cracks spiraled out from the force.

"I think it's time to pay your father a visit," he said as he pressed harder on the gas.

"Do you think that's a good idea?" I asked. He was the one who'd orchestrated my kidnapping and had hidden his agenda.

"We don't have much of a choice. We need an ally."

But was he an ally?

It was our best hope, and I hoped it would work.

SEVENTEEN

When we got off the interstate, we were still alone. The anxiety that one of them was going to suddenly pop out had me still clutching the door so hard my hand hurt, but I couldn't let go.

The area shifted, no longer dirty and run down—everything was pristine and well-manicured.

The Northbrook neighborhood I grew up in was still marked by massive mansions with a few smaller, older homes mixed in. Many of them had been torn down to have the giant structures replace them.

My stomach knotted at the wrought-iron fencing, and I took a deep breath before I stared up at the stone facade, noticing how little had changed in three years.

My hands shook as we pulled up to the house that I had once called home. It was the property my father purchased when he'd climbed his way higher into the organization. A veritable fortress, a gilded cage.

As soon as we stepped out of the car, there were half a

dozen men outside, half of them with their hands on their guns. I recognized the man in front of me. He'd been one of my father's men when I lived here.

"Santiago," Domenico said with a nod.

"Sir," he said with a hint of surprise. He glanced over to the guard on his right, then to me. "Miss."

The guard he'd looked at turned to me, his brow scrunched.

"We need to see Maurizio," Domenico said.

"He's not taking any visitors today," the guy said as he scowled at me.

I quirked a brow at him. While my veins were buzzing with nervous energy, part of me was waking up—the part of me that was a Mafia princess, even if I didn't want to be.

I walked up to him, my jaw locked as I glared at him. My fingers wrapped around his tie before yanking his head down until we were face-to-face. His arm swept up, but before he could strike me, Domenico held one of his arms, while Santiago held the other.

"Get my *father*. Now," I demanded, then released his tie.

His eyes were wide as he straightened, his arms released.

"Go on, Jenkins," Santiago said.

There was something off about Jenkins and the few others who followed him inside. They didn't match the Ferrante men in that they didn't look Italian. They looked more like hired guns, and I wondered why he'd searched out more security than Ferrante provided.

What was my father up to?

Santiago led us up the steps, and Domenico kept me tight to his side as he eyed Jenkins when we entered.

The foyer was just as grand as I remembered, especially the double marble staircase with ornate iron handrail. The memories it held made me shiver, and I hated our pause as Santiago knocked on the door to the left of the grand staircase.

"Sir, Mr. Mancini is here," Santiago said.

"Domenico?" A shiver rolled through me at the sound of my father's voice. Domenico must have felt it because he gave me a squeeze. He released me after that but kept my hand in his as we moved to head in.

Santiago stepped back and held the door open. "There are six roses, sir," Santiago whispered under his breath as Domenico passed. It was so low I barely heard.

It had me confused until we walked through the door to my father's office and I spotted a rose lapel pin on his jacket.

The door closed behind us, but even that couldn't pull my father from his power trip of a pause.

My father sat behind his great carved walnut desk, the scent of cigars still lingering in the air. The room was exactly as I remembered with its rich wood walls, bookshelves, and coffered ceiling, a marble fireplace on one wall and a window opposite that surveyed the front yard.

"You're just about the last person I exp—" He stopped mid-sentence when his head rose and his eyes landed on me. "Arabella."

I held back a shudder as he said my name. "Father."

"Truly the last person I expected to see. It's been three years, Daughter."

"You sent for me, didn't you?" I held my arms out. "Here I am."

He tsk'ed as he stood. "I see you're at least wearing clothes these days, though you look like a hobo."

I scoffed and rolled my eyes. "Donations at their finest."

His mouth turned down in disgust. "You had such potential. Now look at you."

"What do I have now?" I asked.

"An empty cage that misses you," he sneered.

My fear swirled inside me, morphing into the hatred I'd long forgotten. "That's why you had me kidnapped? To slowly kill me in a cell?"

He stared at me, his gaze then trailing down my arm to our

joined hands, then back up. "If I wanted you dead, I easily could have had you taken care of, and nobody would have known of my involvement."

"You wanted her. I have her. Now we need your assistance," Domenico spoke up, cutting him off.

He turned to Domenico. "Because of what you did? You really shouldn't have, Domenico."

"What do you mean? She was running out of days. Shit was getting out of control. You told me to protect her."

My father turned back toward his desk. "Protect her so that she wasn't a shell of a girl. To not let those animals you command destroy her. Not rescue her."

I stared at Domenico, then to my father. Not rescue me? What did that mean?

"You're going back." My father pulled a gun from a drawer and aimed it at me.

I drew in a sharp breath, eyes wide as I stared down the barrel. Domenico stepped forward and pushed me behind him, shielding my body with his own.

"I have a deal with Roman," my father spat.

"What deal?" Domenico demanded.

"He gets to marry Arabella and gets a leg up in the family ranking, taking over the position of underboss from Giovanni's fluff of a brother, Giuliano."

There was my answer. Why I was taken. Why he searched for me then. Why I was kept for so long. It was all to use me to his advantage.

"It's all a power grab. I'm nothing but another pawn in your fucking quest for power," I said. I knew it. Deep down, I knew it wasn't because he missed me or loved me—I was simply a piece to play. Just like my mother. We never meant anything to him.

A dark chuckle left Domenico. "You and Roman are both stupid if you think that will work."

"And you aren't stupid for what you did? You've fucked up. You protected her too well, compromised your position. Now you're just as useless to me as my daughter."

Useless.

Useless.

The word was on repeat. All my childhood memories flashed through my mind, my chest clenching at my early memories of the man who read me bedtime stories and made me laugh, then to the last dreadful years I'd spent as his prisoner. That was all his home had been—a prison.

Long ago, he stopped being a loving parent. Long ago, the monster took over.

"You don't want to do this," Domenico said, but his tone wasn't pleading. It was a warning.

"Giovanni will forgive me. I'll tell him I caught you stealing her away. They are already on the lookout for you."

"Trust me, Giovanni won't be pleased with my death," Domenico growled.

My father shrugged. "I'll take my chances." His finger flexed, and Domenico jerked as the sound reverberated about the room. The deafening shock had me covering my ears.

There was no chance at a second shot. Domenico closed the space between them and grabbed his hand. The gun fired off again, this time lodging a bullet somewhere into the bookcase.

Domenico's fist slammed into my father's face. Then again, and again, just as I had seen before. Hard strikes to quickly immobilize an opponent, the fury of a beast. All the while I stared, my entire body shaking with adrenaline and a line of justice each time his fist connected.

The sounds of feet stomping could be heard from the other side of the door, and I knew there wasn't much time before my father's guards burst in.

"Domenico!" I cried out when my father was slumped into his chair, his body limp.

Domenico's shoulders heaved with each harsh breath he expelled. The gun had tumbled to the ground as he was beating my father, and he bent down to pick it up.

He staggered as he straightened and reached up with his free hand to his abdomen. "Shit."

My eyes popped wide and dread zipped down my spine when Domenico turned toward me. His shirt was deep red and wet, his fingers red as well.

The jerk he'd made had been him being hit by a bullet.

"Oh God."

His eyes squeezed tight, and he shook his head as if to clear his mind. "We have to go. Now."

I nodded, the voices growing louder. "Give me his gun." I held out my hand. Domenico looked at it before his gaze flickered to the door.

"You know how to work it?" he asked as he passed it over.

I released the magazine and glanced at the remaining bullets before seating it back with a pop of my palm. "Yes."

He reached into his waistband for his own piece. His steps were uneven, and I knew that each second that passed, the more blood he lost, the greater the chance I would lose him.

That last thought shook me to my core. They were without thought. Losing him meant more than the protection he provided, and my chest tightened at even the small prospect that he would leave me.

"Come on." He stood for a second, listening with his hand on the door handle, then swung it open.

On the other side stood nine men in suits, guns in hand. Domenico once again placed himself between me and them.

"Stay right there, Domenico," Jenkins called out.

"Besides some hurt pride and probably a broken nose, he's fine," Domenico said.

A few of the men relaxed once Santiago did, their gazes still locked on Domenico. Jenkins glared at those who stood down.

"What the fuck are you doing? Get your guns up, now!" Jenkins yelled to the other men. They refused, which was odd, but then again, they worked for Ferrante in the end. The leader, though, didn't seem to share the same sense of order and obligation, which made me believe he was a direct hire of my father's. "Fuck this," he hissed, returning his attention to Domenico, but before he could do anything, a shot rang out.

Domenico's arm was raised, and a moment later Jenkins had crumpled to the ground. There was a split second of silence before the ones loyal to him pointed their guns at Domenico.

They were so focused on their anger and revenge that they didn't even notice me. Didn't see me as a threat.

But I was, and they weren't going to take him from me.

I fired off multiple rounds, hitting my targets before they could hit theirs.

I stared down at the men. One was gasping for breath, his eyes wide. The other was on his knees, clutching his stomach. Domenico's eyes were on me, but I felt no guilt or remorse. They were trying to take Domenico from me, and there was no way I was going to let that happen.

"Sir, you need to go. Now. Take Miss with you. We will deal with this," Santiago said. He stepped forward and fired off two shots—one in each head of the men I'd injured.

Domenico nodded. "Thank you, Santiago." He took a step forward, but before he could take another, his legs gave out and he crashed to the marble floor. "Fuck."

Santiago rushed forward and called the others over. They got him to his feet and walked him out to the car.

"Miss," Santiago said as I watched in horror as Domenico's strength spilled out of him. My gaze moved away from him to Santiago. "Get him to a doctor. Fast."

I nodded and took the keys he'd pulled from Dom's pocket and moved to the driver's side. With one last glance I peered up at the house I once knew and wished Santiago would burn it to the ground with my father still inside.

There was no room for thoughts of anger or retribution, only getting Domenico help. His head was leaned back against the headrest, eyes drooping. His shirt was completely soaked, and blood was running down his pant leg.

We were more than a mile away from the nearest hospital when his hand reached out and grabbed my arm.

"Not a hospital."

"What are you talking about? Of course a hospital! You need a doctor."

He shook his head. "No hospitals. They'll find you. Too many questions. Police."

My heart hammered. His concern wasn't for himself—it was for me. If no hospitals, where was I supposed to find help? Who would save him?

I need someone to save him!

"Where?"

"Not Ferrante."

Not Ferrante? Then…

My mind whirled, and my eyes widened as the answer came. We were in Northbrook. We weren't far. I slammed the car into a hard left.

EIGHTEEN

It had been years since I'd been cut off from my mother's family, and there was one man I knew who would help. My only hope was that I could reach him before his men opened fire on us. Thankfully we were only about ten minutes away.

"Stay with me. Please," I said as I bit back tears.

Nearly a decade had passed since I'd visited, but I still knew the way. My mother had made sure of it. She'd even made a song of it, a rhyme. It was a little like "Head, Shoulders, Knees, and Toes," but with street names. Maybe she knew one day I would need him and that was how I would remember.

The estate was larger than I recalled but held more warm memories than my father's house. A tall stone-and-iron fence surrounded the property and the gate was open, one guard in the shack, but there was no time to stop.

It had been so long since I'd last seen my grandfather. Would he recognize me? The years apart were not by my choice, but the tighter my father wound the leash around my mother's neck, the more things he cut from her life, starting with her own family. The deeper he got with Ferrante, the more unwelcomed he became with my grandfather.

I powered past the entrance, drove under the guard tower, pulled up to the front door, and slammed my foot on the brake. In seconds a swarm of armed guards surrounded the car. No attention was paid to them as I jumped out and ran to the passenger side.

"Help me!" I yelled.

"Miss, stop right now," one of them yelled.

I shook my head. "No! He needs help."

"Then go to a hospital."

I glared at him as tears welled in my eyes. I didn't care that there were multiple guns pointed at me. All I cared about was Domenico. "I can't!"

The guard came closer and towered over me. "You can't come in here. Leave now of your own will, or leave in a plastic bag."

My lip curled up into a snarl, and I slammed my hands against his chest. "Get me Vitale!" I cried out.

"Miss, I'll give you ten seconds to get back in the car before we open fire."

Anger flared in me, and I whipped back around to him. "No, you listen to me. You have ten seconds to get me Laureano Vitale."

"What is all the commotion about out here, Angelo?" a deep voice rumbled from the door. It was one I recognized despite the years since I'd last heard it. The overflow of my anxiety was wiped away at the calming, familiar tones.

"Please! Please help me, Nonno!" I cried out in hopes that I'd made the right decision.

Hard heels clacked against the stone steps, and Angelo was pushed aside. Light brown eyes matching my own were wide as they stared at me in shock. "Arabella? My Arabella?" His gaze flickered around, zeroing in on the red splotches covering my skin. "Get the doctor!" he yelled out, and a few men ran back into the house. He took my hands and flipped them, his fingers gingerly searching out the source.

"Not me, Nonno. Him." I stepped aside, exposing Domenico. At that moment, his head lolled to the side, and he looked at my grandfather briefly before his eyes shut.

"Dio mio. What happened?" he asked.

"He saved me."

His eyes searched mine. "Saved you?"

"From my father."

My grandfather's expression darkened, almost crackling. Recognition flitted across his eyes before settling again. "Who is he?"

"His name is Domenico Mancini," I said, and I began to question my decision. "You know him."

Of course he would, because they were enemies, and Domenico was la Bestia.

"He is one of Ferrante's men. Therefore, I need you to tell me why I am fixing up one of his men instead of throwing him into a landfill."

"Because he protected me, took a bullet for me, stood between me and my father and beat my father to a bloody pulp with that wound and made sure I got out of there safely."

He stared at him, then motioned at his men to take him inside. "Let's get you cleaned up before we talk more."

"I want to stay with Domenico," I said as I watched four men carry his lifeless body through the door.

"Let the doctor help him, Nipote." He took hold of my arms and guided me in a different direction.

All I could do was trust that he would help him, and I prayed with a depth I hadn't known I possessed that I'd put my faith in the right person.

A maid came forward with a bowl of warm water and a rag as soon as I stepped through the threshold. She helped to rid my hands of the dried blood.

Once she was satisfied, I followed my grandfather into his office. There were two guards standing at the doorway, and I did a double take at one of them.

I blinked in surprise at the familiar dirty blond with a crooked smile. "Mia bella," he said with a wink before closing the door, and my stomach dropped with understanding.

"They were your men, not my father's," I said. Tears filled my eyes, and I blinked them away.

"Yes," he said with a sad smile. "He was supposed to give you his card if you refused to listen again, but you never looked at it, did you?"

I shook my head. "I thought he was sent by my father. I…if I'd known…"

"My informants were made aware of a plot to…dispose of you."

Dispose. The word had my stomach rolling. I added it to the growing list of outcomes my father had envisioned when he'd found out where I was.

"Your father had gotten word that you were stripping and used that as an excuse to tie up what he saw as a loose end."

"That, or use me as a pawn." The tears that filled my eyes spilled over, and I wiped them away with the heel of my hand before willing them to stop. "How could he?"

"That is something I've been asking myself. His ego has grown so much, and he believes he is untouchable. Somehow he even managed to convince himself that I wasn't watching him. That I still hadn't enacted my revenge for what he did to my daughter, let alone what he did to you. That he was safe."

My brow scrunched as I remembered the multiple times his men came to the club. "You've known where I was for years. How?"

"Because strip bars are a great way to launder money."

I balked at what he was saying. It couldn't be…"Do you own Castle?"

He shook his head. "No, but we have a great relationship with Al. One day he was showing me his new girl, and I was shocked to find it was you."

"Why didn't you come?" I asked. Though I had to wonder: If he'd appeared back then, would I have gone?

"Word spread about what happened with your father," he said, his eyes a mixture of sadness and anger. "You needed the moment of independence. I couldn't clip your wings, not after everything you'd been through, so Al kept me informed. The deal I made with myself was that I would let you have your freedom, but if you began to spin out of control, I would bring you in."

"So you were fine with me being a stripper?"

He shook his head. "No. I listened, I waited, and I offered, but besides a few unsavory admirers, you were fine. The most alive I'd ever seen you."

"You didn't watch…"

He shook his head."Never. I am not your father. I sent those I trust most to report back, and Al kept me informed as well."

As he continued, I flinched at the memories of my father's hands on me and drew in a shaky, steadying breath.

"We're in a real mess," I admitted. Defeat washed over me. There was no way out that I could see.

"Yes, you are," he agreed. "You will be safe here."

I would be, but as I glanced to the door, I wondered if some of the men on the other side wouldn't find a reason for that bullet or another to kill Domenico.

I needed him.

"And Domenico?" I asked.

"Will go back to the Ferrante," he answered.

I shook my head."No. He can't. They'll kill him."

His hand slammed down onto his desk, and I jumped at the burst of anger. "And he's killed us! That man is a vicious killer, Arabella. His hands are forever red from the blood he has spilled."

"I know he's a monster. A killer." *But I love him.*

"Saving your life absolves him of that?" He shook his head. "You are being ridiculously and recklessly romantic."

I stared down at my hands, at the tiny remnant of red that remained in the small creases on my fingers. "Maybe, but I'm no saint either. I'm not the pure little girl you once knew. That was taken from me, and it hardened me. And that *monster* is the only thing that makes me feel alive."

He shook his head. "He cannot stay here."

"Then once he is patched up, we will leave," I said. *Just please save him.* "Please, just help him and we will go."

He sighed, his body sagging. "Not everything is as it seems, Nipote."

I shook my head. "It never is in this world of money and power."

He nodded. "I'm sure you're right." He stared at me. "He doesn't know, does he?"

I shook my head. "No." But when he woke, he would find out. My deepest secret—one that I'd kept was also the one few Ferrante knew—I was Vitale blood.

And if I was correct, when it came to the Vitale bloodline, I was now the sole heir to the Vitale family. After all, that was what my father had hoped to use to propel himself further. I wasn't sure what his endgame was, but I did know he would pay when everything settled.

If everything settled. If I didn't make it, I knew the man sitting in front of me would make certain my father didn't either.

"You have choices to make, but for now, why don't you go get cleaned up and meet me for dinner at seven."

"I want to see Domenico."

He shook his head. "It will be a while. You can see him after dinner."

I nodded and stood. If he helped Domenico, I could do as he asked, though my whole body vibrated, desperately missing his presence.

The door opened, and the guard I'd recognized stepped in.

"Luca, show my granddaughter to Francesca's room."

The man I now knew as Luca nodded. "Yes, sir."

"Thank you, Nonno," I said as I stepped toward the door.

"Arabella," he called out, causing me to turn back to him. "I know you are caught up in quite a snarl, but I want you to know I will do everything in my power to ensure your safety. Even if that means making it so he is able to leave here as your escort."

I gave him a soft smile. I knew it was hard for him, but it was all coming from that place of fatherly love that I'd been denied for years.

"Thank you."

NINETEEN

I followed Luca through the central hall with its large marble staircase. A glance down the extra-wide hall, and I was reminded of the sheer size of the estate.

I'd forgotten that, though my grandfather was second, he'd raised his family here alongside my great-uncle. Both were great men who'd lost their wives and daughters early, and I could see the toll in his eyes.

"You know, you could have at least told me who you worked for," I said to Luca as we ascended the steps.

"Would you have believed me?" he asked as we reached the top and continued down the hall.

"Maybe."

We stopped at the third door down. There was no special marking—it looked just like the other doors, but when he opened it, a wave of nostalgia hit me.

"Relax here. There will be a maid up soon to help you." He closed the door behind him, and I was alone in silence.

The room was familiar. One I'd been in long ago, one that

hadn't changed. There was a large four-poster bed against one wall, and a floral duvet spilling over the edges. An image of me being curled up under the soft blanket swirled in my head as the memories flooded my mind.

It was my mother's bedroom. The one she grew up in. The daughter of the second-in-command. A Vitale by birth.

As I walked around, my fingers flitted across pieces of furniture, creating a warmth that settled deep inside me even as the pain from her loss ripped through my heart once again. As the memories flowed, it was almost as if she were still there. I could almost see her sitting at the cream-colored vanity, applying makeup. As I sat on the pink velour stool and looked into the mirror, a tear fell from my eye.

Before I could stop it, a torrent of tears erupted.

I missed her. So very much. Add that to the shitstorm that had been the last five or so weeks of my life, and I let all the pain and anxiety and fear out. Expelled everything but Domenico, all the truths that broke me, and I blanketed myself in the memories, in the still-lingering feeling of my mother within the walls of her home. There was the safety she always shrouded me in, even though it had cost her everything.

The swell of emotions that had built up for so many weeks spilled out of me, and I couldn't hold it back, not when I didn't know how Domenico was. All the what-ifs and negative outcomes circulated through my mind. Thoughts drifting in and out. What would I do without him?

"Excuse me, Miss?"

I sniffed and wiped at my eyes with the heel of my palm. "Yes?"

At the door stood a girl around my age, her hair pinned back in a bun and wearing a dress that fell past her knees, an apron topping it. In one hand she held a large wicker basket. "My name is Amelia. Master asked me to help you get ready for dinner."

I looked down at what I was wearing, at the dried blood that splattered across my body, smears of dark red that still stained my skin. Only my hands were mostly clean.

"I…" I looked up to her. "I have nothing else." Our bags were still in the car.

She closed the door before stepping forward and taking my hand. "Let's get you cleaned up." She guided me through the only other door, which led to a large attached bathroom.

I could only stand and stare as she started the shower and pulled some toiletries out of the basket and towels from a small linen closet.

She moved in front of me and began tugging my shirt up my body. With all that had happened in the past six hours, I had no protest left in me and I allowed her to help get my clothes off.

She placed them in a plastic bag, probably to be destroyed, before reaching up for the chain around my neck.

I set my hand on hers. "Don't."

"I'm just going to set it down on that tray while you shower," she promised, her eyes never leaving me as she slipped the gold over my head. "Miss Francesca and Master Laureano," she said as she looked at the photos in the locket.

"Did you know her?"

She shook her head. "No, but there are photos of her in many places, and Master has a large painting over the fireplace in his office."

He did? How had I missed that when I'd just stood in that very room? I needed to look the next time I was there.

She guided me over to the shower. "I will be back in a moment. Take as much time as you need."

The warm water cascaded down my body in soothing droplets that turned to rivulets riding the curves of my skin. For a long time I just stood there, sighing with each muscle that loosened the death grip they'd held ever since I was taken.

I was safe. The fear still sat in the back of my mind, while the fear that clung to my skin like sweat swirled down the drain.

We weren't really safe, only safe for now.

Domenico's blood, still clinging to my skin, began to melt away. A few days of rest and we would leave, run away from all of it. Feuding families served only as a Romeo and Juliet reminder, and I was not going to be driven to death by them. I wanted to live, to be free, but above all, I wanted to be with Domenico, no matter what.

Somewhere along the way I'd fallen for him. The beast. The demon leader who held so much beneath the surface. His ruthlessness was ingrained, his domineering in his blood, his ability to command a group of men his purpose. But the most important aspect, his secret weapon, was his ability to truly care for someone. He wasn't the man my father was—the villain who would use his own daughter as currency. Or Roman who would do anything to best Domenico.

Domenico's ability to care wasn't flashy or in your face, but was subtle and strong.

And Domenico cared about me. It was there in his touch, in his words of claiming. I still didn't know why he'd risked so much to free me, why he'd put his life on the line, but I was grateful to an extent I couldn't measure.

The click of the door had me drawing in a breath, and I reached for the body wash and washcloth. After scouring everything, I stepped out to find Amelia waiting for me. She handed me a towel for my hair, then used a second one to help dry my body before wrapping a silk robe around me.

I'd never had another help me bathe before, except my mother when I was younger, yet I allowed her to help me. Something about her put me at ease, and I felt that she was trustworthy. A feeling that I had lacked in my life until I'd found Domenico…until I'd been forced to return to the life I'd run away from by coming to my grandfather.

With everything that had happened, I welcomed her assistance. Someone to help me get one foot in front of the other and direct me when I felt lost.

Before we moved on, she clasped my locket around my neck. "Better?" she asked with a small smile.

I swallowed and nodded. It helped, but the only thing that would really make things better would be for Domenico to walk in. Instead I was left waiting, worrying, as the doctor took care of him. Hoping and praying he would be okay, that he would look upon me again with his intense silver eyes.

Amelia opened a door I hadn't even noticed, and my eyes widened in surprise. It led to a large walk-in closet lined with clothing, some of it protected by plastic coverings.

"One of the other girls ran to get you some new undergarments, but while we wait, let's find you a dress."

I had undergarments in the car, but I decided not to mention it.

Bright pink jewels sitting on one side of a bright fuchsia dress caught my eye, and I stopped. The last party my father threw, the last New Year's Eve my mother was alive, she'd worn it. Other dresses were familiar as well.

"These are my mother's," I said in a whisper.

She nodded. "Your grandfather acquired them after her passing."

My brow scrunched. "What else did he acquire?"

She shook her head. "I don't know. I'm sorry."

I stepped back out into the bedroom and looked around, my gaze narrowing on a familiar jewelry box. I walked over and flipped the lid. Sure enough, the box was my mother's.

After her death I'd asked my father if I could have it, but he'd said no. It still held all her jewels. Hundreds of thousands of dollars in diamonds and gold. The two other most prominent jewels were our birthstones—topaz for me, aquamarine for her.

I pulled out the necklace that held both our birthstones and added it around my neck with my locket.

"What about this one?" Amelia asked from the closet.

It wasn't one of the spectacular evening gowns but a tasteful, off-the-shoulder blue A-line dress that hit at the knees. I remembered it—a favorite during the summer. My fingers played with the jewels around my neck.

"Perfect."

TWENTY

Amelia dried my hair, straightening out my waves as she did so, curling the ends as she went. While that was going on, the girl they'd sent to get me new undergarments returned, and we were able to get me fixed up and into my chosen outfit.

It was strange, stepping into a dress that my mother once wore. It was a little large due to my weight loss, but thankfully it had a tie-up back. I think that was why Amelia picked it. Her shoes, however, were nearly a size too large, but we found a pair with clasps that would help keep them on.

When I stepped out of the room, two men were stationed across the hall. They were my guards, but I wondered why I needed them. One started walking, and I fell in line behind him as the second followed me.

As we walked, more staff and members of the organization stepped out of our way.

The respect I was regarded with was both familiar and strange after years of no one showing respect as I walked among them. The men around me watched each step, but their eyes weren't filled with lust and an underlying desire to fuck me. Part respect, part wariness.

We headed down to the main floor, and one of the men hooked my arm in his to help steady me. I was used to six-inch platform heels, but for some reason three-inch heels that were too big were more difficult to navigate.

They led me to a large set of doors and opened one, allowing me to step in.

The dining room was stunning. A large dark wood table that seated at least a dozen people was set for only two. The door shut, and I found myself alone as I stepped to the far end of the table.

A fire crackled in the fireplace, dispersing warmth and a soft glow.

The head was set, and I stood behind the open chair to his right. Placement meant a lot in seating. It was a position of respect.

"Please, Arabella, sit," my grandfather said from the doorway. Once again, the large oak door latched closed, and we were the only ones in the room. "Would you like a drink?" he asked from a bar where he poured a glass of amber liquid.

"Wine would be wonderful," I said as I sat and scooted the chair closer to the table. I didn't really care if it was red or white. It'd been so long, and I needed a drink.

The intricate design of the china was another familiarity that struck me. It held the Vitale family crest in the center and had a scalloped edge. The smaller plates were rimmed with an ivy design.

With two glasses in hand, he made his way to the head of the table and placed one in front of me before setting his own down and taking a seat.

"Thank you," I said before taking a sip of the deep red liquid.

"You're welcome. Do you feel better?" he asked.

"Yes and no. How is he?"

He took a sip and relaxed back in his seat. "Ah, your worry is overwhelming you."

"Please, tell me," I begged. I just needed the relief that would come from the knowledge he was okay.

He blew out a breath. "He is out of surgery and steady."

I drew in a stuttered breath and blinked the wetness from my eyes. He was alive. "When can I see him?"

His brow furrowed. "Later. First, I need you to tell me what happened to you."

I leaned back in my chair. "What do you mean?"

"I mean, you know I'm in contact with Al," he said. Oh, that. "You went missing, and I don't think you were in this state when that happened."

Meaning how did I end up with Domenico, looking like a half-dead human skeleton. Even with my improving physique, it would still take time to reverse the damage.

"If I tell you it's my father's doing, will that satisfy you?" I asked.

"No."

I pursed my lips as I stared at the fireplace across from me.

How many years had it been since I'd last sat in this room? My grandfather had aged since the last time I saw him. His once salt-and-pepper hair was now all salt, and the lines on his face seemed deeper from the burden on his shoulders.

I turned to him. "Answer this first: What happened?"

"What do you mean?" he asked before taking another sip.

"Why didn't I see you anymore?"

He regarded me as he scratched at his short beard. "When I first met your father, he was rising in his practice and was eager to work with our legal team. His ambition was strong, and he had a thirst. I knew when he asked for your mother's hand not a month later that his reasoning was to have a foothold into the family. I would not allow him near the family business, but she was an adult and I couldn't stop her. Shortly after was when he met Ferrante. Having your mother as his wife gave him an in."

"And you are enemies."

He nodded. "I forbid him to come anywhere near our organization. Your mother would bring you here as much as she could. The strain…She wasn't as strong as you are. I feared for her, but the more I tried to remove her from that situation, the more he tightened her bonds until she couldn't take it anymore."

I took a long gulp of my wine. It was always hard to talk about her, especially when my father barely let me grieve her death. "I don't hate her for leaving me, but I do miss her."

He reached over and squeezed my hand. "She loved you so much, with all her heart."

"How did you get all of my mother's things?" I asked. Even I wasn't allowed any of it, so how did he attain it all?

"I have informants. They knew who was tasked with disposing and selling her belongings. I used a third party to purchase as much as I could. I couldn't just watch him throw her things away like he did her life." Tears reflected in his eyes, and he blinked them away before clearing his throat. "The bastard even refused me entry to my own daughter's funeral and kept you as far away from me as he could."

I stared down at the plates, wondering how my life might have been different. "I wish you could have gotten to me. Those years were hell."

His gaze locked onto me, his brow furrowed. "I tried. I lost over a dozen men trying, half of them to the man lying in this house."

My eyes widened. "Domenico?"

He nodded. "He was younger then, still working his way up. The anger in him…there is good reason they call him la Bestia, mia bella."

"There are reasons not to call him that as well," I said.

"Perhaps." He reached over and took my hand in his. "Tell me, how did you come to be with him?"

Where to even begin? It seemed like a lifetime ago when I was surrounded on that bridge. "I'm not sure how long ago, five weeks, maybe six, they abducted me from my car on my way home. I spent weeks in a cage, where they held women to be sold off. Domenico…he had to put a claim on me." My fingers danced around my collarbone.

He released my hand and I could tell he was holding back anger as he stared at the script embedded in my skin. He knew what happened to those girls, and what I wasn't saying. "How did you get out of there?"

"Tensions rose. Roman Ferrante had been riling up the men, turning them against Domenico in a bid to get me. We just found out the whole thing was a plan hatched between Roman and my father. We fled one night and have been holed up in a motel until early today, when Roman found us. Domenico thought it would be safe with my father, that he would provide a place of sanctuary, but he didn't. My father tried to kill me, but Domenico took the bullet. Guards turned on guards, and three men were dead at the end. Two of which I shot myself."

His eyes widened, and I knew the memories of him teaching me to shoot, to protect myself, were surfacing. Skills he no doubt feared I would need. "And your father?"

"Domenico beat half the life from him, but sadly he is still alive."

There was so much to digest, to read between the lines, and to understand the deeper meaning, but I knew he was running through it all.

"I can't forgive all of Domenico's sins against this family. I should have just let him bleed out. However, he did something I tried for years to do and failed—he protected you at all cost and brought you home."

My brow furrowed and I reached out for his hand. "Thank you, Nonno."

I knew it wasn't an easy thing for him to do, and something many of his men would be against, but with his help, Domenico and I had a chance to make it to the other side. Unlike my father, the man sitting next to me was strong enough to stand down against a man who was his enemy. Because he valued my life—and showed it by allowing Domenico his own.

TWENTY-ONE

After dinner I lost the heels and walked barefoot through the marble-lined halls. Once again, I was in awe at the space held under one roof. Each room was huge and decorated with such opulence. Chandeliers hung from the ceilings, large fireplaces filled many walls, and hardwood floors were covered with plush area rugs.

I pulled a throw from one of the couches in one of the many sitting rooms. Luca was a ghost behind me, unobtrusive in my perusal. Oddly, little had changed from my memories. A few new pieces of furniture, an updated kitchen, but for the most part everything was the same down to the small plaster details that decorated the walls and ceilings.

I wanted to change out of the dress, but I had a feeling everyone would be aghast at the state of my clothes in the trunk of Domenico's car.

Winding down to the basement, I found the infirmary next to the spa. There were four guards outside the door, and they blocked me from entering.

"You can't go in," one of them said. They weren't guards like Luca. No, these were associates and capos. Men who had retribution on their minds, and I refused to leave until I saw Domenico.

"I'm not leaving." At that, I sat down in one of the plush chairs a few feet away. I curled up on it, pulling the throw tighter around me.

My stomach was in knots with each minute that passed. I needed to see him, to touch him. I needed him more than I could understand. Without him I had no idea what would happen to me, and I feared the unknown.

"Miss, you can come in now," the doctor called about an hour later.

Immediately I was on my feet and racing through the open door. It wasn't until I saw his face and heard his heart beating on the monitors that I began to relax.

"How is he?" I asked as I took his hand in mine.

"The bullet passed through."

"Passed through?"

He nodded. "There was an exit wound."

I stared at him. If I'd been standing more to the right, would it have hit me too?

"It struck to the far right. He is incredibly lucky all internal organs were missed. Half an inch to the left and there would be damage to his large intestines. He lost a lot of blood, and we've given him a transfusion."

"How long before he wakes?" I asked as I smoothed the hair from his forehead.

When there was no answer, I turned toward him.

The doctor looked over to the guard, then back to me and cleared his throat. "Due to his identity, we've put him in a medically induced coma."

"What?"

"He's a Ferrante," the guard spit.

"Who saved a Vitale life," I bit out between clenched teeth.

"Are you a Vitale?" he questioned.

That was the moment I knew I needed to assert the authority of my identity. The identity I'd kept hidden for years. I stomped over to the guard and swung my hand back before whipping it across his face, then slammed my knee into his crotch.

"Ask me something stupid like that again, and I will kill you with your own gun," I growled into his ear.

"The tactless ass said it because you've been under Ferrante control," the doctor said to clarify. "Your father is high up in their internal hierarchy."

I turned to him. "And how did I have any control over my situation? I fled years ago to get away from him."

"And you showed up with a Ferrante in tow," the doctor countered.

"A man who took a bullet for me! Who pulled me away from them."

"We have to take every precaution," he argued.

"He's been shot! What kind of danger is he in this condition?" I sat down in the chair next to Domenico and took his hand in mine. "Take him out of the coma."

The doctor sighed. "I'll stop the medication, but it may take some time for him to wake."

I nodded, paying careful attention to everything the doctor did. I didn't trust anyone near Domenico, even if my grandfather gave his word. There was bad blood, and I wouldn't put it past any of them to seek retribution.

"Wake up," I whispered as a tear slid down my cheek. "I need you."

I awoke to the soft caress of fingers trailing up and down my arm. It lulled me awake, and I remembered where I was. I sat straight up and looked down to find Domenico staring at me.

My heart skipped, and all the anxiety of him waking up flooded out of me. I draped my arms across his chest and held him close.

"You're awake."

"Where are we?" he asked, his voice hoarse. The once lax muscles beneath my touch began to coil.

"At my grandfather's house," I said.

His head cocked to the side. His gaze bounced around the room, at all the medical equipment, then back to me. "Ari, who is your grandfather?"

"So many secrets between us," I whispered as I met his eyes. "Laureano Vitale."

Domenico's eyes widened and he sat up, a strangled groan escaping as he threw the covers from himself and frantically began pulling at the tubes and wires.

"What are you doing?" I asked as I clamped my hand down before he could pull out the needle pumping him with much-needed blood and medicine.

"I have to leave. I can't stay here. They will kill me. It's not safe here for me or for you." He was frantic to get out. I'd never seen him anything but cool and collected.

I cupped his face, trying to get him to focus on me. "They aren't going to hurt you, I promise you."

His eyes were wild. "I trust you, but I don't trust him, not with my life. Vitale hates me, and with good reason."

"He promised me he—"

"A promise one of his men will break!" he yelled, his thoughts mirroring my own.

"What is going on?" I'd never seen him so unraveled. There was something he wasn't telling me. The answer to a whisper that had sat in the back of my mind for weeks. The last secret that needed to be revealed if we stood a chance of getting out of our cursed situation.

Domenico gritted his teeth and ran his hand through his hair. "You've handed the Vitale a bargaining chip."

A bargaining chip? It made no sense, especially with the rose with his name on it losing petals daily. "What the hell does that mean? You said the Ferrante would kill you."

"My truths lacked some critical information, much like yours," he ground out.

The blood in my veins turned cold. "What information?"

His eyes flitted between mine. "My name, like yours, is a half truth."

I blinked at him. That was the moment, the moment all secrets would be revealed. "What is your name?"

His gaze locked on mine. "Giovanni Domenico Mancini Ferrante. My father is Giovanni Ferrante, head of the Ferrante family."

My stomach dropped. The room seemed to spin and I grabbed hold of him, my eyes never leaving his. "You're a Ferrante?"

Of all the secrets, I was not expecting that.

"Technically, yes."

"Technically? If he's your father, if your true last name is Ferrante, you are."

He blew out a breath and sat back on the bed but refused to release me. "I am the second-youngest son, but born of his mistress, Ileana Mancini. Illegitimate. Bastard."

All the stories clicked, the animosities and fighting. "That's why they all hated you. That's why they picked on you and your mother could do nothing." So much made sense, and all bad thoughts of his mother disappeared.

He nodded. "My siblings have hated me for not only being

the child of a mistress, but because our father gave me his name. I've gone by Domenico since I was six, unable to stand being called Giovanni. Then started using Mancini as my last name when I was eighteen."

"That's why you command so much respect." Santiago had called him *sir*. At the time I thought it was odd, but there was too much going on to think on it for long.

"Not everyone knows. When he put me to work, I dropped Ferrante, determined to make a name for myself, and not because of who my father is."

"Why did he give you his name?" I asked. With three other sons, why give that name to your bastard child?

He shook his head. "He married out of family loyalty and obligation, but it was my mother he loved. Divorce wasn't an option, and neither was denying that I was his son. Sure enough, my older siblings and Roman grew up to be disappointments, just like their mother."

"What do you mean they are disappointments?" I asked. For all the years my father worked for them, I may have seen all of the Ferrante children once, maybe twice, and mostly due to them being older than me.

"There are four with his wife, Renata. Antonio is the oldest and thinks with his temper and not his brain. I've had to clean up more than a few of his messes. Manetto is all about drugs and partying. Valentina is a spoiled bitch with only materialism on her mind. And Roman you know."

Oh, I knew Roman. "He's a two-faced bastard who can't seem to do anything on his own."

He nodded. "Roman is Renata's *baby*, and two months younger than me. He wants what he wants, but he expects others to give it to him. And Renata coddles them all, giving them whatever they want."

"What about you?" I asked.

"You already know how I grew up," he said. "Yes, I grew up with the best of everything, including education, but I worked for everything I have."

The status of our births should have pitted us against each other, and maybe it would have—if pieces of the puzzle had been reshaped or the chessboard skewed. Yet, while we were supposed to be mortal enemies, trapped in an epic battle between families, circumstances had made us so much more. Regardless of our hidden identities.

Everyone around us was either a monster in the form of a man, or a man in the form of a monster.

"Did my father know?"

"At one point, before the scar, but after Roman's attack is when I started using *Mancini*. In Maurizio's arrogance, I think he forgot."

That sounded about right. "What are we going to do?" I asked.

He shook his head and pulled me closer. "We have to get out of here."

"And go where? Do what? You were just shot. You shouldn't even be moving this much."

His skin was pale and sweat littered his forehead. How much pain was he in that he was keeping inside?

"Lie back," I ordered. The last thing I needed was him passing out, and he looked close to it.

He let out a breath as he relaxed against the bed. "I knew there was more to you, but I didn't expect this."

"I haven't seen my grandfather since I was thirteen," I said in explanation.

"Your father didn't want Laureano interfering with his plans." He tugged on my hand. "Closer."

"You're hurt," I argued. I wanted to be closer, but the last thing I wanted to do was cause him to be in any more pain.

He sat back up and swung his legs over the side. "Then I'll come to you." He wrapped his arms around me and pulled me until we were chest to chest.

"I don't want to hurt you."

He pulled back and brushed a lock of hair behind my ear. "I don't care if you do." Leaning forward, his lips pressed against mine.

A small moan left me. I was cocooned in the security of his embrace. I felt the rise and fall of his chest beneath my hands, the warmth of his arms, and the gentle caress of his breath across my skin.

"Lie back down," I said after a few minutes.

He begrudgingly followed my instructions, but I could tell when his head hit the pillow and his eyes closed that he needed it. I crawled up onto the bed, keeping clear of his right side, and nestled into his left side.

I rested my head on his chest. His arms wrapped around me, holding me close.

"It's a good thing your father is a shitty shot," he grumbled.

I couldn't agree more. "I can't lose you."

"You won't. I promise you I will keep you safe. No matter what. I will burn the Ferrante empire down to the ground, kill everyone, if that's what it takes."

"You'd go that far?" I asked.

He tilted my head back until our eyes met. That reserved calmness, the one I'd seen so many times, burned deep in his eyes. The intensity was staggering up close and caused me to swallow. "Io sono tuo."

I am yours.

I pressed my lips to his. "From this life to the next."

TWENTY-TWO

It was officially me and la Bestia against the world. However, I had a feeling we had an ally in my grandfather—a grudging one that came about because of the cameras in the infirmary.

He heard Domenico's declarations, and though he still didn't like him, it was his promise that struck him.

"La Bestia doesn't give false promises," he said as we sat down for breakfast. "I will help you two."

I stared at my grandfather in disbelief. "Did you know who he really is?"

He nodded. "I do. I've been around too long not to know. He was still using the Ferrante name when his brother gave him that scar. That is why his words struck me so. To go against your father is no easy decision. He loves you, more than his family or his own life."

I froze and turned to him. "Loves me?"

A light chuckle left him. "Nipote, you are just as bad. Think of the way you charged in here demanding help. You assaulted a capo for questioning your allegiance."

"He was a capo?" That man had nothing on Domenico.

"You're stuck in a trial by fire that only the two of you can escape. I will help, but your love is what will get you through."

"You're not upset by our relationship?"

His lips formed a thin line and his eyes darkened. "I'm trying not to think about the fact that la Bestia is in my home. The house is in an uproar with him here, and I'd just as soon put a bullet in him. I'm not pleased with it by any means, especially with how it began, but he protects you, fights *for* you. For that, I will tolerate his existence. *For now.*"

I was so thankful to him, to have an ally on our side, even begrudgingly. Deep down I knew others wouldn't have the same sentiment, but hopefully they would respect their leader enough to follow orders.

When I'd returned to my room the night before, there were a few bags of clothing waiting for me. Jeans, tops, boots, flats, a coat, and loungewear tagged with names I hadn't been able to afford over the last few years. I was pretty sure the sum was more than I'd made since I'd run away, just for what was in the bags. They must have taken my clothes and used them as a size template.

I also had a feeling they'd gone through the car and quite possibly thrown out my other clothes, as only Domenico's bag was in the room.

I spent the remainder of the morning in the infirmary with Domenico. He was asleep, and I nestled into his side, staring at his scar.

It was unbelievable that his own brother had done that to him. It was more unbelievable that my intuition of Roman had been so off. He'd sold it. An Oscar-worthy performance. I was aware now of the monster he really was. Vile and inhumane, someone who got off on the torture of others.

At some point I drifted off and was awoken by a soft kiss to my forehead.

"How are you feeling?" I asked as I tilted my head to look at his face.

"I'll be okay, princess. Don't worry."

I clenched my jaw at his deflection of my question. "How am I supposed to do that?"

"By telling me what you did this morning."

I sighed, realizing he wasn't going to admit to me his pain level. "Well, I learned there is a camera in this room that is always monitored."

His jaw tightened. "I hope they enjoyed the show."

"It has sound as well."

His lips formed a thin line. "Expected."

"He already knew who you were, all of it."

He nodded. "I went to school with some of the Vitale men."

"When you shot Elio, you said he betrayed the family…isn't that what you've done?"

Again, he nodded. "There was no time. I was to meet with my father later that day. I was going to tell him that I wanted you, that I'd claimed you, but then Roman put his plan into action. My focus shifted to getting you out of there."

"Couldn't you explain to your father what happened?" I asked.

"Roman had it right, and he timed it perfectly. I stole goods, and the punishment for that is severe. My father already gave me leniency that dwindles with each day."

The rose. How many petals remained?

"I hate being referred to as a product," I grumbled.

He reached up and cupped my face. "You have always been so much more than that to me. From the moment I first saw you on the bridge, I wanted you. The spirit and strength you showed as you fought."

A knock on the door interrupted us, and I sat up as Luca stepped in.

"Your grandfather would like to see you," he said.

I turned back to Domenico and placed my hand on his chest. "I'll be back."

He nodded, his gaze moving to Luca. "Take care of my princess, Vin."

"Worry about yourself, Dom."

I looked between them as I stood. It was good-natured banter, something I hadn't experienced in the Vitale versus Ferrante conversations.

"You knew him, I take it?" I asked Luca as we left the room.

Luca nodded. "He was a grade above me. Most of the guys idolized him. It was back then people started calling him la Bestia, before the scar." Our pace was slow, meandering, allowing us time to talk.

Hearing it from another point of view just intensified how horrifically he'd been treated.

"Why was he idolized?" I asked, desperate to hear more, to know more about the man who owned me more with each passing day.

"He was a legend. Unstoppable," Luca said with a smile. "It didn't matter how many guys ganged up on him—he went off in all-out beast mode. He destroyed them time and time again, and they still came back for more. Then Genevieve happened."

I scrunched my brow. "Who?"

He turned toward me. "The catalyst. Roman was always jealous of Dom, but when he became infatuated with a girl named Genevieve, it only got worse. See, she only had eyes for Dom. He didn't seem nearly as interested in her, but he let her hang around him. One day Roman decided he was going to make sure Genevieve didn't want Dom anymore."

I'd studied his scars, seen the depth of them, the damage done. The hatred Roman had. He could never measure up to a brother he felt he should have never been in competition with, a brother he felt superior to.

"Four guys tackled him, sending him down to his knees, but he couldn't shake them off. One held his head while Roman broke a glass bottle and raked it over Dom's face." Luca shook his head. "His screams…It was only his first swipe, but they underestimated Dom. They relaxed, while he gained focus despite the agony he was in."

The explosiveness of la Bestia was one I'd seen before. The way he moved was disarming in its speed and force.

"Blood spilled down his face and soaked into his clothes, but that didn't stop him. He broke one guy's arm, bashed some ribs of another, but Roman ran away. Once he was done and the four guys were on the ground, Dom blacked out. He didn't return to school for weeks, and when he did, he wasn't the same."

My heart hurt for him. His whole life he'd been tormented by Roman. All their encounters I'd witnessed—Domenico throwing his weight around, making Roman do menial tasks—served only to remind Roman who was the stronger brother. Claiming me, a tool that Roman wanted to use, was all he could take.

It was Genevieve all over again, only Domenico wanted me, and I reacted only to him.

Don't touch what's mine, Roman.

Luca knocked on the door to my grandfather's office before showing me through.

I stopped and stared at the man towering over my grandfather. While my grandfather was not a short man, he seemed so in the shadow of the giant next to him.

"Ah, Arabella. Come," my grandfather beckoned.

I stared at the man, his own eyes staring back. "I know you."

He remained stoic as he stared at me. "Are you sure about that?"

I nodded as I shifted my weight. "I was with my father, downtown, after my mother passed. At Asher Holdings. My mother had an account, and you refused to release any information about it to him."

"You're Francesca's daughter," he said in understanding. "He was quite incensed. The account was left to you, and I couldn't discuss the contents with him present."

"To me?" I asked.

He nodded as he took a sip of amber liquid in his glass. "Come to my office sometime and we can pull it up."

I looked to my grandfather. "Do you know?"

He shook his head. "My guess is Francesca wanted to make sure you were able to take care of yourself." His gaze moved up to the painting above the fireplace.

I followed his gaze, and my heart sank. She was so beautiful. Hair so dark brown it was almost black, clear brown eyes, and soft features. Too fragile to survive in this world of death and power.

"You called?" I asked, turning back to him.

He cleared his throat. "I was going to introduce you to Malcolm, but it seems you've met."

"Word has it you're in a bit of a bind," Malcolm said as he picked at some lint on his jacket.

I nodded. "We are." I looked back to my grandfather. "I want you to let Domenico out."

Malcolm's eyes narrowed. "Mancini?" He looked from me to my grandfather. "*You* have Domenico Mancini in your home?"

My grandfather's expression tightened. "Much to my chagrin. It's drained me of every ounce of goodwill I've ever possessed."

"Is he chained in the basement?" Malcolm asked, clearly intrigued as to the reason for Domenico's presence.

Malcolm. As I thought about the name again it triggered a memory.

"Domenico owes you," I said as I remembered the words Javier had said.

Malcolm nodded. "You're the girl from the cage Javier recognized."

Whatever Malcolm did, it was obvious he held no familial allegiance between the different organizations. It was all business.

"With regards to letting him out, that is up to his doctor. He sustained a major injury," my grandfather said. "Once he is released, I will allow him to stay with you, but he can't stay for long."

Malcolm's brow creased. "He was shot?"

I nodded. "He was blocking me, keeping me safe from my father."

Malcolm tilted his head as he appraised me coolly. "That explains the uproar in the Ferrante camp, and why a red-faced Maurizio stormed into my office yesterday."

"I hope you didn't see him," I said.

He finished off the last sip in his glass. "Unfortunately, I did. However, I couldn't help him."

I quirked a brow. "Couldn't, or wouldn't?"

Malcolm set the glass down. "I wish you luck. Once you get settled, come see me."

"Can you at least tell me what it is?" I pleaded. "She's been gone for over six years, surely you can tell me."

"No."

"Please."

He stared at me, his jaw clenching and unclenching. "I deal in money, Arabella. I'll tell you how much when you come to my office."

I nodded, knowing there was more he wasn't mentioning, but I did know one thing my mother left me—money. Something that might be able to set us free.

TWENTY-THREE

I walked the halls, letting memories wash over me, giving me something to do while Domenico healed enough to be released. Dozens of doors lined the halls. Large wooden panel doors, some with intricate carvings, others plain, but all were heavy and solid.

I stopped at the detailed tree sculpted into the thick wall of a set of double doors. They were familiar. They led to the best room in the house—the library.

As a child, during the rare times we were allowed to go to my grandfather's, I had loved visiting the library. It was one of my favorite places in the house, a place where I spent a lot of time—so much so that my grandfather kept a shelf of children's stories for me, then later young adult novels.

With a twist of the handles I was able to push the great doors open, exposing one of the grandest rooms I'd ever been in. It was one of the many rooms that dripped elegance and prestige. Dark, rich woods held vast volumes of books.

It held both a cozy and expansive feeling. A fireplace sat

against the outside wall framed by two large leaded glass windows. The ceiling opened into a second story, an ornate crystal chandelier centered in the open space above a few wingback chairs and leather sofas. I ran my hand across the smooth leather surface and breathed in the scent of the thousands of books that lined the walls.

Books had always been my escape. My way to see the world in a way I was never allowed to. Reading was my comfort, my greatest joy—and the stories inside my savior.

Books got me through the hard times. Let me live in a world full of wonder and happy endings. As a teenager I used partying, sex, and alcohol as an escape, but even outside of those times I still read. In the days I was trapped inside, I used books to explore other worlds.

Shelves were labeled with placards showcasing the language or genre.

A wooden spiral staircase was built into a corner, and I climbed up to the second story. The view of the ground was spectacular. Over the treetops I could see the sun reflecting off Lake Michigan.

If it had been warmer, I would have taken a walk down the path that led to the shore. I could barely recall what was down there anymore, but I remembered a beach area and a boat house, both protected by jetties.

On the second floor was where my shelf was located. I loved going up the staircase, so that was where my books were kept.

I didn't expect it to still be there—I was just curious what was—but I was shocked to find it fully stocked. The young adult novels still sat, but the collection had expanded to two shelves. Classics from Charlotte Brontë and Jane Austen, the entire Harry Potter series, and many others lined up together.

One in particular caught my eye—*La Belle et la Bête* by

Gabrielle-Suzanne Barbot de Villeneuve. The origin of the Beauty and the Beast fairy tale.

I pulled it from the shelf and returned to the first floor and the comfortable furniture. The binding was quite old, but I was surprised by the pristine pages inside. Written in its original French, I didn't get very far before my eyes grew heavy.

A hand gripped my arm, and I drew in a sharp breath as my eyes popped open.

"I'm sorry. I didn't mean to startle you," my grandfather said as he took a seat in one of the wingback chairs.

I straightened and rubbed my eyes. "I didn't realize I'd drifted off."

"When nobody knew where you were, I knew you'd be in here," he said with a smile.

"Not much has changed. It even smells the same."

He nodded. "I see you found your shelf," he said with a smile.

I glanced down to the book in my arms. "Thank you for keeping it stocked."

"My pleasure. How interesting, though, that you picked that book."

"It called to me," I said as I ran my hand across the gold lettering on the front.

"It's quite fitting, given your situation. A beast of a prince, and a beauty of a princess. Speaking of, your beast is asking for you."

I wondered how long I'd been asleep. "Would it be all right for me to take him some books?"

He gazed out at the shelves and the collections. "Avoid that wall," he said before pointing to the tallest bookcase in the room.

I leaned down and pressed my lips to his cheek. "Thank you, Nonno."

He took my hand in his and gave it a squeeze. "There is little I wouldn't do for you."

I pulled a few books down, everything from history to classics, mystery, and even romance. The stack was ten deep, and Luca was called in to help me.

At the infirmary, I glared at the men guarding his room, wishing they would just go away, and entered.

Luca followed in behind me, and we set the books on the table. The doctor was talking to Domenico, examining his wounds, and it was the first time I'd seen the doctor since the day we'd stormed in.

"How much longer am I to be secluded inside these four fucking walls?" Domenico cursed. His expression was one of clear aggravation at his situation.

At least he was out of the hospital gown and into some sweatpants and a T-shirt.

"Your swelling is starting to go down, but your pain is still high," the doctor said, which surprised me. Did he get Domenico to admit to it, or was it purely observation that he was in pain? "You seem to be healing well and could be out in a day or two. With restrictions." He pulled Domenico's shirt down, then marked something in a chart. "I'll check back in tonight."

"Thank you," Domenico said begrudgingly. Luca followed him out, and I leaned over and pressed my lips to Domenico's.

He reached up and fisted my hair, deepening the kiss and taking control. When we parted I could feel the warmth spreading through my body from my cheeks down to my toes.

"Hi," I whimpered as he nipped at my neck.

His breath was harsh against my ear. "I want to fuck you so hard."

I swallowed. That was exactly what I wanted as well, but he needed to get better before bursting open his stitches. "Just a little longer."

I had to pull away, and he was reluctant to let me go.

"I have something for you," I said as I shoved one of the books at him. "Here."

He took it from me, his brow furrowed. "What's this?" he asked as he looked down at the book in his hands.

"I thought you might be bored," I said, a little uncertain whether it was a good move. I pulled a few more up. "There are others if you aren't interested in that."

He looked through the titles and pulled a book out—*Qualcuno volò sul nido del cuculo.*

One Flew Over the Cuckoo's Nest by Ken Kesey, in Italian.

I set the other down, just in case he finished that one or wanted to switch.

"Thank you. This room is like a tomb, and I've been bored out of my mind when you're gone." He linked his fingers with mine and pulled my hand to his lips. His teeth grazed against my knuckle before his lips soothed.

"Resting is good. It will help you heal."

"Resting, yes, but can't I rest where there's a fucking window?" He closed his eyes, his agitation getting to him.

I ran my hand across his chest. "I know this sucks, but soon you can leave here."

"And we can get the fuck out." A tic of his jaw told me that was his main concern. Being caged by an enemy had the beast pacing.

"He's going to help us."

He scoffed. "If they don't kill me before I make it to the front door."

"Grandfather said—"

"It's not him," he said, cutting me off. "I trust Laureano's word. But there is bad blood between me and many of the men here."

"Heal, and we can go." I needed him to get better, and leaving right then was not in our best interest.

"We can go now, is what we can do."

I shook my head. "Stop being stubborn. You can't go how you are now."

"The hell I can't," he growled as he sat up. He tried not to let the strain show, but it bled through.

I pressed my hands against his chest. "Stop. You're fucking hurt, and you need to heal. Lie to me all you want, but I can tell you're in pain. Think about it—can you protect me like this?"

His brow furrowed and his jaw clenched as he stared at me. "No," he ground out.

"Then lie back, read a book, and heal so that you can."

"Why do you have to be so fucking logical?"

"Because I need you, I want you, and for both of those things you have to be able to move around. Do I need to ask the doctor for a sedative?" I asked. His gaze narrowed at me. "Then just believe that we are safe—for now—and focus on getting better so that we can leave."

I still had no idea what we were going to do when we left, but my focus was on getting him better. He complied, and I crawled up on the bed with him, a book of my own in hand.

Being close to him, even just while reading, calmed my frayed nerves. A few more days and he would be healed enough so that we could formulate a plan. I knew I could take care of myself, but I also knew I could use his protective nature to get him to comply.

The better he was, the better chance we had of making it out of this mess.

Two days and three books passed before Domenico was released and moved into my room. He kept his right arm close to his body and there was a hitch in his steps.

"Your mother's?" he asked as he looked around the room.

I nodded. "He didn't change anything. It's exactly like I remember."

"How long has it been since you've been here?" he asked as he rested on the edge of the bed.

"Almost a decade. I was thirteen."

"That was around the same time…" He waved his hand toward his face.

"The same time?"

"A year or two after. There were a lot of changes going on at that time. The most important being when your father became consigliere."

"He wasn't before?" I asked. When I was younger, I was never really told what was going on. My mother shielded me from a lot.

Domenico shook his head. "He was counsel and Giovanni's friend. When Agostino, the former consigliere, retired, your father slipped right in."

"How does it go? Boss, Underboss, Consigliere?"

He nodded. "Then me."

"And you are fourth because you are the most powerful capo."

"I am."

My gaze moved to the window. "That was when he bought that house." One small period of time that seemed to shape the course of both of our lives. "And the last time I saw my grandfather or this house."

"To show allegiance, he cut ties." He blew out a breath and shook his head. "Why do I get the feeling even then your father was formulating how to use you to get even further into the Ferrante family?"

"Because that is his modus operandi." I slipped my hands in his. "The doctor said you could shower."

His eyes scanned my body. "Are you going to be my nurse and help me?"

"Do you think I'd let anyone else?"

His lips twitched up into a smirk and he pulled me closer. "It's been six days since I've been inside you, and I'm not going another fucking day without feeling you come on my cock."

"You still need to rest."

"I'll rest when I'm dead."

I rolled my eyes as I pulled up his shirt. "We need to take these off." I gently peeled up the tape holding the gauze pads in place. The hole was scabbing over, the skin around it a myriad of colors—purple, blue, red, and yellow. Some swelling remained, but it was receding. The wound on his back was the same.

A little to his left, and he would still be lying in that bed. Instead he was up and walking, even if it wasn't the fastest. It would take months for him to fully heal.

I leaned forward and rested my head against his shoulder blade. It was only for a moment, but it was enough to soak in his warmth, to remind myself he was alive.

He reached back and rested his hand on my hip—a simple gesture of reassurance and one I desperately needed. Having him out of that room and with me dulled the buzzing in my veins that had vibrated my core since I saw the blood on his shirt.

I blew out a breath and pulled back. He turned, his eyes meeting mine as his fingers slipped under the hem of my shirt. His hands opened, running up my sides, pushing the material up. I drew in a breath at the feel of his hands on me again, at the flames that ignited my skin.

A groan left him when he reached my breasts, cupping them and squeezing.

"You're a tease."

He shook his head. "Nothing is going to stop me from fucking you."

I bit down on my lip as he pulled my shirt the rest of the way off. The fire in his eyes, his touch—he knew exactly how to light me up. To turn me on until I was begging for more.

"We should get in," I said with a shuddered breath.

A moan slipped from his lips as he popped the button of my jeans. "You're still wearing too much."

I reached out and pulled at the elastic waist of his sweatpants, my fingers sweeping across his warm length. My thighs clenched as I realized he wasn't wearing anything underneath. A groan left him as his hands slipped into my jeans and cupped my ass. He squeezed the flesh beneath and pulled me closer.

A squeak left me as we crashed together. He leaned down, his lips ghosting mine.

"There are a lot of fuckers around here that have been too close to you lately. I need to re-stake my claim. Remind them all that only I command your body."

"Only you."

"You're mine and mine alone." He closed the thin thread of a space between us.

I melted into him, into the softness of his lips and the roughness of his tongue against mine. It was like the frayed wires since he was shot fused together again, our connection solidifying as the kiss intensified.

A moan left me and I pulled back, my eyes heavy and my brain clouded with the need for more.

"We need to shower," I reminded him as I pushed at his waistband again.

I stepped out of his arms, earning a growl from him, which subsided as he watched me strip out of my remaining clothes.

The walk-in shower, with a bench and multiple showerheads, was large enough for both of us with room to spare. After the water warmed, we stepped in. We both let out a sigh as the heat relaxed our muscles.

I was still incredibly turned on, but iodine and blood still stained his skin. After washing off, I grabbed a cloth and began to gently dab at the skin around his wound.

"How does it feel?" I asked, careful not to touch the entrance and exit.

"Would it make you feel better if I told you it didn't hurt at all?"

I glanced up at him. "No."

"It hurts like a bitch, but I'll live." He turned his head to look at me. "It's not the first bullet I've taken, and it probably won't be the last."

I glared up at him. "That doesn't make me feel better. Are the meds helping?" I asked. I didn't like that he was hurting.

He looked forward again as a muscle jumped, indicating a sore spot. "I'm just on the antibiotics and ibuprofen. Had the doc wean me off the heavier stuff."

"What? Why?" There was no reason for him to be walking around in pain.

"I don't trust them, and I don't want anything impairing my mind."

With the armed guard that led him upstairs, that didn't really surprise me. My stomach knotted thinking about how bad he probably felt, and I prayed for it to heal faster.

I continued cleaning the area until all that remained was the discoloration caused by the bruising. When I was done, he grabbed my wrist and pulled me until we were chest to chest.

He cupped my face, his thumb brushing against my bottom lip. "I've missed these lips," he said before leaning down. A small, restrained peck, then his hand was knotted in my hair at the base of my head as his urgency kicked up. His lips and tongue demanded, and I could do nothing but drown in his desire.

"Wait," I said as his lips moved down my jaw.

"No," he growled against my neck. His teeth nipped and his hips flexed, pushing his hard length against my stomach.

"But you're injured," I tried again. It wasn't that I didn't want him, because I did. I craved him inside me, being one with him, being dominated by him as I came around him. I just didn't want him to hurt more.

"I can still fuck you."

There was going to be no deterring him. "Don't make me call you by your full name."

"Go ahead. I'm not stopping until I've emptied myself inside you."

He spun me in his arms and pressed on my back, bending me over until my hands rested on the tile bench. His hands gripped my hips, pulling them back as he pressed his forward, his length running across my pussy lips.

I felt the hot head of his cock at my opening before he pushed forward, slamming all the way in. My eyes popped wide before rolling back, an intense wave of pleasure crashing through me. I was still riding the wave when his pace picked up.

Grunts and groans sounded with each time he bottomed out, but there was no indication of pain. So, I let it go and gave in.

His grip was intense as he guided my hips. Each cry of pleasure that left me earned a growl and a hard slam into the same spot.

Over and over again, he took me higher and higher until all there was in the world was the two of us locked in a sea of pleasure.

As always, I was overtaken with nothing but him. Completely owned until I was nothing but a captive to his lust.

"Dom!" I cried out, unable to even finish his name.

"Who am I?" he asked as he knotted my hair and pulled me back, his thrusts never letting up.

"Mine."

His pace increased and I cried out. I was close, so close.

"Who are you?"

"Yours," I panted. "Only yours."

"Damn fucking right." His teeth pressed into my shoulder and

I froze, my muscles snapping as the building pleasure released. A silent scream from my parted lips erupted into an echoing, high-pitched moan as I broke, my body shaking as I pulsed around him.

"That's it, princess." His thrusts picked up, drawing out my orgasm before he slammed in. A roar left him as he exploded inside me.

It was moments later when his grip on my hips let up and he pulled back. His cock slipped from me, and I instantly missed it.

"Fuck, that's a great view."

My muscles started to give out, so I turned and sat on the bench. He was staring down at my pussy, watching as his cum slipped out. That edge of possession in his gaze had me biting down on my lower lip to suppress the fire that wanted to spark again.

As I looked at him, all possible ideas of going again left me and I gasped at the trail of red leading from his wound. "Oh my God!" I cried out, still too weak to jump up.

He followed my gaze. "Damn. Guess I broke open the scab."

I shook my head. "You just *had* to fuck me."

He stepped forward and leaned down, one hand resting beside me on the bench while the other slipped between my thighs. I drew in a sharp breath as he slipped two fingers inside me.

"Always."

I wrapped my arms around his neck, pulling his lips down to mine. "Come on, we need to finish cleaning up and get you bandaged up again."

He pulled his fingers from me and raised them to my lips, pressing them inside. That fire-filled light in his eyes burned brighter as I rolled my tongue around his fingers, cleaning them off.

When he pulled his hand free, he helped me to stand but held me close. "I'm never letting you go."

My heartbeat sped up, and I reached up and cupped his face. "You never have to."

TWENTY-FOUR

After our shower, we got dressed for dinner with my grandfather. I was both excited and terrified by the prospect of the two of them in a room together, but it was a necessity.

Armed guards lined the halls wherever Domenico went, a huge leap in security. They wouldn't pause in taking him out if they perceived him as a threat.

When we arrived in the dining room, my grandfather was already waiting for us. However, instead of it just being the three of us, there were two guards at the door, and I was certain another dozen were just outside.

"How are you feeling, Domenico?" my grandfather asked as we headed to the two table settings that were thankfully next to each other.

There was more to the question than politeness, but I wasn't sure the extent.

"Sore, but I should be ready to leave soon." Domenico nodded and held out his hand. "Laureano, I cannot thank you enough for your hospitality and generosity."

My grandfather stared at his hand before giving it a shake. "Hmph, so you are like your father? Ever the diplomat."

Domenico moved to his seat. "I don't think I'd ever really considered myself that, but I am very aware it would not be wise to anger you, not after what you've done for us. And I am grateful for your assistance. Without it, I might not be around to protect her."

He shook his head. "I helped you for her and her alone, make no mistake. Unfortunately, you two need each other, and as much as I dislike that, I know you are the only one who can keep her safe."

"With my life."

"And that is why I helped you. However, I ask that you don't make me regret it."

Domenico nodded. "I will do my best."

"Good." My grandfather gave a strained smile. "Then let's have a pleasant dinner."

It was a bit stilted and awkward as we ate, especially with armed guards practically breathing down our necks. Having meetings with your enemy was one thing, but having them staying under your roof was another.

The next afternoon, we took a tour and I showed off my favorite places. We were constantly followed by at least three men, and more were in every room we went.

In the library I showed him my shelf and the view from the second story.

"I can see why you have such good memories of this place. Your grandfather loves you. There is a warmth here you never received at home."

"My father's house was a prison, and he was the warden. Here was always a place of wonder and love. It was the only time I remember seeing my mother truly smile."

He nodded. "My father's house didn't feel like a prison, more like a gauntlet. A constant onslaught, with few safe areas. Even my grandfather despised me for being a bastard child."

"Why did you stay?" I asked.

He shook his head. "We eventually left. At fourteen my grandfather passed away, and my father became the new boss. That's when the fighting greatly picked up, when Roman was determined to beat me, to feel superior to me, and my mother had had enough. We moved out. It was only to another Ferrante property, but it was away from Renata and my siblings."

"I'm surprised she waited that long."

"It was a decision a long time coming. I had a place I could finally relax in. Giovanni would come to visit almost daily, and for a few hours we were like the family he always wanted."

"That sounds really nice."

"Until you remember I was a hormonal teenager who hated everything and everyone and was constantly being attacked at school." He blew out a breath and shook his head. "What I wouldn't give for those days now."

Because of the death glares from many of the men roaming the halls, we decided to head back to our room, where we stayed for the next day. Amelia brought us up meals, and we read, had sex, and relaxed as best we could.

I needed him to heal, to get better, but the tension was thick outside the confines of our room. All in all, though, it was better than the hospital room in the basement.

Domenico was napping, so I decided to take a walk. Of course, the moment I stepped out there were three men standing there. However, when I started walking, they stayed right where they were. I wasn't the issue—Domenico was.

I returned to my favorite room to replace some of the books we'd been reading. As much as I loved the space and the happy memories it evoked, I was getting a little tired of the unknown. The constant waiting, then running, then waiting again. And while safe where we were, I was tired of being watched constantly.

I shelved the books, then curled up on the couch to soak in the atmosphere as I stared out at the gardens.

"What are you doing in here?" a voice called from the doorway.

I turned to find the capo I'd hit in the infirmary, the one I'd threatened to kill with his own gun.

"And who are you?" I asked. I hadn't gotten his name. All I knew was that he was blocking my way out, and I didn't like the way he was looking at me.

"Salvatore," he said, but his stance remained rigid. "Again, what are you doing in here, traitor?"

"Traitor?" I stood and stepped up to him. "I am no traitor."

Between his black suit, the black of his hair, and his dark eyes, he struck me as an ominous figure. He reached out and wrapped his hand around my arm. "You may have Vitale fooled, but I see right through you."

I pulled back, but he was too strong. "Let go of me," I growled. I didn't think he would do anything while in my grandfather's home, but I was beginning to doubt that.

"You're just a fucking whore giving it up to the nastiest dick you can find." His lips curled back, exposing his teeth.

Every warning bell inside me went off, screaming sirens that begged me to run away from the heightened anger that rolled off him.

"Fuck you! You have no idea who I am."

"Saying you're a Vitale when I know you're a bargain-basement stripper, showing your body for a dollar, is a fucking disgrace to the Vitale name."

I couldn't wrench free from his grip, and he wasn't backing down. Without pause I swung my leg forward, right up into his crotch.

"I told you to let go of me!" I screamed out.

He cried out, his grip loosening, but the fire in his eyes only increased. I pulled away, but he was too fast.

"You fucking bitch!" His hand jumped up to my throat and he squeezed, silencing me. He pulled me up until just my toes touched the ground.

I gasped for air as I clawed at his arm, trying to get him to let go. I swung my legs, kicking him over and over until he'd had enough. He released me, dropping me to the floor, where I coughed and drew in deep breaths.

My gaze moved to the open door, waiting, begging, for someone to walk in, because I knew I'd angered him, and I wasn't strong or fast enough to escape him.

"You'll fucking pay for that," I hissed. My only way was to strike fear into him. If he let fury take control, I knew things would get bad.

"If your precious la Bestia tries anything, they will all open fire on him. Then what will you do?" he taunted.

I glared up at him. "I'll fucking kill you."

At that, he laughed. "You're weak. I can do whatever I want to you, and you can't stop me. Maybe I should try that pussy out to see if it really is worth getting shot over."

I stood, my gaze never leaving his. "Lay another finger on m—" His hand swung back and lashed out across my face. I cried out as pain radiated through my bones.

"Don't fucking touch her!" Domenico roared, appearing at the door with at least four of my grandfather's men in tow. He shoved Salvatore back and turned to me. "Are you okay?"

I could feel the sting of tears in my eyes as I held my face, but I managed to nod. Domenico's eyes were slits as he looked to where Salvatore's hand had been, then he turned back around. I could feel the rage racing to the surface, his muscles tightening. "You son of a bitch."

"I will fucking end you, Mancini," Salvatore growled.

Domenico made sure to shield me. "Lay a finger on her again, and they'll never find your body."

A gasp left me as Salvatore pulled out his gun and aimed it at Domenico. "The body they'll never find is y—"

Domenico's fist slammed into his face with such force Salvatore fell to the ground, his gun skidding across the floor.

Domenico hissed and clutched his side, bending over. Worry knotted my stomach as I placed my hand on his back. He looked to me, his jaw clenched, and nodded.

"I'm okay," he said before straightening.

"I'm going to do what I should have fucking done when you were dragged in here," Salvatore spit as he stood and reached into his jacket for another weapon.

"Enough!" my grandfather's voice boomed out, vibrating around the walls.

There was a scramble of men kneeling, and Salvatore glared as he bowed his head.

"There will be no more of this, understand? If anyone lays a hand on either of them, they will answer to my bullet. Do I make myself clear?"

"Yes, sir."

Domenico wrapped his arms around me, holding me tight with one arm as he gently examined my cheek with his free hand. I had no idea how it looked, but I did know how much it hurt. In all the weeks I had poked at Domenico while I was stuffed in a cage, he had never once hit me.

My grandfather looked to us before ordering everyone out. "Let's talk in my office," my grandfather said.

I was pressed tightly to Domenico's side as we followed. When we entered, my grandfather immediately picked up his phone and called for the doctor.

Domenico's nostrils were flared, his eyes locked with mine. "I thought she was safe here."

"Trust me, there will be penance for laying a hand on her. I'm shocked by his behavior. Salvatore is one of my most loyal and level-headed men."

"It seems not all of your men accept Ari."

"I'm so sorry, Nipote."

"We all know whose fault it is, Nonno, and it is nobody's in this room," I said to assure all present. My father was the one to blame. It all fell back on him. He was the reason I hadn't seen my grandfather in so long.

Amelia entered with an ice pack in hand and pressed it against my swollen jaw. The doctor came in a few minutes later and poked around the area, making me cringe more than once.

"It's not broken, but it will be sore for a few days. Keep the ice pack on, and I'll get you something for the pain."

"Thank you," I said, wincing as I pressed the cold pack against my skin. The doctor headed out, and we were left in an uncomfortable silence. The confrontation would only intensify the already-strained tension.

Domenico's jaw clenched, anger radiating from him, and I reached over and ran my hand up and down his chest to try to soothe him.

"He bruised you," Domenico bit out between clenched teeth.

I blinked up at him and looked to my grandfather. His eyes dropped down to my neck and I reached up.

My grandfather let out a sigh. "And Salvatore will be punished for it, but not by you. This was never going to be a long-term solution, but I think it's time for you to go. Arabella can stay, but you need to go."

My eyes widened as I looked at him. "What?" Over one mishap?

"He's right. This only causes more strain on the already-thin alliance."

I shook my head. "But you're still healing. Regardless, where you go, I go too." Where would we go?

"He's good enough to knock a man to the ground," my grandfather pointed out. He looked to Domenico and gave him a nod. "Thank you for not killing another of my men."

"That would be a foolish move if I had. He deserved the hit, though," Domenico said.

"I don't disagree there. Tensions are high with you here. Even without a weapon and wounded, you are formidable."

"Has there been any chatter?" Domenico asked.

I tried to understand what he meant.

My grandfather's lips formed a thin line. "Some. The trail went cold when Arabella came here. It is the last place they would suspect."

Domenico nodded. "Especially since the only people who know who she is are Roman and her father."

"I can't convince you to stay, can I?" my grandfather asked, his gaze beseeching.

I shook my head. My place was with Domenico. I couldn't and I wouldn't abandon him.

With a sigh, he stood and stepped over to reveal a hidden wall safe. Once open he reached in and pulled out a wrapped stack of cash. "Take this." He held it out to me. I stared at it, then back to him. "You will need it. He will need more rest before he can continue being your monster and savior. That requires safety."

I nodded and took the offered stack, but Domenico stopped me.

"Thank you, but we have money," he said.

"There are no strings attached," my grandfather stressed.

"I understand, but it still is not necessary."

He nodded and replaced the cash. "Where will you go?"

"I have a safe house," Domenico revealed. "Few know about it."

A safe house? Why hadn't he mentioned it earlier? And why didn't we stay there before?

"Won't they be watching it?"

"That is where we could use your assistance. I'm not sure they are, but a distraction to pull any potential spotters away would be helpful."

If they were watching, then it wasn't as safe as the name implied.

My grandfather moved back to his chair and sat. "What can I do?"

"Call Giovanni. Talk to only him, and tell him you have me," Domenico said.

My grandfather looked to me, then back to Domenico, his spine straightening. "He didn't know."

Domenico shook his head. "The entire ordeal was orchestrated by Maurizio and Roman. My father is unaware of her true identity."

He nodded. "It interests me that your father has not been informed."

"He hasn't been told because I claimed her—and because I also only recently found out."

"If Roman had her?"

A growl vibrated in his chest. "She'd be a prize he would be parading around. On a leash if he had to."

"And you?"

"She is mine," Domenico answered plainly. "Before I knew she was from your family, she was mine. And I will protect her. Always."

The conviction in his tone set the butterflies off in my stomach.

That seemed to satisfy any last doubts my grandfather held. "I will call him right away. How long will it take you to get where you need to go?"

"Half an hour."

My grandfather gave a curt nod, then stood and pulled a set of keys from his pocket. "I had the bulletproof windows replaced and repaired the body damage. It also got a new paint job to help. They'll never notice it's the same car."

"Thank you again," Domenico said as he took the keys from my grandfather's palm.

"I'm leaving her in your hands. Don't make me regret it."

"I won't."

I stepped forward and wrapped my arms around my grandfather, taking in his familiar warmth. "Thank you, Nonno."

It took only a few minutes to pack up a bag of our clothes, and we were back in the foyer. The doctor handed us a bag and gave instructions. The bandages would still need to be changed, and he had to make sure to continue the antibiotics. There were also pain meds for me.

"Good luck," Luca said as we passed.

I gave him a smile while Domenico nodded. We would need it.

We stepped outside and my mouth dropped open. What was once an all-black Mustang was now matte gray with a black racing stripe.

Domenico's lips formed a thin line, but he didn't need to say anything. I knew he wasn't happy about the paint job, but it really did change the look. Not the body shape, but Ferrante's men were looking for a black Mustang.

His steps were a little stunted from his healing wound, and I could tell he was holding back the pain. I gave one last look to my grandfather, then slid in the front seat.

I was shocked. There were no traces of blood anywhere in the car, and all the windows had been repaired. It looked like a completely different car.

Sadness washed over me as we passed through the gates, not knowing if I would ever see my grandfather again.

"Where are we going?" I asked.

"My house," he replied.

"Your safe house?"

He glanced to me, then looked back at the road. "My house."

I turned in the seat to stare at him. "Your *house*. You really don't think they'd be watching that?"

"No, but for now it's the best place to be. There are fortifications and supplies there. If we keep the lights low and the blinds closed, it will be days before they notice."

"They are watching." That was why we had to sneak in.

"It's possible, which is why there are a few rules," he said, glancing at me.

Ah, his beloved rules were coming out.

"Don't open the curtains or blinds. Don't turn on any lights at night."

"How are we going to get around?"

"I have a standard set of lights that are always on, so we'll be fine."

I bit down on my lower lip. "How long will we be there?"

"A few days," he said.

"Will the phone call work?" I asked. Anxiety was thrumming through me. If they were watching, if they did see us, what then?

"I don't know."

That was the unanswered question. The only thing I did know was that we were sailing on a fucking wing and a prayer.

TWENTY-FIVE

The air was tense, Domenico's guard up as he surveyed every street, which indicated we were close. He crept down one street and pointed at a ten-foot-high brick wall that surrounded a box-like structure.

"This is your house?" I asked as I stared up at the modern structure.

He remained silent as he hit something on his phone and a large gate slid open. He arranged the car and backed up through it, hitting the button again as soon as we were in. Another button and the garage door opened and he slipped the car in, then shut it as well.

"Quietly," he whispered when his eyes met mine.

I nodded and grabbed the bags from the back seat and climbed out of the car, shutting the door as quietly as possible. He held his hand up, listening, then took my hand. We walked through a door that led to the backyard. And while it was surrounded by a huge privacy fence, he still walked quickly to the back door. Another press of something on his phone and he ushered me in, following right behind.

I drew in a deep breath, not even realizing I'd been holding it.

He led me through another door, and suddenly we were in a kitchen and I understood what he was talking about. All the under-cabinet lights were on, as well as two lamps in the living room.

"Why do you keep so many lights on?" I asked.

"Habit. That, and it makes people unsure if I'm here or not."

Everything on the interior was as minimalistic as the exterior. The kitchen was all clean lines and shiny surfaces. The family room held a couch, chairs, lamp, and table, with one painting on each wall, and that was it. There was nothing homey about it, but at the same time it seemed very much him.

I turned to say something, but he was missing. "Domenico?"

A blue glow came from a doorway on the opposite side of the house. Inside was an entire bank of screens. Cameras, dozens of them, captured every angle on the outside of the house, and another dozen captured the inside.

Fortifications was right. I understood why he wanted to come here. It was his house, but it was also his sanctuary, the one place he could relax, and he made sure that nobody could sneak up on him and disturb that.

"The doors are armed with a strong electrical current, and I'm alerted to anyone who gets too close."

"This is a fortress," I said in awe.

He scanned the screens, one of which was on rewind. After a few minutes of watching the images fly past, he stopped.

"There," he said as he pointed to a car sitting on the opposite side of the street from the front door.

"When was that?"

"Two days ago. It doesn't look like anyone has been by since."

I leaned against the desk. "So we were fine. He didn't need to call."

"He needed to call."

"Why?"

Sometimes talking to him was like pulling teeth. I knew we weren't flying completely blind, but he also had a habit of not telling me things.

Domenico turned to me. "Because my father needs to know who you are. If this goes all sideways, if we don't make it…it's the only way your father will go down with us."

"And Roman?"

His jaw clenched. "Roman is my problem. Roman has always been my problem, and I will take care of him."

"If we get through this, I think we're both owed some retribution."

He took my face in his hands. "And we will get it by any means necessary. I meant it—I will burn my family to the ground if it means you're safe."

I relaxed into his touch and wrapped my arms around his waist. "Just promise me you won't burn with them."

He pulled me close. "Tutti ui vogliono morta ma dio non vuole, perche chi ha tonti nemici non muore mai."

"I don't care if God doesn't want to see you die—our enemies are numerous, and I don't want them taking you from me."

He cupped my face, his thumb brushing against my bottom lip. "I have ideas, thoughts, partial plans, but everything requires a sacrifice. It just depends on what we are willing to pay."

When Domenico mentioned provisions, what he really meant was weapons. Food wasn't in large supply, but I was able to make some pasta for dinner.

When we were done, he gave me a tour of the second floor:

two bedrooms with a shared bath and a large master suite. As soon as we entered the master bedroom I fell down on the bed. The last few hours at my grandfather's house had been exhausting, and I was ready for sleep.

There was little lighting on upstairs compared to the main floor. A bright night-light in the bathroom illuminated enough to get around, but blackout shades in the bedroom allowed us to turn on the bedside lamp.

After stripping down to nothing but my panties, I sat down on the bed and an odd feeling settled in me. A sense of normalcy after months, a sense of right. We were where we were supposed to be.

I watched him walk around with ease and comfort, the constant hackles of la Bestia relaxed. Just a man, if even for a few fleeting minutes.

This was *his* castle, his sanctuary.

I wasn't dirty or hungry or cold. I was warm and clean and… relieved. We were far from out of the woods, the edge still miles away, but for the first time we were able to relax a little.

"What?" he asked as he stopped in front of me.

Slowly I trailed my eyes up his body, taking in each piece of ink that covered his skin. The rose to signify his family sat right over his heart. A crow, a skull, and other shapes folded in sharp lines and splashes of red and black from his shoulder down to his wrist. A lion sat on his right pec—a nod to his persona.

Each muscle was pronounced, and when I finally reached his gaze, a shiver rolled through me. I blew out a breath and fanned myself.

"Just admiring the view." I smiled at him.

He tilted his head to the side, those silver eyes studying me. "Do you realize you did that while lying on my bed almost naked, right?" I nodded. "And that in doing so, you are making sure that I fuck you in said bed."

I bit down on my lower lip. "Oh, I was counting on it. Do you think you're up to it?" I asked, eyeing the gauze that still covered his wound.

He followed my gaze, then stepped closer, looming over me. "I don't care if I break open again. I *will* have you."

I scooted back as I bit down on my bottom lip. The excitement thrummed through my veins. He stalked each inch I moved, waiting for the right moment to strike, which only lit me up more.

A game of cat and mouse, and I couldn't wait until he caught me.

I smiled at him, teasing him with a cup of my breasts, a flick of my nipples, and an undulation of my hips. I drew him in just as I had done to so many others from the stage, waking the beast with each tease.

A growl vibrated in his chest as he grabbed hold of my ankle and pulled me to the middle of the bed. A giggle escaped me, my body heating with each heartbeat of anticipation.

He crawled up the bed, his body covering mine, caging me against the bed.

"You think you can get away from me?" he asked with a quirk of his eyebrow as he gave a playful nip to my lower lip.

"What are you going to do if I did, la Bestia?"

A growl vibrated in his chest and he crashed his lips to mine. His lips demanded, his tongue caressed, and I melted into it.

"You shouldn't have called me that." There was a hard edge to his tone, but before I could ask why, he moved to my neck and bit down.

I drew in a sharp breath, shuddering in his arms. Another bite to my shoulder and my nails dug into his back.

Each inch he trailed down my body was punctuated with a kiss or lick. The closer he got to where I desperately needed him, the slower he went.

"Domenico," I whimpered, my hips moving of their own accord, trying to draw him in.

He growled against my hip bone as he ran his hands down my thighs. He grabbed my legs just above my knees and pushed, pressing my legs open until they were flat against the bed. A swift tug of my panties and the fabric ripped.

I could have easily slipped them off, but the raw energy radiating from him was intoxicating and I loved all of it. His nose brushed against my clit, his breath brushing against my sensitive skin. I shook in anticipation, desperate for more, but he was taking his time.

He nipped my thigh, moving slowly down to my knee, then back. My muscles tensed in anticipation, only to be denied as he skipped to my other leg, progressing in the same slow, teasing path.

I was so worked up, desperate to grab hold of his head and put his mouth right when I wanted it. A flick of his tongue against my clit sent a jolt through my body, and my head fell back to the bed.

Another whimper. "Fuck!" I cried out.

Again he denied me, his mouth continuing its slow assault to my nerves. When I felt his breath against my clit, I was near tears.

"So wet for me," he said with a moan of appreciation before he ran his tongue up the length of my slit.

My body was shaking, my pussy pulsed, and I was on the verge of crying from sheer desperation.

"Please," I begged.

He nuzzled my clit, then gave it another flick. "Please, what?"

I shook my head, my eyes fluttering closed as I fisted the bed sheets. His whole mouth covered my pussy, his tongue lapping at my juices. My whole body tensed, muscles locking down as I reached the precipice, but before I could fall he pulled away.

"No!" I cried out.

He was smirking down at me, at the misery he had me in. Moving up, he nestled his hips between mine and pushed his length against my wet pussy lips. I dug my heels into the bed and raised my hips, grasping for the friction I desperately needed.

His hand wrapped around the side of my neck, his thumb running across my bottom lip. "What do you want, princess? Tell me."

A whimper left me as I pressed up harder. "I want you to fuck me."

His thumb moved down and joined the rest of his fingers around my neck as he leaned down. The intensity of his eyes boring into mine sent a shiver down my spine. I was so close, and he kept denying me.

I reached for him, but before I could pull him closer he grabbed my wrist and pinned it to the bed.

"I don't want to fuck you," he whispered against my lips.

I blinked at him in confusion. I was desperate for him, near madness, but he didn't want me?

He shifted his hips, and I drew in a ragged breath as the tip of his cock pressed in.

"Yes," I hissed as he slowly entered me. My eyes rolled back and I shuddered when he was fully seated inside me.

"I'm going to savor you."

Slow, deliberate strokes stoked the fire, building me up again while denying me release. It was torture, sweet torture.

Each stroke further intoxicated me until I was drunk on him, on the pleasure only he could give me.

"You're mine, Ari, and I'm not letting you go."

He pulled back and slammed back in, making me cry out. He changed his pace to long, hard strokes. Every muscle tightened and my back arched.

"Sempre."

Always.

No longer slow and savoring, Domenico pounded into me like it was his purpose in life.

Everything snapped as he drove me over the edge, never letting up as I pulsed around him. My vision whited out and I was lost in pleasure, unable to comprehend anything around me except the groans against my ear as he slammed in a final time.

His head fell into the crook of my neck and it was minutes before either one of us moved.

"I think I'll keep you," I whispered, earning a chuckle against my neck.

"You're never getting rid of me."

The next morning I woke in my favorite spot—nestled in Domenico's arms. There was a security there, a peace I didn't know I had so desperately needed for years.

His eyes were focused over my shoulder, and I realized he was staring at his phone.

"Anything?"

He shook his head. "Nobody last night. Nobody today."

That was a good thing. "I know you need the break, but I hate not knowing what the next step is."

"Because the next step isn't written."

"What does that mean?" I asked.

He blew out a breath and set the phone down. "I'm cursed into this life. An heir and an abomination, turned into a beast and shackled to the role of executioner."

"If you weren't shackled, what would you do?" I asked. Could we break the chains that bound us? Run away from this life that hunted us down and start anew?

"If I was to ever get out of the life, I would go to Italy. Live on a boat and sail around the Med."

My eyes widened. "That was fast."

He shrugged. "When I was a child, I longed to be free of the Ferrante name, to leave the confines of this city."

"What if you can never break free?"

"Then I will live as long as I can, live as much as I can, but only if you are beside me."

I stared at him, at what he was saying, what he was offering. "No offer will sway you?"

"None that do not include you."

I wrapped my arms around his shoulders and drew him close. "Why do you want me so much?"

"I don't know. Perhaps it's because we're both trapped. Perhaps you are one of the few who could ever understand."

"Perhaps it's fate."

He nodded. "But fate is often cruel and demands a price."

"Then we will pay it. Together."

"Princess, if you aren't with me, there's nothing to stop me from finding Roman and having a deathmatch. Keeping you safe, loving you, is all I have."

My life was a wreck, the road behind me completely destroyed in a crumbled heap and unnavigable. The road ahead filled in with each step I took, with no forecast. A gamble with no security of a future.

"You have one hell of a way of getting a girl's attention, Mr. Ferrante."

TWENTY-SIX

It wasn't a sound I'd heard in days, though I'd kept it plugged in while we were at my grandfather's. After a day there I'd remembered his phone and located it in a tray full of his things. One of the maids had been able to get me a charger, and I'd kept it on me. I wasn't sure why I had, but I remembered Domenico saying he was waiting for word, and I didn't want to miss it. Anything that could help with our path forward.

After he was released from the infirmary, I gave it back.

A week had passed in silence, but it was going off nonstop.

"What is it?" I asked as he picked up the phone.

"Marco."

I froze. "What about him?"

He mashed his teeth together, the sharp angle of his jaw even more severe. "Roman tortured him to get information on us."

My eyes widened. It shouldn't have surprised me. Marco was Domenico's closest ally, and Roman would assume he knew where we were. "Is he okay?"

He stretched his neck to the side, letting loose a cacophony of pops. "He's in the hospital. Loyalty has been split between me and Roman."

"And your father?" I asked. Surely he would have some influence over the fight between his sons.

"Is uncharacteristically quiet," he said. "He has been the entire time. He should be sending more men out to find us, but he's been leaving it up to my crew."

"And here we sit right under their noses." That thought was a bit unnerving.

"Because this is my castle, not my father's. Few know where it is."

"And why didn't we come here sooner?" I asked.

"Because it was the first place Roman would have looked."

"You just said few know," I pointed out.

He nodded. "My family knows, which was why we couldn't come here. It was being watched, and it will probably receive visitors again in the next few days."

"If it wasn't Roman, who has been watching it?" I asked. There seemed to be more working parts in the Ferrante family that I knew of.

"Those were my father's guards."

I shook my head. "I feel like there's something you're not telling me again."

He remained silent.

"By the way, whatever happened to my phone?" I asked. It wasn't in my Louis Vuitton bag.

His lips formed a thin line. "After I told your fucktoy of yours you were leaving and not returning, I put my heel through it then threw it in the river."

My eyes widened as I stared at him. "You told Mac I was leaving?" No wonder nobody was looking for me. It wasn't uncommon for girls at the club to leave suddenly.

He pulled me close. "You were mine, even then."

The whistle of the teapot brought me to my feet, and I pulled it from the burner. I was a little surprised he had one, but I was thankful. Reaching up, I pulled two teacups, actual teacups and not coffee mugs, down from the cabinet.

My skin caught on a sharp edge, and I inspected the rim.

"This teacup has a chip," I said. "You should probably get rid of it."

In two steps he was in front of me, and in a move of gentleness I'd never seen, he lifted the cup from my hands.

"That was my mother's favorite," he whispered as he placed it back in the cabinet. His fingers lingered on the fine china.

That was why he had a kettle. His mother must have been a tea drinker, and he'd gotten it from her.

"Why her favorite?" I asked, desperate to know everything I could about him.

He leaned into the counter. "When I was six or seven my parents were having a bit of a rough patch, probably due to Renata. In an effort to cheer her up I decided I would help out. As I was washing the cup in slipped and fell back into the water, hitting another dish. I was so upset when I pulled it from the water and saw the chip, but when I showed it to her she hugged me and said it was her favorite now because I'd washed it with love."

He was silent as he stood, his gaze still locked on the cup.

"What happened to her?" I asked, and chastised myself for not asking before. He knew all about my mother, but I hadn't even asked where his was.

The muscles in his back coiled. "She died."

"How?" I stepped up behind him and placed my hand between his shoulder blades. The muscles relaxed under my touch.

"Fucking cancer," he spit. "I was seventeen when she was diagnosed. They gave her two to three months, and at two she was gone."

I stepped forward and wrapped my arms around his waist, placing a kiss against his skin. "Who are you, Domenico?"

He was silent as he thought about what I was asking. "I'm *la Bestia*. I want to be a man for you, Ari, but I don't know how. I've been the beast for so long, covered in the blood of Ferrante's enemies, that I don't know how to be anything else."

"There's more to you than that," I said. I had seen it first-hand, felt it.

"Is there?"

"Even my grandfather saw it. Diplomacy, respect, order… there is a reason you were so high in the ranks at such a young age."

A chuckle left him. "You don't even know how old I am."

I hummed against his skin and ran my fingers up his chest. "Twenty-eight?"

"Twenty-nine."

It felt so good to have skin-on-skin contact. It was calming in a way I'd never experienced before, filled a void of longing I didn't know I had.

"I have a question," I said, earning a wary look.

"That I'm probably not going to want to answer."

I shrugged. "I can give you a hand job while I do it if that makes it better."

His tongue swiped against his bottom lip. "Snug inside your pussy would be better."

"Deal." A small chuckle left me. "You're a Ferrante, and you marked me, so why did we have to run? Couldn't you have gone to your father?"

"Yes and no. There was a lot going on you weren't aware of."

Being seen as little worth, Domenico would probably be surprised with how much information I'd caught. "I know there was grumbling in the ranks. Roman's plotting."

"It was more than grumbling, and you know it. Roman

gained supporters. Now that we know he was in league with your father, it makes sense why he would try to overthrow me."

"Would that have worked?" I asked.

His brow furrowed. "If they killed me, yes, but Roman isn't subtle. The larger the crew, the more unruly they became. Roman was angry when I marked you with my name."

When he marked me? "Why, then?"

"Because I laid claim that you were my property. Once ownership is established, I can defend my property."

Property? Was I an object?

"I really don't like being referred to as property."

He shook his head. "That is the best way for me to make you understand. If he had tried to take you again, I would be in my rights to get retribution."

My gaze moved to his scar and I reached up and trailed the path with my finger. He didn't flinch or pull back, but let me explore and understand. "Shouldn't you have gotten that for what Roman has already done to you?"

"Hurting me is one thing—my property is another."

I shook my head. It didn't make sense to me, but if I had to be referred to as an object for us to get some leniency, so be it.

"Time for a bandage change," I said as I pulled at his shirt.

"What happened to my relief?" he asked with a huff of annoyance.

"It'll have to wait until this is done." I'd made sure that he kept up on his meds. An infection was the last thing we needed.

His fingers curled around my neck and he tugged me to his chest. "You're treating me like an invalid. Do I need to remind you what I am physically capable of?"

I quirked a brow at him as I lowered to my knees. "Oh, I know. You're supposed to be taking it easy, but you just can't stop, can you?" I worked the edge of tape with my finger while he set his hand on my head and rocked his hips forward.

"Never," he said through clenched teeth as I pulled the tape from his skin.

My brow furrowed as I looked over the area. I needed to find a new place to tape, as his skin was getting raw from the constant application, and subsequent tearing off.

"How does it look?" he asked, not flinching as I probed the area around the scab, then the one in back. The bruising was still bad, but fading. The wound itself seemed to be healing and the swelling had gone down.

"It's looking better. You still need to keep it wrapped." I dug into the bag of supplies the doctor had sent us with, but soon became frantic. "Shit."

"What is it?"

I shuffled things around, hoping it would appear. "We're out of gauze."

"There is some in the master bath closet."

I nodded and ran up the steps. Scouring the shelves and containers of medical supplies, I saw there was only a small strip of gauze that remained.

"Out," I said as I reached the last few steps, holding the remaining strip.

He blew out a breath. "We're also out of food." The fridge doors were open, showcasing the bare shelves. The pantry was down to the dregs.

Half the food in the fridge had gone bad by the time we arrived, and there wasn't much to begin with. We'd come up with some interesting concoctions for more than one meal. The pantry hadn't been fully stocked, so we wiped out what little was in there in no time.

It was obvious he was a bachelor who wasn't home often.

At least there was a lifetime supply of tea.

The idea of leaving had my stomach in knots, but the truth was it had to happen at some point. Whether it was to the next step in this game of chess or for provisions, we had to brave the world at some point.

After getting dressed, Domenico checked the feed of the surveillance cameras. "They're gone again."

Whoever was watching had stopped by once and stayed for a few hours. While they were here, we spent time in the basement watching TV, curled up on the couch like a normal couple.

We were anything but normal, and that was okay, but it made me appreciate those moments more. There was safety, love, and protection in his arms—things I never would have believed six weeks ago.

Another hard thing to wrap my head around—only a month and a half had passed since he'd pulled me from the street. I never imagined we would end up where we were. That I couldn't imagine my life without him by my side.

Desperate times called for highly amped reactions, and as secrets spilled out, as I realized how much we had in common, the closer we grew. It wasn't just physical, even though that was strong.

Domenico heaved a sigh, clearly agitated as he stuffed his gun behind him. He looked over his weapons stash and groaned.

"What?" I asked.

"I don't like leaving so ill prepared, but carrying ten guns isn't going to help when I only have two hands."

"I have two hands," I pointed out. He already knew I could handle a gun.

"It's not that."

I nodded. "You're always in the know, in charge. The unknown claws at your chest as what-ifs run rampant and you want to stay locked up in safety until you feel like you have some measure of control of the situation."

His brow knit as he nodded. "Exactly."

"You may have upended my life, but this isn't the first time I've dealt with those emotions. When I was planning on escaping,

I was crushed by the same thoughts. The fear of the unknown is powerful, but we can face it together."

I slipped my hands in his and watched as he relaxed. He pulled me close and pressed his lips to my forehead. "Sei il mio inizio e la mia fine."

Beginning and end. No truer words could describe the whirlwind that was our fucked-up love story.

It began with Domenico, my life forced anew, pulled back into the world I'd fled. Somehow it felt like the pieces were coming together, despite being unable to see the path. We would walk it together, fight it together, and live it together.

He took one last glance at the monitors before I pulled on my wool coat and we headed out.

As we sat in the car, he turned to me. "I can't go in with you, but I'll keep a lookout. Go in, get supplies as fast as you can without drawing attention, and get out." He pulled a wad of cash out of his pocket and handed it to me.

I checked the bills, wanting to make sure I didn't overspend, but when I saw there was at least two hundred, I slipped it into my pocket.

The drive was tense, both of us keeping a lookout for anything or anyone familiar. A few miles away was a small grocery store. It was older, hence its size, and I felt better knowing it wasn't some huge mega store.

He parked along the side, where he could view the rest of the parking lot.

"Food, supplies for a week."

"Anything you want?"

He shook his head. "Be watchful and hurry." He slammed his lips to mine, and I hated when he pulled back too quickly.

The adrenaline pumping through my veins increased my heartbeat, and I was acutely aware of everything as I entered through the automatic doors.

I glanced around, taking stock of the order as I grabbed a cart and headed over to the pharmacy section. I loaded up on gauze pads and medical tape, along with some over-the-counter pain medication, then moved on to food. I tried to appear relaxed as I loaded the cart up with fresh fruits and vegetables. Some ground beef, chicken, and steak. Bread, pasta, and rice. Cans of soup and vegetables.

Everything was going great. I moved through with ease, but at a faster than meandering pace. The frozen food aisle was my last stop. I pulled out a pint of ice cream, trying to decide which flavor when I felt someone behind me.

"Hello, Ella," Roman whispered in my ear.

I froze and the pint fell from my hand, dropping to the floor with a thud. A shudder of panic rolled through me and my muscles tightened as he ran his arm around my waist.

"After I kill him, I'm taking back what is rightfully mine," he hissed as he shoved his hand between my legs.

I glanced around, trying to figure out if there was anyone else around. I mapped out where the door was and the path to get there. He wasn't the only one—I just knew it—but I hoped I'd be able to make it to Domenico before they got me.

I slammed my head back, his cry of pain signaling I'd hit my target, then swung the cart around, knocking him off balance and into the glass door. I didn't pause and didn't look before I took off down the aisle. The sound of footfalls stormed behind me as I burst through the doors.

I ran all-out toward the Mustang but was knocked off my feet, my head slamming into a windshield before the car stopped and I rolled off onto the ground.

"Ari!" Domenico yelled.

My vision was blurred as I looked toward him, seeing him struggle to fight off multiple men.

"Get her and let's go!" Roman said as hands grabbed me.

"N-no!" I screamed, but my limbs felt sluggish and I was unable to fight against them.

"Don't you fucking touch her!" I could tell he was still struggling against them, his injury hindering him and allowing them to gain the upper hand.

"Domenico!" I screamed as they loaded me into the car.

I still struggled, but my head was spinning and pain radiated through me.

Roman put a cloth over my mouth as the car sped off. My eyes widened as I tried to pull away.

"Not this time," he hissed, his lips pulled up in an eerie smile. "Sleep tight."

That was the last I heard before the slightly sweet chemical smell from the cloth took me under.

TWENTY-SEVEN

I awoke gradually, and awake was entirely subjective at that point. My eyes were heavy, but I felt the familiar cold sinking into my bones.

Bars. Cold steel. The stale smell of decay.

My head pounded and my body ached. I wasn't even sure the words *at least I'm alive* were relevant. The sinking in my stomach confirmed that, because things were about to turn out very differently than before.

The scene before me was familiar, eerily so. A sort of déjà vu.

I sat up, and darkness enveloped the room. My heartbeat skyrocketed because I knew Domenico wasn't hiding in the shadow. A fate worse than death slithered in the black.

"Awake now?" Roman said as he emerged from the shadows.

"Let me out of here," I growled.

"Oh, kitty got her claws, huh? A little bit of freedom and suddenly you're a badass?"

My lip twitched up into a snarl. "I always was. You were just too stupid being nice not to notice."

"You bitch!" He slammed his hand against the cage, but I didn't flinch. I wasn't going to give him the pleasure.

It was all an act with him. A role he wanted to play but could never measure up to. Not for lack of desire but for lack of wanting to put in the work. Killing for him was all a game. He was going to play with me first, hurt me. That was why he'd set up the kidnapping—to break me, to make me believe in him as my savior, and if he couldn't do that, he would break me.

He was the one who'd given me the ecstasy. Planning for me to be taken by every man in the place and appear as my savior as he pulled me away. But I wasn't as stupid as my father told him I was, and neither was Domenico.

"You will never measure up to him," I taunted. "You don't have the strength. You're weak."

He reached through the bars and knotted my hair in his hand, pulling me closer. "Shut your mouth before I fucking break your jaw."

I smiled up at him. "Truth hurts, doesn't it? You never could compare to him. You manipulate, but you can never strike fear or respect in men like he can."

He yanked me forward, slamming my head into the bars. "I fucking told you to shut up! I am Roman motherfucking Ferrante. You are nothing!"

My head was splitting from the impact, pain radiating through my face, and I could feel blood trailing down from my brow. Still, it couldn't stop the laugh that left me.

I couldn't stop it.

Maybe I'd hit my head one too many times in a short period, or maybe I could hear the fear in his words, the insecurity.

"Scared, little boy? You should be." I smiled up at him. "La Bestia is coming for you. Will you play dirty again? Play the spoiled brat enacting revenge because you didn't get what you wanted?"

"You *will* be mine. You were supposed to be mine, and I will make it happen."

I glared up at him through the bars. "Good luck with that."

He shoved me back and stood. "Get comfortable, Ella. You're going to be here a while."

"Minutes?"

He glared down at me. "Domenico isn't coming for you. He can't."

"You killed him?" I asked.

I expected him to flinch, to be angry I caught him in his lie, but instead his lip curled up, and a dark look took over his eyes.

My stomach dropped, as did my expression.

"Not yet, but he won't be going anywhere anytime soon," he said before snapping his fingers and heading toward the stairs. "Don't go anywhere."

The group of men broke out into a cascade of laughter before disappearing.

I watched after them and held back the despair that was trying to surge through me. Did they have Domenico? Was he downstairs? Were they going to kill him?

I took deep, steadying breaths to keep the panic at bay.

Don't believe him. Roman is a liar. A manipulator.

Still, in the back of my mind, there was a small scratch that sent a nagging seed of doubt.

What if?

I swallowed hard and focused on not panicking that I was back in the cell, that Domenico was hurt, that I had no idea where he was.

What if nagged at me again.

I had faith in Domenico. He promised he would protect me, and I had no doubt in him keeping that promise, but how was he going to find me? Even if I had to take a few hits, he would make them pay, and I would happily watch him enact that justice.

What if he couldn't?

A sob caught in my throat. Without him, there was nobody to stop Roman. Without him, my future was nothing but pain and torture, and there was no longer a card to play.

I had nothing and no way out.

The despair that thought caused rolled through me. Was this what the girls felt when they were brought in?

The cage was exactly how I'd left it when Domenico had taken me away, when he'd freed me and showed me what love could be. Dirty and dingy and even colder with the November air, it didn't feel the same without Domenico sitting in the shadows or a group of men sitting at the table watching a football game.

Was that what it was like normally? Were girls just left in the cages unattended?

The fear was real and bone deep. There were things before that allowed me to not feel helpless, but those things were gone.

I pulled the blanket tight around me. At least my coat helped to hold in the warmth.

There was no way to tell what time it was, especially since the sun set around four thirty. For all I knew it was only minutes after that.

I expected them to come back, for anyone to, but as time wore on, the silence stretched. Hours ticked by and nothing. The feeling of being alone, trapped, only made my anxiety grow.

Eventually my eyes grew heavy, and I relaxed down into the mattress.

I drifted in and out of sleep all night long. The sun moved higher in the sky and when it finally hit the skylight, I heard a clanging of doors.

I froze, my gaze on the stairs as I begged it to be Domenico, but there were multiple voices. Their pace was slow and casual, no worries. That scared me more.

Domenico.

Roman emerged first, followed by two other men I recognized, and made his way over.

"Did you have a good night?" Roman taunted as he stood in front of me. "All alone with nobody coming for you, waiting for your knight, who is lying in a ditch somewhere."

I glared up at him. "You don't know where he is, so stop trying to pretend you do."

"He's not coming for you, Ella."

"My name is Ari."

"Still so feisty, I see." He leaned in closer. "I can't wait to break you."

The clang of the lock turning echoed off the walls, and my teeth mashed together as I watched every little movement he made.

"Don't you fucking touch me!" I hissed as he grabbed me. It was easy for him to overpower me.

Roman's grip released with a hard push, and as I regained my balance, his hand whipped across my face, sending me down to the debris-covered floor. I reeled from the shock and pain.

"I do love to destroy the things my brother loves."

I looked up to him, my eyes widening as he pulled his belt through the loops, a sneer on his lips.

I pushed myself up and started to run, but my path was blocked. I ran the other way and the other one blocked me.

"Don't wear yourself out too much. I want you to still be able to struggle."

I gritted my teeth and tried to find a path, but every direction I chose, they immediately blocked. One of them gave me a shove in the direction of the other, who shoved me as well. I fell to the ground at Roman's feet and looked up to find his belt looped in his hand. He pulled his arm back, then whipped it forward.

I cried out at the sting across my hip. Another one across my ass and stomach before he stopped. My eyes watered from the pain, and I could feel welts rising up from where the belt snapped, even through my coat.

"Hold her down," Roman instructed as he opened up my coat. One of them grabbed my arms, but I swatted him away. The other joined, and together they were able to pin my arms above my head. Something brushed against my skin, and I looked up to find them wrapping a zip tie around my wrists.

Roman held a knife up in front of my face, and my eyes widened. "Don't move unless you want to get sliced up."

I wanted to kick him in the balls, but as the tip slipped under the fabric of my shirt and tank top, I froze. The knife sliced right through the cloth, slicing it in half and exposing my chest.

He wasted no time repeating the action on my bra, and I drew in a sharp breath as my breasts met the cold air.

A groan left him, and he palmed one with his free hand. My stomach rolled as he was one step closer to his goal. He threw the knife down, and I returned to my struggle to get him away. He straddled my thighs, his weight holding them to the ground.

His tongue peeked out to wet his lips as he stared down at me. "I'm going to enjoy breaking you."

My heart was slamming, my mind in total disbelief of what was happening. I was about to be raped. Forcefully held down.

"N-no!" I cried out as he pulled the zipper of my jeans down.

"Mmm, there it is." He grinned as he yanked on the waist, tugging them down my hips. "Come on, baby. You creamed all over his cock. I know you love it."

"Fuck you," I hissed as I glared at him.

He yanked hard, and my jeans and panties were over the swell of my hips and ass. I drew in a shuddering breath and pulled at my arms again, but they didn't budge. A tear slipped from my eye, running across my temple.

"Such a pretty pussy. I'm going to enjoy wrecking it."

"You don't have the equipment for a job like that," I spat.

The back of his hand crashed into the side of my face, and I cried out. The hit dazed me, and he took the opportunity to drag my pants all the way off and toss them aside, then he balled up my panties and shoved them into my mouth.

"Let's see you talk through that," he said as he gripped my knees and forced them open, pressing them down to the floor. I wasn't strong enough to stop him.

A sob broke through me, and I closed my eyes, unable to watch what was about to happen. I could still hear him fumbling with his pants and the sigh as he freed himself.

I braced, waiting, but the next sounds I heard were two loud bangs, followed by the release of strain on my arms. I tilted my head back, my eyes widening as I saw both men dead from two perfectly aimed headshots. I blinked away the tears just in time for a sob to rip from me.

He'd found me.

"Son of a bitch!" Roman cursed, but that was all he got out before Domenico's fist connected with his face.

Roman grabbed hold of him, and they crashed to the floor. They wrestled, each trying to gain the upper hand before Domenico pinned him to the floor and slammed his fist into his face.

I sat up and pulled the fabric from my mouth, watching in satisfaction each time Roman's face flew to the side. The blade he'd used to cut my clothes was a few feet away and I scooted over to it as Domenico's beating began to taper off.

Loud groans and pleading croaked out of Roman and earned him a fist to his stomach. He whimpered and fell to his side, his arms wrapping around his waist.

Domenico turned to me, and I was captured by the burning rage in his eyes. Another tear fell from my eye as I looked at the cuts and bruises that littered his face. His gaze moved down to the knife, which I was trying to use to cut my bonds. He stepped over and took the knife from me and slipped it across the zip tie, freeing me before moving back to Roman.

Domenico delivered a swift kick to Roman's stomach before straddling his chest, one foot resting on one of his arms, pressing it to the ground before squatting down, trapping the other arm with his knee. He wrapped his fingers around Roman's neck, holding him in place, then pressed the blade against his forehead.

Roman screamed and struggled with all his might, but he couldn't knock Domenico off. I watched the motion, the curve of the blade's path. Roman's cries echoed around the dank walls, reverberating across the hard surfaces.

"Now we match, *brother*," Domenico hissed into his ear.

He maimed him. Carved into his flesh the same way Roman had done to him years ago.

Domenico straightened and stared down at his brother.

"You don't touch what's mine."

"You're a fucking dead man, Dom. I'll make sure Father has you killed for this."

"Then I better make it worth his while," Domenico spit before plunging the blade into Roman's chest.

Roman sputtered, his eyes wide, a silent scream that became shrill when the blade entered him again. Domenico sank the knife into Roman's chest again and again in escalating fury.

All Roman's fight died down, his head lolling with each plunge, eyes unfocused.

He was dead.

Domenico's mania subsided, and he dropped the blade to the ground as he stood. He turned to me, and I gasped at the blood covering him.

He was breathing hard as he stepped over Roman's body, then fell to his knees in front of me. I stared into his eyes as he cupped my face, the blood on his hands still warm, and drew me closer. He pressed his lips to mine, and I sighed into him.

He was there—he was real.

He saved me.

I sobbed as he gathered me up into his chest, unable to take the flood of relief that washed through me.

After a moment, he pulled back and his nostrils flared as he took in my mostly naked body. His lips crashed to mine again, and he leaned me back against the floor.

I didn't need to ask, to beg him to erase the memories of Roman's touch. He reached between us, and after a moment I felt the hot head of his cock press against me, then thrust inside. A low moan escaped me, his eyes never leaving mine as he set a furious pace. Silent as he took hold of my hips and drove into me over and over again.

I worried briefly about his wound, but just as that thought began to take hold, he found that perfect spot that sent me flying.

"You're mine," he growled between clenched teeth. "No other man will touch you. Ever."

"I'm yours," I said with a whimper.

He rested his forehead against mine. "Ti amo."

I drew in a sharp breath as I searched his eyes for any false pretense, but there was none.

"I love you, too."

His breath was harsh against my neck as he continued to thrust into me, harder, faster. Every muscle tensed, and my hips rocked against his, drawing him right to the spot I needed him.

"Domenico," I whispered, needing just a little more. Nobody knew my body like Domenico. He was in tune with every part of me.

A groan vibrated against my neck before his tongue swiped across my pulse point. My eyes rolled back as his teeth sank into the meat of my neck, and I exploded around him.

A moment later a moan left him, and his hips stilled against mine.

We were both breathing hard, and I was trying to come to terms with all that had just happened. So many emotions heaved inside me, but relief was the biggest one.

Roman was dead.

He couldn't hurt either of us ever again. We were free of him.

The silence was interrupted by the crashing of footfalls up the stairs and the yelling of men.

Domenico pulled out and tucked his dick away before retrieving his gun from his waistband and standing, taking me with him.

I feared for what was about to happen as a dozen men in suits charged up the stairs.

TWENTY-EIGHT

omenico's arm swung out as he stepped forward, putting himself between me and the men storming in. The arm pinned me to his back and a hissed "fuck" slipped between his lips.

I couldn't see around him, but I knew it wasn't good.

Thankfully my coat was long enough to cover my ass as my jeans were across the room, and also still able to close.

"Domenico," a smooth voice said. The tone was stern, reprimanding.

"Father," Domenico replied.

I drew in a breath and pulled back, but he kept me tightly to him. I was able to peer around his arm to see the near-dozen men with their guns pointed straight at us.

In the center was a man in a crisp charcoal three-piece suit, his expression pulled tight and framed by short salt-and-pepper hair. His eyes were the same silver as Domenico's, and his gaze was just as piercing. His eyes locked with mine, and I stared back before sliding fully behind Domenico again.

"You've been causing quite a stir," Giovanni said.

"And? If you've come to kill me, just get it over with, but let Ari go."

"Is that what you want?" his father asked. "To exchange your life for hers?"

"Yes."

I gasped, my stomach sinking. Life without Domenico wasn't a life I wanted to live.

"Interesting. However, I don't want your death." He paused and stepped to the side, his gaze finding Roman's body behind us. "I've already lost one son today."

"Roman got what he deserved," Domenico hissed.

"No doubt there," Giovanni said with a sigh. "He always was driven by his selfishness. I thought maybe he would learn something from you, but alas, he only stayed the sociopath he always was."

"What does that make me?"

"That depends. You've stolen my goods. She's worth a lot, being Francesca Vitale Santoro's daughter."

A deep growl rumbled in Domenico's chest, and he pulled me tighter against his back.

"She's mine."

I peeked over his arm again, curious as to his father's reaction. My grandfather had obviously told him who I was, but had he told him everything? One eyebrow was arched high as he regarded Domenico. Those familiar eyes studied Domenico in the same way Domenico always studied everything around him.

"Are you sure you want to take that tone with me?" Giovanni asked.

"I'm tired of this game," Domenico bit out. "What do you want?"

"What I want I'm not sure you can give me," Giovanni spoke. "I want my son back."

"He's a bloody fucking mess, and I have no remorse for putting him down."

"I wasn't speaking of Roman." He sighed. "You are so strong willed, just like your mother."

"My mother has nothing—"

"She has everything to do with this. She took you from me—that was the start."

"She just couldn't stand to breathe the same air as your wife."

"I wanted you both in my house."

"Treated like a bug beneath Renata's heel. Living with my half siblings who bullied me for being the bastard son," Domenico spat.

"You will stop this rebellion, and you will release Arabella," Giovanni said, the warmth gone from his tone.

"I told you, she's mine. The only way you will take her from me is by prying her from my cold, dead grip."

I held on to him tighter, my eyes sealed shut.

"Is that the only way? Does she mean that much to you?"

"Yes to both."

"Worth dying for?" Giovanni asked. "Your death would only serve to put her right back in the cage you freed her from."

"It is the only way I will ever give her up, and even then I *will* be with her."

I gripped his shirt harder and suppressed a sob. Snaking my arms around his waist, I wrapped him tightly in my arms, my hand covering his heart, protecting it and him. His heart beat fast under my touch.

"It would be a pity. Of all my children, you are the only worthy one."

"Worthy of what?"

"Of succeeding me."

Domenico faltered, his aim on his father lowering as a snap rang through him like he'd been slapped.

"They are all spoiled, self-absorbed brats. You remind me so much of myself, including your attachment to her. It was the same with your mother. I married out of obligation, but my heart belonged to your mother." A long sigh left him, his shoulders folding in for just a fraction of a second before straightening out. "Let us go home and talk."

"About what?" Domenico asked.

"About your future. Bring the girl."

TWENTY-NINE

The house was grander in design and opulence than my father's, but different than the ornate details of my grandfather's home. The grounds were much larger and secluded, the halls wide, and there was a flurry of staff walking around.

Domenico kept me close to him, hugging me tightly to his side, glaring at anyone who even glanced at me. I was practically naked, my coat barely hitting my thighs. There hadn't been time to grab my jeans as we'd been practically pushed out the building. Thankfully I had been able to grab my panties, and Domenico had zipped up my coat, concealing my destroyed shirt. I was thankfully covered, but my legs were cold and on display.

The looks could also have been due to the blood that covered us both.

We followed his father into a room walled with dark wood, a fire glowing in the fireplace, and bookcases filled with antiques and books. It was similar to my grandfather's office, and that fact put me somewhat at ease.

Giovanni strode across the room and pulled a stopper from a decanter before pouring an amber liquid into two glasses. The doors closed with a hard thud, and I jumped. Glancing around, I saw there was only one other person in the room with us, and based on his posture, he was Giovanni's guard.

Giovanni held out a glass to Domenico, who glanced down at it but didn't move. After a momentary stare-down, he turned to me.

"Arabella, would you care for a glass?"

I nodded, not caring what it was, but I was in desperate need of something to calm the thumping in my veins. There had been too much happening too fast, and my emotions were still playing catch-up.

I glanced up at Domenico as I tipped the glass back, our eyes locked. A burn trailed down my throat with each sip.

"Please, sit," Giovanni instructed as he stepped around his desk.

I moved to do as instructed, but Domenico pulled me down onto his lap, refusing to let me go.

An amused chuckle danced across the space from father to son. "I'd like to tell you a story, and perhaps together we can figure out how it ends."

He waited for any response, but Domenico's only indication of his father's words manifested as his hold tightened.

"How do these things begin? Once upon a time, is it?"

Still no response.

"I've long known Arabella, though we haven't seen each other for many years."

There was a familiarity about him, but I had brushed that off as the similarities he shared with Domenico. However, when I scoured my memories, his face popped up multiple times, the clearest being at my mother's funeral.

"Once upon a time, her father used her as a bargaining chip

to get a further hold into the family. I entertained it, especially when I remembered who her mother was. We even set up to arrange her marriage into our family."

A gasp left me, and my nails dug into Domenico's arm as his fingers held fast.

"To whom?" Domenico asked, never taking his eyes off his father. There was a lack of trust in him, but I wasn't sure if it was a fissure in their relationship or his fierce need to protect me above anyone.

"Roman."

My breath stuttered, and I let all my weight relax onto Domenico. The thought that I would have been bound to Roman, to *Roman*, made my stomach roll. I turned my face into the crook of his neck, the spicy cinnamon scent calming me.

"I thought I could tame him with a wife, and Arabella's father thought he could tame her. It seems your dear girl had other ideas. Not days before the announcement, she slipped her security detail and disappeared in plain sight. It was quite an impressive trick, Arabella."

With another inhale of Domenico's familiar scent, I turned to his father. "And not a moment too soon, it seems."

"Perhaps you are correct."

"Forget all this time-wasting speech and tell us what our fates are." The words almost signaled a resignation, a giving in, but they weren't. Domenico was calculating his next move based on his father's response.

"Fine, story time is over. Here is your ultimatum—you will step up and learn how to become my successor, and Arabella will be your bride."

"Amicizia di signore non è retaggio; chi troppo se ne fida non è saggio."

It was a proverb that meant *A king's favor is no inheritance.*

"A caval donato non si guarda in bocca," Giovanni said,

warning him not to look a gift horse in the mouth. "Right now you have few options, my son."

"Shouldn't I get a say in this?" I asked.

"Is that your wish?" Giovanni asked.

"Yes."

"Then let me remind you what is in store for you if my son does not agree. Domenico will quite possibly be killed due to his part in Roman's death. You will be returned to the cage to await the sale of your body to the worst of the bottom dwellers and perverts who will fuck you until you stop moving, because that's the type of death your father requests."

I flinched at his words, the last bit of my heart that still held feelings for my father shattering. Domenico's fingers brushed against my jaw, drawing my eyes to his. Anger flickered in their silver depths, and I realized I was shaking.

"What did I say, princess?"

"I am yours," I whispered.

"That's right. No man will ever touch you, even if it means I have to kill you myself." His gaze flickered to my mouth, his thumb rubbing against my bottom lip. "Antonio, Manetto, and Valentina won't be happy."

"Do you wish me to sing your praise? Antonio is hot headed and will burn this organization to the ground with his impudence. Manetto is a coke head. And Valentina is as much of a spoiled bitch as her mother."

"Good to know we are in agreement," Domenico said.

"You are like me, more so than any of the others. I despise that you weren't formally acknowledged under my father's rule as my son and able to take your rightful seat in the family. That will change."

"I am now the youngest."

"I decide who my successor is, and everyone will fall in line or I will put a bullet in them, no matter who it is. Besides, isn't this what you were aiming for when you had Vitale contact me?"

My eyes widened as I turned to Domenico. "Did you?" I asked in a whisper, but he didn't answer.

"Very diplomatic move, I must say," Giovanni said. "A worthy mind to succeed me."

Domenico let out a hard breath and caught my eye again. "It was the only way."

"Why didn't you tell me?" I asked. He'd been so secretive in his plans, keeping my anxiety high with the thoughts of what was going to happen to us. There was no direction, but like always, Domenico was working out pathways in his mind, trying to choose the right direction.

"Because it was a gamble," Giovanni answered. "Roman fed the family lies, and Domenico had little faith in me."

"Why would I? You've always sided with Roman, even after what he did to me," Domenico gritted out.

"Your mother, God rest her soul, would have killed him for that had she still been alive."

Domenico's jaw twitched. "And you did nothing, so again, why would I?"

Giovanni sat back and took a long pull of his drink. "I long ago saw all my sons for who they were. There is a reason none of them are ranked very high in the organization and you are. Roman wanted to beat you down, to make himself feel superior to you, but with each fight, you rose. Even when he disfigured you, well, that was when la Bestia came out, unrestrained. You were strong, fierce, and unstoppable—the very things our family needs to survive, to grow."

"What did you talk about with my grandfather?" I asked, pulling the conversation back to that reveal.

"He told me how Domenico came to be in his care, of his granddaughter's sudden revival, and how you two ended up together." Giovanni's eyes flickered with the same anger I'd seen many times in Domenico. "He also told me of your feelings for each other. Then he offered me something that only you two can give me."

Domenico's eyes widened as he stared at his father. "He didn't."

Giovanni nodded. "The Vitale were the first family to come up in Chicago, but sometimes families die out. Laureano Vitale has only one heir." Giovanni's eyes met mine. "Arabella, you are the last Vitale, the last of the bloodline. Like royalty, we pass the mantle down to our children, not outsiders. Your union will join the two families and make us the most powerful family in Chicago."

"He offered a merger?" I asked, understanding. The family had thinned through the generations, and I was all that remained. "To his greatest enemy?"

"There will be strife in the ranks at first, yes, but the empire the Vitale built will continue on, and the Ferrante will run that empire."

My heart beat wildly as I processed everything. When it came down to it, the choice was simple—die or be together as the most powerful couple in Chicago.

The answer was also simple—live.

I had tried to get away from everything that the Mafia stood for, but Giovanni's offer was different. I wouldn't be some powerless doll.

"It won't be easy for either of us, but this is the only way I can protect you," Domenico said. "You will trade one cell for a different kind, but I will be beside you. Marry me."

Only two months had passed since I was trapped on that bridge. Such a short time for my life to be completely turned upside down to the point that I was right back where I started three years ago.

Leaving Domenico wasn't an option. No matter how horribly we'd started out, I knew the reasons behind his cruelty, and when we were free it had morphed into a passion like I've never known. He'd taken a bullet for me, freed me from being sold like an object, and shown me a level of caring I'd never experienced.

"If I am your equal as your wife, as both a Vitale and a Ferrante, then I still have freedom."

"You will still have to follow my rules."

"Of course you'll have more rules," I said with a shake of my head.

"Will you tame the beast in me?"

I cupped his face and met his eyes. "Never."

Domenico sighed before pressing his lips to mine. "Da questa vita a quella successiva."

From this life to the next.

I turned to Giovanni. "What about my father?"

He nodded. "Maurizio will pay for what he did. His actions, had Domenico not intervened, would have sent us into a war with the Vitale, one I'm not sure we would survive."

I knew how he would pay, and I also knew I wanted to be the one to do it. I needed retribution for all that he'd done to me. "Please, let me take care of him."

Giovanni nodded. "Of course…Daughter."

THIRTY

Once everything was settled, Giovanni released us to clean up, assuring us he would send the physician to tend to our wounds. I didn't even want to look at myself in a mirror. In twenty-four hours I'd been hit by a car, had my head slammed into metal bars, and had been beaten with a belt. Domenico didn't look much better. I hadn't really gotten to focus on much but the presence of him, and I had a feeling there was more to be seen under his clothes.

When we stepped out of his office, a woman in slick black heels and tears streaming down her face stomped toward us.

"You murderer!" I recognized her as Renata Ferrante, Giovanni's wife. Domenico stepped in front of me, but when I watched her pull her hand back to strike him, I moved in front of him and grabbed hold of her wrist.

"Don't you fucking touch him, you witch," I growled.

"Get your hands off of me, maggot!" she screeched.

In her heels she was easily six inches taller than me, so I turned her wrist outward, bringing her down to my level.

"I would watch what you say to us. Your son got what he deserved, though he deserved so much more torment," I spat.

I had no remorse in me for Roman's death, and she would never touch Domenico again.

"Get this thing off me!" she screamed, but nobody moved.

"They won't help you. If they touch me, Domenico will kill them." I pushed her away and released her.

"Giovanni! Do something!" she hissed at her husband. "He killed our son!"

"And as my underboss, and a Ferrante defending what is his, it is his right."

"W-what?" she stuttered. Her eyes were wild.

Behind her a man that looked eerily like Roman emerged. The second she saw him she called him closer.

"Manny, baby. You have to kill him."

His eyes met mine, and I inwardly cringed. Domenico drew me behind him again.

"Kill whom, Mother?"

"That *bastardo* that killed my poor Roman!"

"Roman is dead?" He looked to his father for confirmation before pulling a gun from his jacket.

"Think with your head, Manetto, or are you too high to use your brain?" Domenico taunted.

"You little shit," he hissed before pointing the gun at Domenico.

Immediately the rustle of guns being raised as men stepped in front of Domenico echoed around the marble floors.

"What the fuck is this? Stand down!"

"Loyalty is earned, Manetto, but you never did care for that lesson, did you?"

"Father, let me kill him," Manetto pleaded.

"No."

Manetto stared at Giovanni in anger. "You always favored

him—now you're letting him get away with killing Roman? He isn't even a true Ferrante!"

"He is as much my son as you are," Giovanni's voice boomed out, echoing against the marble floors. "I gave him my name to ensure that. You're just angry because you were taught from your mother to hate him. If you want to live, Manetto, lower your weapon."

"Are you serious?" Manetto asked.

"Where are your siblings? I really do not wish to have this conversation over again."

Renata lunged forward and snatched the gun from Manetto and turned it on Domenico. One of the guards was on her and threw her arm up, the gun firing off into the ceiling as he wrestled it away.

She fell to the floor as she let out a scream.

"I believe dinner should be ready shortly. Domenico, Arabella, why don't you go upstairs and clean up," Giovanni said.

With a nod Domenico wrapped his arm around my shoulders, keeping me close, and we followed a guard upstairs. The tension was thick, and I was waiting for another gun to go off or more hysterical screaming from Renata.

My grandfather's house was huge, but as I stared down the hallways, I was certain the Ferrante house was larger.

I was paying more attention to the details than where we were going when Domenico opened a door and we stepped in. The bedroom was large and complete with its own en suite. It was well appointed with leather chairs and dark woods, deep navy blues and creams.

Once the door was shut, I unzipped my coat, freeing the awkward, shredded layers beneath.

A hiss left me as I pulled my arms from my jacket. "Do I even want to know what I look like?" I asked.

Domenico's brow furrowed, answering my question. "I wish I could kill him again right now."

I turned and got my first good look at him since I left him in the car what felt like days ago.

A deep red stain covered his shirt and I immediately pulled the hem up. "It's Roman's," he assured me as I ran my hands across his skin. While the blood was Roman's, the bruising underneath was caused by someone else. It was obvious he'd been punched and kicked, but I had a feeling there were more corpses out there.

The skin around his bullet wound was still a rainbow of colors that seemed to be spreading. His fingers brushed against my skin, and I hissed when he hit a spot on my cheekbone.

"Stay still," he said, and I did as he requested. I ground my teeth as he probed the spot, then relaxed as he drew his hand away from it. He touched my jaw and moved it around. "Nothing is broken." He took my hand and pulled me toward the attached bathroom.

My eyes widened as I got a look at myself in the mirror. Dried blood was splotched all over me, my skin swollen and turning purple from where Roman had struck me, welts left from the lashing of his belt. On my cheekbone and bottom lip were two scabbed-over breaks in the skin, and there was at least one gash in my hairline. Then there were the bruises that littered my body from head nearly to toe in splotches of dark and deep colors. I even had a black eye.

Streaks of rusty red stained my hips and sides from Domenico's bloodied hands.

"I look like a nightmare," I said as I looked in the mirror at Domenico. His arms were covered in the same red. His knuckles were split open from all the punches he'd delivered.

He was silent as he pulled me into the shower. The water stung the places where gravel bit into my skin and scratched, making me hiss. For a few minutes I just stood under the spray, letting it dissolve and wash everything away.

"Thank you," I said as Domenico ran a washcloth across my skin, taking special care of any tender areas.

"I will always protect you."

It began to settle in then. Domenico promised he'd figure out a way, and I knew it when he said it—this was the only way. Taking up the mantle, merging the families, was the only way we were ever going to survive.

It was never a position he wanted, nor expected would ever be his, but from what Giovanni said, it was one he was groomed for from the beginning. Above all others, Giovanni knew, possibly even from the moment he named Domenico after himself.

I was moving to step from the shower when Domenico's fingers curled around my neck and he whipped me around to face him. I drew in a sharp breath at the intensity of his eyes.

"Hades himself will not take you from me. Ever. You are mine from this life to the next."

"Always."

His lips crashed to mine and he backed me up against the wall. I drew in a sharp breath when my skin hit the cold tile, but that didn't slow him from pulling my leg up and positioning himself at my opening, then slamming in. My head fell back as I cried out. It was a moment of necessity, of need. To drive out the whirlwind of emotions and settle the adrenaline back down.

He didn't last long, soon spilling inside me. His forehead rested against mine as he regained his breath, my leg still hooked in his arm. "Arabella Santoro, will you marry me?"

A tingle exploded in my chest and my lips curled up into a smile. "I want nothing more than to walk this life with you beside me."

He pressed his lips to mine. "Ti amo."

"Ti amo."

When we exited the shower, there was an assortment of toiletries sitting in a basket, and I grabbed hold of the brush immediately in an attempt to move through my tangles. I no longer looked like death, but I did look like I'd been in a brawl. Domenico had the same look about him. We were quite a mess.

After drawing the excess moisture from my hair and drying my skin, I looked to Domenico, who had a towel around his waist and was sifting through the basket. He pulled out a tube of something and stepped over to me. His eyes met mine before his fingers pressed against my cheekbone, the cut on my forehead, and the welts.

"This will help," he said, then spun me around to dab it on my butt and the backs of my legs.

"How do you know all this wound care?"

He quirked a brow and pointed to his body. "Who do you think took care of me after all those fights?"

I shrugged. "I guess I assumed your mom."

"In the beginning, yes, but as we got older and the punches got stronger, I started taking care of myself."

"You didn't want her to worry."

He nodded.

"We seem to be in a predicament."

"How so?"

I looked down at my naked body. "I don't think I want to go to dinner wearing the emperor's new clothes."

He nodded, then opened the door to the bedroom. In the middle of the room stood a woman about twice my age. As soon as she saw movement, she stepped forward.

"For Miss's modesty," she said as she held out a basket.

"Thank you," Domenico said as he took it from her, then turned to me. I blinked down at the items—a variety of panties and an assortment of bras, all with the tags still on them.

"I like the red," Domenico whispered.

I shook my head as I sifted through, finding something that would not only fit but that I'd like.

In the end, I did choose a pair of red panties and a mismatched—but not really noticeably so—red lace bra.

The door to the room swung open just as I finished putting them on. A young maid scurried in with an armful of clothes, and I blinked at the stack.

"What the hell are these?" Domenico asked.

"I'm sorry, sir," she squeaked. "All Miss Valentina wears is dresses."

"It's better than what I was wearing," I said.

He gave me a side-eye before shuffling through the stack until he found one he was satisfied with.

"What does she wear in the winter?" he asked.

"Still this, sir," the maid responded. "With thigh-high boots."

"Of course," Domenico said sourly.

"What are you going to wear?" I asked Domenico as he pulled open a chest of drawers.

I blinked, watching as he slipped on some underwear and an undershirt, then moved to the closet, emerging with a charcoal suit.

My mouth popped open and I looked around the room. By the blankness of it I'd assumed it was a guest bedroom, but then the familiar sterility reminded me of his house.

"This is your room," I said as I stared at him.

He nodded. "I don't stay here often anymore, but I keep it stocked for when I do." He furrowed his brow at me. "What?"

I shook my head. "I'm just thinking about the difference a few months make. What I thought when I first met you."

"You were frightened."

"Yes, but even then I could tell you were different. You were a ruler, and you've remained a ruler."

The physician arrived and looked us both over and ruled everything superficial, but he said we should call him if any symptoms arose, especially with the hard knocks my head had taken.

Thankfully Valentina's shoes were about my size, just a half size smaller, but the maids found a pair that fit before they left. The dress, however…

I stared at my reflection, eyes wide. "This was the longer one?"

He stepped behind me in the mirror to adjust his tie, his eyes caressing my reflection. "Sadly."

I was fairly certain my coat covered more than Valentina's so-called dress.

My hair was drying in waves, and I had no makeup, so I looked underdressed in comparison to Domenico's crisp three-piece suit.

I turned to look at him. One day, somewhere in the middle of my time in the cell, he arrived wearing a suit, but I didn't get a very good look before he changed his clothes. Full access to the image made my thighs rub together.

"Is there anything you don't look hot in?" I asked, wetting my lips at the delicious way the suit hugged his body.

He grinned at me. "I could ask you the same."

"Umm, I'm pretty sure torn jeans and an over-stretched sweater that hadn't been washed in three weeks answers that question," I reminded him.

A groan left him, and he dipped his head down, his tongue brushing against my tattoo of his name. A shiver rolled through me as he pulled me close.

"Even then."

He took my hand and I drew in a deep breath, preparing myself for the coming battle. Because that was what dinner was going to be. The rest of the Ferrante family were about to learn of their brother's demise and their half brother's rise.

THIRTY-ONE

It felt like whiplash—and quite a role reversal. At my grandfather's Domenico had been heavily guarded, and as we walked down to the dining room I couldn't help but notice all eyes were on me.

When we arrived, Giovanni was sitting at the head of the table. He looked up from his drink and smiled. "Much better. You no longer look fresh off the battlefield."

The rest of the table was empty.

"Where is everyone?" I whispered to Domenico.

"They like to be fashionably late," Domenico said with a sigh of annoyance.

A chuckle came from Giovanni as he stood and pulled out the two chairs to his right. "Sit here. They'll be in shortly."

"Has Manetto or Renata spread the word about Roman?" Domenico asked as he pushed my chair in for me.

Giovanni returned to his seat and swirled the brandy in his glass before taking a slow sip. "I forbade them, so it is possible, though I think Manetto returned to his line of cocaine, and Renata is probably plotting some manipulation."

Just then there was yelling at the door, and we all looked to find a dark-haired man in a black suit spitting mad as he handed over his guns.

"Really, Father?" he snapped as he walked in, a scowl etched deep into his forehead. His features were closer to Domenico's, with a strong jaw and sharp cheekbones, and he had the same glowing silver eyes. His hair was black as night, and his obvious disgust of Domenico was apparent the second he noticed him. It was clear he was the last of the brothers—Antonio. "The whelp is here? I thought he was on the run with his tail between his legs with some bitch." His gaze moved to me. "He brought her here?"

"Sit, Antonio," Giovanni commanded.

"What is going on?" he asked as he looked from his father back to Domenico and me, lowering into the seat across from Domenico.

"Wait until everyone is here."

Domenico was rigid beside me as he stared at Antonio, almost as if he was on guard, waiting for him to strike. I rested my hand on top of his, and I felt some of the tension bleed out.

I took a sip of water, and the sound of heels clicking cut through the silence. The woman who walked through the door was the physical embodiment of a stuck-up socialite. Her hair was long, her dress short, and her makeup flawless. She even carried herself with a holier-than-thou, nose-in-the-air attitude.

"Father, Antonio," she said as she approached the table, completely ignoring Domenico. She gave me a brief glance, then did a double take.

"Is that my dress?" Valentina's eyes were wide as she looked at me before letting out an awful screech. "Take it off right this minute."

"She'll do no such thing," Giovanni said as he stared at his one and only daughter. "Sit."

Valentina huffed and glared at me before taking a seat next to Antonio.

Next to arrive was a portly man who bore a resemblance to Giovanni, only shorter and squatter. His eyes pinched in confusion as he looked to our seats.

"Giovanni?" he asked.

"At the head, Giuliano."

He nodded and took a seat.

More shouting from the doorway and another screech before Renata slammed something and stomped in. She shot daggers at us as she took a seat at the other end of the table, near Giuliano.

Manetto floated in after her, clearly high as a kite, and, at her prodding, sat next to his mother.

There was a divide at the table, which was fine by me, though I was getting sick of Valentina's glares pretty quickly. I snapped to face her and glared right back without flinching.

"Welcome, my family."

"Roman's not here yet," Valentina said, stopping Giovanni from continuing.

"Because that fucker killed him! He killed my baby!" Renata roared before throwing her knife at Domenico.

It headed right for me, and I threw up my hands to block it, but there was no impact. Domenico was crouched around me, the knife securely in his hand.

He straightened and pointed it at her. "I warned you, Renata."

"I wasn't aiming at her—I was aiming at you." Another item, a spoon, crashed into a wine glass, and it exploded, sending shards all over the table. Valentina screamed, and I scooted back to avoid any pieces.

"Enough!" Giovanni boomed. "Even think about throwing another item, Renata, and I will tie you to that chair."

Her eyes popped wide before narrowing. "You wouldn't dare."

Giovanni leaned forward, his eyes slits. It was the same expression I'd seen on Domenico when the anger surged in him. "Try me."

It took a moment, but Renata finally sat back in her chair. Attendants came around and quickly dealt with the glass shards, replacing all the table settings.

"Is it true?" Valentina asked, her voice cracking. "Is Roman dead?"

Giovanni nodded.

Antonio shot up from his chair, his eyes alight. "You did it?" he accused as he glared at Domenico.

Domenico reached over and brushed the hair back from my collarbone, exposing the elegant script of his name. "He hurt what's mine."

"Your brother laid claim to the girl. She is his property, but more importantly, she is my new daughter."

"A whore?" Antonio hissed. "You brought a whore into the family?"

My lips drew up into a smile as I looked at him, a giggle escaping. I wasn't sure why it made me laugh, but it did. The dysfunction of the Ferrante family, the over-the-top antics, was amusing. Insinuating I was a whore for no reason was simply laugh inducing.

"What's so funny, whore?" Valentina asked, mimicking her older brother. Her lips turned down as she looked at me with disgust. "Ugh, I'm going to have to burn that outfit."

"I would hold your tongues, all of you," Giovanni warned. "I was lied to about one of our products. Important information withheld. It was in Domenico's right to kill Roman, but make no mistake, I would have done it myself for Roman's grievances."

Everyone settled after that revelation. They knew the kind

of person Roman was, and if their father was saying he would have pulled the trigger himself, it was justified.

Valentina sniffed as she mourned the passing of her brother, while Antonio's jaw clenched.

"I was told there was a stripper that Maurizio wanted. One he wanted to break. I assumed he'd had a bad experience. What both he and Roman told me was a series of lies to gain a boost of power within the organization, or to get rid of a loose end. They failed to tell me the girl was Arabella Vitale."

I turned to him when he omitted my real last name and was met with his steely gaze. There were some secrets he wanted to remain secrets, it seemed. He wanted them to feel the power that came with my Vitale lineage. Even though the truth would eventually surface, I knew that his point came through loud and clear.

There were shocked gasps, and more grabs for guns, but Giovanni had had them stripped upon entering the dining room—hence all the yelling before they entered.

"You have lost your mind!"

"Kill her!"

"You can't allow this!"

All of the Ferrante children were up in arms, as was Renata. However, Giuliano sat at the end of the table with a smile on his face as he held up a glass of wine.

"Does this mean I finally get to retire, brother dearest?" Giuliano called over all the yelling.

It clicked then—Giuliano was the underboss. It was his position that Domenico was taking, and it was obvious was ready to relinquish his duty to the family.

Giovanni held his glass in the air. "Enjoy the beach and the cabana boys, brother."

They both drank, ignoring the screams that I couldn't even make out anymore. I looked to Domenico, his jaw locked tight.

Every muscle was coiled, ready to spring, ready to take down the first person who came near either one of us.

He was higher strung than I'd ever seen him before, and I knew it was due to his siblings.

After a few minutes of us sitting there, they finally settled down.

"How can you be in bed with the enemy?" Antonio spat at Domenico.

His lips curled up in a sinister grin. "Very easily. Her thighs are quite soft."

"Arabella is not the enemy," Giovanni said in an attempt to silence his boisterous family.

"How can he just sit here with what he's done?" Valentina yelled as she crossed her arms in front of her and glared at Domenico. Her eyes flickered to me, and I stared back. She didn't like that I didn't back down, and she returned her gaze to her brother. Domenico glared back, an eyebrow cocked as if he was begging his sister to start something. Eventually, she looked away, upset she wasn't able to get us to bow to her *superiority*.

I looked around the table and noticed something missing… there were no spouses. Not a single one of them wore a wedding ring. Were they all that dysfunctional?

"Question…do any of them work? Make their own money?" I asked. For the first time in years I wasn't running, wasn't trying to be free. No, I was taking back that which I'd been denied, and that which I'd used every day for years—my power.

I held the power in the room, and that knowledge surged through me.

We were the new rulers, and I wanted to make damn sure they knew from the very beginning who ran their world.

"I work for the family, bitch," Antonio spat.

"Watch your tongue before I cut it out," Domenico growled.

"Anytime, whelp. You think you're the indestructible la Bestia, but you're nothing."

I thought maybe his words would rile Domenico, but instead he sat there, a deep chuckle from that wicked grin. "You're all talk, Antonio. You always have been. A hothead with a gun. How many of your episodes have I had to clean up? How many of your whores have I had to make disappear?"

"That's your job as the help."

Domenico leaned back, the smile never dropping. "Go on, princess."

I turned back to Antonio. "And what do you do? For the family?"

"What the fuck does it matter to you?"

I looked down to my fingernails. It was meant to be a pausing gesture, to make him stew, but it only highlighted how desperately I needed a manicure. "Because my money isn't going to let any of you continue in this lifestyle of overindulgence. I will not coddle you or be your piggy bank." I turned to Valentina. "Especially not you."

Giovanni chuckled. "You're just as brash as I remember."

"What is she talking about?" Renata asked, finally calmer than earlier.

"A toast." Giovanni held his glass up. "To Giuliano. I hope you live out the rest of your years in the paradise you've so yearned for. Thank you for being a trusted and loving brother all these years. To Giuliano."

"To Giuliano," Domenico and I spoke before taking a drink.

"Who is becoming the underboss?" Antonio asked, finally listening to the words being spoken.

Giovanni sat back and pulled a gun from his jacket and set it on the table in front of him, his hand resting atop. "The three of you have been such disappointments. I don't blame you for it, but I do blame your mother."

"Giovanni!" Renata spat. "You don't speak about our children that way."

"It's never been a secret that our marriage was one of convenience, Renata, dear."

"Perhaps, but you cannot tell them such things."

"I can and I will, because what I am going to say next is very important, and if anyone at this table disagrees with *my* word, which is law in this family, I will put a bullet in them right here and right now," Giovanni said. "Roman deserved Domenico's justice. It was long overdue, and I know there are scars that litter his skin from each of you."

"Not me!" Giuliano chuckled as he drank more, becoming quite tipsy.

"Domenico is my successor." He paused and looked at all the faces at the table. Antonio shook with anger, his expression locked down as he worked to rip his napkin in half. Valentina looked distraught, while Manetto stared on in confusion.

Renata's hands were white knuckled on the edge of the table. "You can't be serious, Giovanni. You can't mean you appointed the murderer of our son as your successor."

"I am extremely serious, and I did. He has shown great characteristics of a leader. He has the loyalty and respect of the men, and instilled fear in those Roman turned against him. He knows when to be diplomatic and when to explode in physical rage. He thinks before he acts, calculates before he moves. He is the best and only man for the job."

"And her?" Antonio bit out.

"Oh, I wouldn't touch her. That is your queen. She brings with her the whole of the Vitale organization. They will be married shortly—"

"As soon as possible," Domenico interjected.

Giovanni nodded. "They will be married this weekend, and we will begin merging the families. Domenico and Arabella are your new rulers. You will abide by their word as if it was my own while we transition over the coming years. Death by my hand to anyone who opposes or even thinks of harming them."

"You always loved him more than us," Valentina sniffed. "All Roman wanted was your attention."

"All Roman wanted was what he couldn't have. His actions nearly sent us into war with Vitale," Giovanni corrected.

The air was thick, and everyone held their tongues, though Antonio stewed as he glared at Domenico.

"I've already lost one son today. Tell me, am I losing any more children?"

"No, Father."

"No."

"No."

"Good, but know this—if Domenico or Arabella is injured, you get nothing. Not only do you get nothing, you will be kicked out with only the clothes on your back. If any one of you tries to cause a revolt, anyone involved will be gunned down. There will be no dissension in the ranks."

It was clear they weren't used to such ultimatums, but they were used to obeying Giovanni.

"Renata, this extends to you as well. However, if you wish to continue throwing knives at my son, you can go crawling to the Volkovs. I'm sure you remember how they like to marinate their women in vodka."

The name sparked, and I remembered Domenico issuing me a similar threat the day I bolted from my cage. By Renata's response, it was a serious one. Her expression fell, and she dropped her head in defeat.

It was acceptance by only a thin thread, and I wasn't sure it would last. But that thread was all that we had at that moment.

THIRTY-TWO

The days passed quickly as Domenico and I took hold of our new roles. The Ferrante household was strained, to say the least. The uneasy acceptance from his siblings ratcheted up the tension, and my presence didn't help.

The household held a buzzing energy that I was desperate to get a reprieve from. I knew it would take a while for everyone to accept Domenico's new position as well as our marriage, but I also knew it was only going to get worse when it was announced to the rest of the organization.

Giovanni didn't seem concerned, especially not after his ultimatum.

After my encounter with Salvatore, I knew we were going to have an uphill battle of trust with the Vitale side. They didn't know me, and to some it mattered that my mother was a Vitale, but to others it didn't. Salvatore was going to be a problem that would have to be dealt with if my grandfather hadn't already.

I didn't wander the house without Domenico or a guard, so while I waited for Domenico to finish his meeting with a still-healing Marco, I decided to give Giovanni a visit in his study.

"Big day," he said when I entered.

I nodded. "Bound to be one of the most memorable of my life."

"The first often is."

"Who was your first?"

He leaned back in his chair. "An associate who crossed the family. In the middle of a weekly poker game."

"What did he do?" I asked.

"He stole money and bragged about it. During the game he was in high spirits, and every time he looked at me he had a little smirk. For an hour I let him think he'd gotten away with it, but really it was me working myself up to doing it." He studied me. "Do you think you're ready?"

I gave him a strained smile. "I honestly don't know. I never thought it would be something I would ever do."

"Domenico will be with you if you need help." He stood and picked up a frame from his desk and walked around to me. "I know this is quite an adjustment for you after the last few years, but I know that you will rise and the two of you will be a force no one will challenge."

I smiled at his praise and blew out a breath. It wasn't a life I was ever expecting to have, but I had love, and that made it all worth it.

Giovanni presented the frame, and I was struck by the blonde beauty in the photograph.

"She was to me what you are to my son."

"Is that his mother?" I asked, noticing some of the similarities. Domenico's hair was a dirty blond and lighter than his father's, which I guessed was once as dark as his other children's.

He nodded. "My Ileana. She should have been my wife," he

said as he looked longingly at the framed photo. "I was already married with two children when I met her. We Ferrante men accept duty over love, but when we do love, it is fierce and eternal." He looked up to me. "Domenico has that same ferocity when he looks at you."

I smiled. "He's quite intense in all things, and it's one of the many things I love about him."

"Am I interrupting?" Domenico said as he entered.

Giovanni smiled at his son. "Not at all. I was just introducing Ari to her mother-in-law."

Looking past Giovanni, I noticed another frame on the shelf behind him. It was hard to see, but it was Giovanni with Ileana, and a much younger Domenico sitting on his lap. That was his heart's true family. Renata was an obligation, and while I was certain he loved the children he had with her, it paled to his feelings for his second family.

I reached out and slipped my hand into Domenico's. "She was beautiful."

He nodded. "She was. Are you ready?"

I drew in a deep breath. "As I'll ever be."

The anticipation of finding that last piece of the puzzle left by my mother had far surpassed simple curiosity. It had become a dire need, akin to taking a breath.

Malcolm wouldn't tell me about anything other than hinting it was money, but I knew there had to be more.

There were no guards with us, but about halfway into our trip downtown, I spotted a black Escalade a few cars back. Domenico confirmed that we were being followed, but it didn't seem to bother him.

"They're just making sure nothing happens to us."

I pursed my lips as I glanced at the mirror again. "Are we ever going to be able to go out on our own again?"

"Probably not. I told you, it's just a different type of cage."

"At least I get hot showers and cute boots," I said as I glanced down at the high-heeled, knee-high black leather boots.

That made him chuckle, a sound that made my chest clench. A relaxed Domenico was a beautiful sight.

We pulled into a parking garage and found a space before walking into the lobby of the high-rise office building that held Asher Holdings.

Finally, I was going to find out what my mother didn't want my father to know about.

When we reached the top floor, the butterflies in my stomach kicked up. Thankfully there was no wait, and we were ushered into Malcolm's office.

"You came," Malcolm said as he rose from his desk. "And you brought a still-alive Domenico with you."

"I should take that shot as the favor I owe you," Domenico said as he held out his hand.

Malcolm gave him a strong shake. "Just a jab between friends. It really is a miracle he let you out alive."

"Precious cargo," Domenico said as he pulled me tighter to him.

Malcolm sat back down. "Would you like something to drink?" he asked and we both shook our heads and thanked him. "I take it things have settled down in the Ferrante camp?"

"More or less," Domenico said with a nod. "Speaking of, I will be taking over management of some of our overseas accounts."

"Moving up, la Bestia?" Malcolm asked.

"Why ask questions you already know the answer to?"

A grin slid onto Malcolm's lips. "Confirmation." He picked up his phone. "Mariah, I need you to retrieve a safety deposit box. Two-two-eight-nine." He hung up the phone and held out his hand. "Please sit."

We took the two chairs opposite his desk, but I stayed on the edge. "What did she leave me?"

I had a feeling he'd revisited the account after we talked, and so there was no point in drawing it out further.

"Your mother left you many things, the least of all being an offshore account worth almost ten million dollars."

My eyes widened as I attempted to process the number. Where would she even get access to that kind of money? With my father constantly watching her, I couldn't imagine it possible.

"How?"

"It was money that had been accruing since she was young. An account your father was not aware of and did not have access to. When she came to me…I knew something wasn't right. She insisted your father could never know what the contents were, which was why I couldn't show you all those years ago." The door opened, and his secretary walked in with a box. "Thanks, Mariah."

She smiled, then the door closed again.

"She also left you this. I am unaware of any of the contents. It hasn't been opened since she left me the key years ago." Malcolm handed over the box, then reached into his desk and retrieved the key.

My hands shook as they ran down the sides of the box. The butterflies kicked up again as I turned the key and pulled open the lid.

Tears welled in my eyes as I recognized the top contents: my baby book and my teddy bear that I thought I'd lost sat on top along with an envelope with my name on it.

I picked up the letter, transfixed on my mother's handwriting, and slid my finger under the seal.

Arabella,

My sweet, precious daughter, I'm sorry that you are reading this. I imagine your father will insist he be present, but these items aren't for him, they're for you.

I don't know how much time has passed when you read this, but you must know one thing—I love you. With my whole heart, my whole soul, I love you.

Are you free? I hope so. I hope you are soaring through the clouds, that you find love and happiness.

I know you're mad at me for leaving you. I wish I could have stayed, but I'd had enough. He broke me, tore me down, used me to his advantage, and threatened me into compliance.

You have always been my strong little girl, so fierce. You are a Vitale through and through. I wish I had half your strength, but I never have, and what I had has been beaten from me over time.

Over the last year I've stolen away precious things. Hid them where he could not get them. They are for you, kept safe until it was time.

Tell your grandfather I love him. I love him so much and I wish I'd been able to break away, but Maurizio threatened to kill you if I did, and I couldn't risk that. You never knew, but I tried to smuggle you out when you were thirteen. He found out and told me that if I ever tried to take you to my father's again, he would kill you. That was why we never went back. I couldn't even call him because your father was keeping tabs on all phone activity.

This is my last-ditch effort to free you, that my father can rescue you.

If he fails, heed my final request and get out of there any way you can.

I love you, Ari. You are my greatest treasure, and I only wish I could have protected you better.

If you ever need anything, go to your grandfather. Remember that rhyme we used to sing when we would visit him? That's all you need to find him.

I love you, to the moon and back.
Mom

I swiped at the tears streaming down my face. It felt like I had her back for one brief moment, only to lose her once more.

It was all my father's fault. He was the reason she couldn't take living anymore. What had he done to her that she kept from me? What horrors did she hide on a daily basis?

No matter what, I was certain of one thing—he was going to pay.

For everything.

We left Asher Holdings with a box full of mementos and a whole lot of pain-filled anger that was desperate for an outlet.

There was no need to tell Domenico where to go when we exited the parking garage.

We had a loose cannon to deal with. A man whose ego made him think he was invincible, and I was going to show him just how wrong he was.

It was time for retribution.

When we pulled up to the house I'd spent my teenage years in, the boiling of my blood increased. It was a monument of his success that my mother had paid the price for.

Santiago was waiting when we exited the car.

"I've cleared the premises, sir," he said.

"Thank you," Domenico said as we walked up the steps to the front door.

We entered my father's office, which was devoid of his presence. I took a seat at his desk chair and kicked my feet up onto his desk.

There had been a last gift that sat buried at the bottom of the safety deposit box—a gun.

It was my mother's, a gift from her father—a 9mm Glock with filigree detail, the Vitale family crest, and a white pearl handle.

It was beautiful.

And it was going to serve justice for her.

Domenico moved to stand behind me, his hand resting on my shoulder as he kissed the top of my head. "I'm right behind you."

He knew what was about to happen was mine, but I loved that he was there to support and protect me.

"Where the fuck is everybody?" I heard my father call out, his footsteps echoing on the marble floors.

The knot in my stomach tightened as I stared at the door, listening as he drew closer. I swallowed when his shadow drifted into the room a step before he did.

After a few steps he came to a halt, blinking as he stared at us. "Arabella. Domenico. I'm surprised to see you here."

I took in the faint bruises that still lingered on his skin from Domenico's hits.

"Father."

He sneered as he stared at my boots up on his desk. "Get your feet off my desk."

I shook my head. "I came to tell you I did it, Daddy."

"Did what?"

"I merged the families, just like you wanted."

He stared at me, his eyes growing wide. "Did you marry Roman?"

I shook my head. "No, not Roman. He's dead."

"Dead?" he asked.

"I killed him," Domenico said from the corner of the room.

My father sneered at Domenico. "I see you survived."

I held up my hand featuring some random ring. It was a prop, our wedding not until the weekend. "As I was saying—I merged the families, just like you always wanted."

The wariness melted and his lips drew up into a smile. "You really did it. I am now up there."

"No, you're not. It was a merger of families. A merger between the Ferrante and the Vitale. Not you."

His gaze narrowed at me. "I'm your father."

"And neither a Ferrante or a Vitale."

His brow furrowed. "If Roman is dead, who did you marry?"

"The next in line, of course."

He scoffed and rolled his eyes as he shook his head. "All Giuliano is interested in is getting dicked down and not exploring pussy."

"Just because he has same-sex preferences doesn't make him less of a man, Father," I said. It was getting more difficult to keep myself calm. "He's probably a better man than you are."

"He's older than me and gay. There is no way you married him."

"I never said I married Giuliano."

"He's next in line."

"Was," Domenico said. He'd remained mostly silent, but I knew he had an affinity for his uncle and wasn't going to stand for my father talking down about him.

"What?"

"He *was* next in line. Giuliano retired."

My father's eyes narrowed on the man behind me. "I'm having a conversation with my daughter, Domenico. Why are you still fucking here?"

"Because I'm here to protect her from you."

My father glared at him before turning toward the door. "Santiago!" he called out.

When Santiago entered, his posture straightened when he saw us, and he bowed to me. "Missus."

At that, my father's eyes widened as he stared at the leader of his guard. It was the confirmation he needed, knowing all that I said was true.

"Sir?" Santiago asked as he looked at my father.

"Kill Domenico," my father said, glaring at the man in the corner.

My heart beat wildly in my chest, but I tried to appear calm. His callousness as he tried to get rid of Domenico was staggering. If it had been Jenkins I doubted there would have been any pause, but Santiago wasn't some hired gun—he was a loyal Ferrante member.

Santiago failed to move, which only angered my father. He thought he had a one up, but he didn't know, or rather, he forgot.

"I told you Giovanni would not be pleased with my death," Domenico said, reminding my father of our last visit.

"Just what is going on here?" my father asked Santiago. "I told you to shoot that man."

"I can't do that, sir," Santiago replied.

"Why the hell not?" My father's face was turning red, his muscles tight.

I knew my father—he wasn't happy that his order wasn't followed.

I uncrossed my legs and set them down on the floor, moving to stand tall, proud that I knew nothing he said or did could hurt me anymore. Nothing he said or did could frighten me anymore, because this was the end of the road for my father.

After all he'd done to my mother and me, it was no less than he deserved.

"As I said, Daddy, I married the next in line."

He looked between the three of us. "I don't understand what you are saying."

"Think of it this way. Why would Giovanni not be pleased with Domenico's death?" I asked.

His eyes widened as he looked at Domenico, really studied him for probably the first time. I was fairly certain my father had always brushed him off as nothing more than another hired hand.

"How did you become next in line with his three sons?" he asked.

"I know it has been a while, but I'm surprised you have forgotten his fourth son. It was out of wedlock, but that makes me no less a Ferrante than Roman was."

My father's eyes widened and he froze as the realization of what he'd done to a Ferrante family member set in.

"We've found that your services are no longer needed, Father."

Domenico started to raise his hand, but I stopped him.

"No, my husband, let me." I pulled the gun my mother had left me, the one her father had given her, and leveled it at my father.

It was fitting. Ending the life that destroyed her with her own gun. Poetic, almost.

"Where did you get that?" he said.

"This?" I asked as I opened my palm, exposing my mother's initials carved into the side. "I'm surprised you remember it. You sold off all her belongings, leaving me with very little to remember her by."

"That gun disappeared before she killed herself."

I hated the way he said it, like he was trying to absolve himself for the part he played. He was the star, after all.

"Yes, it did." I aimed the gun and fired, hitting him in roughly the same position he shot Domenico.

"Fuck!" he cried out. His face scrunched up in pain, his mouth open, brow furrowed as he looked at me.

"That was for Domenico."

Any trepidation I'd had about shooting my father ebbed away with each vile word that had come out of his mouth. My first kill would be the man who gave me life. The man who drove my mother to kill herself. The man who touched me in a way no father should touch his child.

"Are you fucking happy now, you little bitch?"

I aimed higher, pulling the trigger. My ears were still trying to recover from the first shot, but I pushed that away so that I could finish what I came to do.

The bullet entered his chest, breaking through his ribs.

"That was for me," I said as I walked around the desk.

His eyes widened as he fell down to his knees, one hand on his stomach trying to hold the blood in, the other on his chest failing to do the same.

I stopped in front of him as all my hatred boiled up. I'd been powerless under his roof and knowing the future he'd had in store for me, he hadn't paid enough.

He stared up at me with pleading eyes, but it wouldn't sway me. He had to pay the final price for my mother's death.

"Arabella."

I leveled the gun with his head. "This is for my mother."

I flexed my finger and the gun fired one last bullet. The force sent him down to the ground on his back, and I couldn't look away as all movement came to a stop and he was still.

I was breathing hard when I felt Domenico's hand on my waist and his lips against my forehead. "How do you feel?"

How *did* I feel?

Overwhelmed, overpowered with emotion, but most of all, I felt free. A tear slid down my cheek. There was no more looking over my shoulder, no more fear he would find me. There was nothing he could ever do to me again.

"Like I can breathe for the first time in years."

"We'll deal with this," Santiago said.

"Thank you." Domenico guided me out into the foyer. "What do you want to do with this house?"

"Burn it to the ground for all I care," I said, my gaze flicking back to the open door and my father's body. "I don't care. I just never want to be here again."

It was the place both of my parents lost their lives. The gilded cage that I escaped.

THIRTY-THREE

From the moment Giovanni showed up, our lives had been nothing but a whirlwind. From the choice we'd had to make, which was really no choice at all, to getting retribution on my father and releasing him from service, to pulling up to the Vitale stronghold in a Ferrante vehicle.

My life was no longer the standard *life* by which I was accustomed to living.

For the last several years, I'd stripped to put a roof over my head and food on my table just to be out from underneath my tyrant of a father. For the first time in my life, I was free.

Now, I'd willingly traded my freedom for a cage—one that would give me a lifetime with the man I loved. My father was dead, and the structure of the organization was a little unstable. Time was critical, and all moving parts had to be settled before we would be given even a moment to adjust to our new roles.

For Domenico, there was less of an adjustment. He already knew everything the Ferrante organization was doing, as he had orchestrated many of the moving parts on a daily basis. For years

I had floated in an abyss, and because of that my learning curve was steep. I was disjointed as I soaked in as much information as I could. I knew some basic workings, but there were points I had trouble keeping up with.

I didn't even get to shop for a new wardrobe—clothes were brought in by the bagful. We were staying at the Ferrante house, and while I feared that might change Domenico, it didn't. He was the same as always. It was me who was struggling with my identity.

Domenico squeezed my hand as we sat in the back of a large SUV. I turned to him, biting down on my bottom lip as I took in the vision of him in a suit. It got to me every time.

"Are you okay?

I nodded. "It's just…"

He pulled my hand up to his lips. "It will take a while. I will answer any questions you have, no matter what."

"Any?"

He nipped at my knuckle. "Do you have some already?"

I nodded. "Where are we going to live?" I was hoping he wouldn't say the Ferrante house, because after a few days I was ready to leave.

"My house. For now. We can figure the rest out later."

I picked at my dress and the white fabric. To the fashion police it was too late in the year to wear white, but it was a special day.

We were getting married.

Married.

The word didn't sound right, foreign to my tongue, but it was the truth nonetheless. It was the first major step toward our future, and while it wasn't a grand event, it was still an event, a merging of families. White felt right, and the knee-length sheath dress was classic and elegant.

I only wished my lace looked as nice. Our skin still held the evidence of our battle, and I tried my best to hide what I could with makeup and the style of my hair.

There were no reservations about tying myself to Domenico—it was everything that came with it. What we were undertaking to be together was monumental.

My heart jumped at the familiar fencing signaling we'd reached the Vitale property. A calmness washed through me. We weren't on the run. We were not there to fight. We were there to come together in a way our two families had never thought possible.

The car came to a stop, and Domenico exited and held his hand out for me. The dress restricted my movement, so he took hold of my waist and helped to lower me to the ground.

My grandfather appeared, and my whole body lit up as he held his arms open.

"Nonno!" I cried out as I stepped into his waiting embrace.

"Arabella," he whispered as he wrapped his arms around me.

I wasn't sure I'd ever see him again, and I held him tight.

"Come," he said as he pulled back. His gaze met Domenico, and he held out his hand.

There was a wariness in Domenico's eyes as he stared down at it, but he pushed those feelings aside and took hold of his hand. It would take some time for those ingrained reactions to subside.

"Thank you for keeping her safe."

Domenico nodded. "Always."

"Good to see you again, Laureano," Giovanni said after emerging from another car.

"You as well. What a day we have."

My grandfather led the way, heading straight for the dining room. Inside two men sat, enjoying what looked to be a glass of brandy. Upon our entrance they stood, both giving a bow of their heads.

"Arabella, Domenico, this is Matthew Cleary and Daniel Wright from the county clerk's office. We've worked hand in hand with them for many years, and they are both trusted advisers."

My grandfather and Giovanni had found some workaround for filing at the courthouse, which shouldn't have surprised me.

They both stepped forward and shook our hands before Matthew spoke. "We have everything ready for you. I'd like to be the first to say congratulations on your nuptials, and I wish you a long and happy marriage."

The butterflies kicked up in my stomach. It was an odd thing to be nervous about, because it was what I wanted.

He shuffled papers, and we took our seats around the table. "We've taken care of everything. The only thing we need from you are your signatures."

Included were copies of all my pieces of identification, items I wasn't sure I would ever see again. Some I hadn't seen since I was sixteen when my mother helped me to get my license, like my birth certificate. I didn't know at the time the license was to help prepare me for her departure.

I looked to Domenico. It all seemed so formal. There were even multiple trays scattered about the surface, holding ring after ring.

"Before that, we need to discuss some more pressing matters," my grandfather said. He signaled to the butlers standing by the bar. They came around, getting drink orders from everyone, and I requested a glass of wine.

Once everyone had something, Giovanni raised his glass in the air. "To the end of an era—and the beginning of a new one as a unified family."

"To the end of war between our families," my grandfather added.

Domenico's eyes met mine. "To our future."

I smiled at him. "To love."

Everyone took a sip, and then Domenico leaned forward and pressed his lips to mine.

I turned my attention to the heads of the families. "A few things before we finalize this," I said, gaining everyone's attention. Domenico was already aware of my one request and had agreed. "I want to stop the sex trafficking."

Giovanni shook his head. "No."

My grandfather lifted his hand. "I agree. If you want this merger, the sex trafficking stops."

"There is a lot of money to be had," Giovanni argued.

"With the Vitale empire you will have no need. Drugs, weapons, and secrets fetch a far higher price."

Giovanni looked to Domenico. "What are your thoughts?"

"It ends. Now."

Giovanni clenched his jaw. "If it wasn't for that, you wouldn't have her."

"What would my mother think?" Domenico asked.

Giovanni blanched and hung his head. "Ileana would have agreed with you."

"Let it go so that we can expand past that."

Giovanni nodded. "Today it ends."

I smiled and nodded, happy to have my say acknowledged, considered, and agreed with. I'd been afraid they were going to push me aside, that I had no real say and would be treated as a showpiece, as my mother had been.

Giovanni signaled to the men from the county courthouse, and they set papers in front of us. "Arabella, I need you to sign here and here—then Domenico signs here."

"And then what?" I asked.

He blinked at me. "And then you're officially married."

"That seems so anti-climactic."

"This is only a legal formality so that we can begin merging the organizations. It will help dispel animosity in the ranks," my grandfather said. "I thought this summer would be good for a public wedding."

I nodded. We were doing it to proceed with the merger. This was the business end of our marriage. In doing so, old grudges would be laid to rest.

I picked up the pen and stared at the signature line. Years had passed since I'd written my real name, but as I pressed the tip to the paper, the letters flowed out like no time had passed at all. I handed the paper to Domenico and watched as he wrote out his full name.

Matthew smiled as he gathered the papers. "Fantastic. We will run and get these filed right away. Congratulations."

"Thank you, Matthew," my grandfather said, shaking his hand before they headed out.

"What are these, then?" I asked, signaling to the trays of rings.

"Your wedding bands. I assumed an engagement ring would be chosen by Domenico."

I pulled a tray forward, scanning the different styles and colors. I stopped on a delicate-looking sculpted crescent band of diamonds. My fingers gripped the band and pulled it from the tray. Domenico plucked one of his own, then set it on the table.

He grasped the one I was holding and took my hand, his eyes locked with mine. "With this ring, I promise to protect you with my life. To love you and only you for the rest of my days."

I blinked back a tear as he slid the ring on my finger, seating it in place.

"I promise to love you, to stand beside you and support you, until the end." I couldn't stop smiling as I slipped the ring on his finger.

There was nobody to pronounce us man and wife, but it was fine. I threw my arms around his shoulders and pressed my lips to his.

My Bestia.

My husband.

As I stared out over the lake, I marveled at my new life. I had nothing and everything at the same time. My entire life had been accounted for in only a handful of possessions until a few days ago, when I was handed an empire. I didn't even have any form of identification, but I did have a name and a title that commanded respect.

The wind whipped around me, and I pulled my coat tighter. A sigh left me as large arms circled my waist and pulled me to a solid chest.

"What are you doing out here by yourself?" Domenico asked.

"Just musing. And I'm not alone." I pointed to Luca silently surveying the property fifty feet away. "What do you think about this spot for the wedding?"

I tripped up a little on the last words. It was such an odd sentence for me to say—and one I never thought I would.

A chuckle at my ear confirmed he had similar thoughts. "Whatever you want."

I turned in his arms and looked up at him. "I already have what I want. A wedding is simply a formality, a show for everyone."

"There are going to be a lot of changes happening soon. I want you beside me during it all. To show that it's not just me running things."

I ran my hand across his chest. "Of course. Besides, I have to let all the ladies know you're mine. No mistresses for you."

"Why would I ever need one when I have you?"

"You could get tired of me."

"Never." He leaned down and pressed his lips to mine. "You're mine and I'm yours. Forever."

There was still a lot to work out, but after everything we'd been through, I knew we could do it together.

They said love was blind, but my eyes were wide open.

I was in love with a murderer, a killer. Married to a monster.

One only I could command.

La Bestia.

My love.

EPILOGUE

A year and a half later…

The whirlwind that was our marriage didn't allow for things like a honeymoon, even after our wedding for the masses. However, we both needed a break. Desperately.

For a year I'd gotten an in-depth schooling of the inner workings of organized crime. It made me realize all I'd gleaned before was just the tip of the iceberg.

There were so many pieces constantly at play to keep track of.

My grandfather was wonderful in reminding me of my Vitale lineage and history, and I was ready to carry on our dynasty as a Ferrante.

Four weeks ago we boarded a plane and left Chicago, bound for a boat and the sea. Domenico once told me his dream, and I'd wanted to make it come true.

While I had a feeling the three-hundred-foot yacht we chartered was not the sailboat Domenico had envisioned, the size was necessary due to the amount of staff we were required to travel with.

Business never stopped, and it was difficult for Domenico to relinquish control, but when he did, when he opened his eyes to the world around him, I fell even more in love.

We celebrated his thirty-first birthday on the boat.

Luca and Santiago accompanied us, along with a few other guards. While Santiago was the Ferrante guard Domenico trusted the most, Luca had also become the same for us on the Vitale side.

There had been some dissension in the ranks, but things had begun to settle as old grudges were buried. Truthfully, it would be years before things really settled, but we were on our way.

Salvatore, the Vitale guard who assaulted me, did not fare as well. My grandfather terminated him for what he did, and it was a great relief when I found out. He'd already harmed me once, and there was no way I could trust him. I didn't want someone like that in the ranks, wondering if I had to watch out for someone who was supposed to be a loyal associate.

Marco had stepped up with Domenico. After all, he was Domenico's most trusted. He now held Domenico's old position and orchestrated all the other capos and crews.

"I am not going home," I declared with a shake of my head as we lay on one of the loungers on the upper deck, my head resting on his chest.

We were on the tail end of our month-long Mediterranean tour and I had fallen head over heels for Greece, despite my Italian heritage.

The crystal-clear blue of the water was hypnotizing and the history amazing. We did get a few odd looks though, when we entered the Acropolis with an armed guard.

"We have to go home sometime."

I tilted my head back. "As long as you promise me we can do this again."

He brushed the hair back from my face. "Anything for you."

There was a commotion coming from the couches not far from us. I couldn't help but laugh, watching as Luca and one of the shipmates raced to see who could chug a bottle of lemonade the fastest.

It was a stupid game, but neither could drink while on the job, and they'd found some interesting ways to entertain themselves when the threat level was low.

"Mr. Ferrante, there is a call for you on the ship phone," one of the cabin stewards said.

Domenico scrunched his brow as he sat up. "Thank you, Alexa, I'll take it inside."

He pulled me up with him and we stepped back into the air-conditioned interior. At the bar was the nearest phone, and I stood beside him as he answered.

"Ferrante," Domenico said into the receiver.

I couldn't hear anything from the caller, but it was very strange that whoever it was didn't call his cell phone. Domenico's lip twitched and his eyes found mine. They sparkled and danced, making my stomach spin. "Thank you so much, doctor."

Doctor.

"And?" I prompted as soon as he hung up.

"Pregnant."

I froze before launching myself into his arms.

For a few weeks I hadn't felt quite right, and there was a reason for that. I'd had the IUD birth control implant removed six months earlier. It was only a matter of time.

I stepped back and turned to the mirror, my gaze locked on my abdomen. He wrapped his arms around me, his palms stacked flat against my midsection as he pulled me close.

"So I guess I got knocked up with your kid, after all."

He chuckled against my neck. "I told you I would."

I met his gaze in the reflection. "If it's a girl, we could name her after our mothers."

He turned me in his arms and pressed his forehead to mine. Those silver eyes that always captured me bored into mine. "I think that is perfect. But if it's a boy, we are not naming him Giovanni."

A giggle left me and I smiled up at him. "Deal."

"Now, my queen, where do you want to sail to next?"

I stretched up onto the tips of my toes and pressed my lips to his. "I don't care, just as long as you're beside me."

He pulled me closed. "Always, my love. Always."

AFTER ALL THE WORDS AND ALL THE THINGS...

When I started writing this, well, it was an idea I'd had on the backburner, so when I was approached to become part of the Sinister Fairy Tale Collections, I was like "Ya know, I have this start of an idea and about 3 scenes."

It exploded from there.

Oddly, the scene where she wakes up in the cage and when Domenico comes out of the shadows was the one scene that stayed from that original idea.

I hope you loved Domenico and Ari as much as I loved writing them.

To Jo, thank you for escaping.

The beginning scene on the bridge was a real life incident that happened to one of my oldest and dearest friends. While she was able to get out of the situation before they got her stopped due to flashing lights nearby, it could have turned out horribly wrong for her.

Please be aware of your surroundings. If something doesn't seem right, call the police. It's better to be discovered as nothing than something happening to you.

Stay safe!

Easter egg (ha! I'm literally writing those words on Easter Sunday, how fun!)

Some of you may have recognized a certain side character.

I LOVED Malcolm Asher in Sin by Elena M Reyes, and seeing as my setting was also in Chicago and also in the world of organized crime, he was the perfect character to borrow for a couple of key scenes.

Thank you to Elena for letting me borrow my man!

Interested in finding out who exactly Malcolm Asher is? Find out more here—books2read.com/sin-sin

SOUNDTRACK

Afterlife—Hailee Steinfeld

Teeth—Five seconds of Summer

Won't Go Down Easy—Jaxson Gamble

Gasoline—Halsey

Heathens—twenty one pilots

Arsonist's Lullabye—Hozier

Hold Me Down—Halsey

I like trouble—Jailbreakers Ltd

Blinding Lights—The Weekend

Take What You Want—Post Malone feat. Ozzy Osborn &
Travis Scott

All the good girls go to hell—Billie Eilish

My Love Will Never Die—Ag feat. Claire Wyndham

I'm a Wanted Man—Royal Deluxe

Not Afraid Anymore—Halsey

Wolves—Sam Tinnesz feat. Silverberg

Lions Inside—Valley of Wolves

I Can't Get Enough—Jaxson Gamble

Animal—Chase Holfelder

Until We Go Down—Ruelle

The Baddest Man Alive—The Black Keys

Control—Halsey

Lux Aeterna—Clint Mansell

Graveyard—Halsey

ABOUT THE AUTHOR

K.I. Lynn is the USA Today Bestselling Author from The Bend Anthology and the Amazon Bestsellers, Breach and Becoming Mrs Lockwood. She spent her life in the arts, everything from music to painting and ceramics, then to writing. Characters have always run around in her head, acting out their stories, but it wasn't until later in life she would put them to pen. It would turn out to be the one thing she was really passionate about.

Since she began posting stories online, she's garnered acclaim for her diverse stories and hard hitting writing style. Two stories and characters are never the same, her brain moving through different ideas faster than she can write them down as it also plots its quest for world domination…or cheese. Whichever is easier to obtain… Usually it's cheese.

Website—www.kilynnauthor.com

Facebook—www.facebook.com/kilynn.breach

Twitter—twitter.com/KI_Lynn_

Instagram—www.instagram.com/k.i.lynn

Get my Newsletter—http://bit.ly/1U9NSoC

MORE BOOKS FROM K.I. LYNN!

That Night

I got pregnant on New Year's Eve.

That night was hands down the best night of my life. A magical night with the man of my dreams.

The aftermath changed everything.

After weeks of silence from him and a positive pregnancy test, it was safe to say I was in full out panic mode.

Until I walked into a conference room only to find Mr. Man-of-my-dreams-father-of-my-unborn-child at the head of the table.

Turns out the VP of finance isn't an old boring guy with white hair.

Two different cities.

A baby on the way.

An intense attraction.

And he's technically my boss.

Life just got even more complicated.

Find out more here—books2read.com/ThatNightKILynn

Domenico

The mafia never lets you go.

I thought I was safe, free, but I never expected to find myself locked in a cage.

I'm in his territory. His prison.

The beast.

A fate worse than death awaits me if I can't get away, so when the opportunity of salvation presents itself I grab it, even if I'm unsure if I can trust the hand I'm holding.

The only way out is through, exposing secrets and spilling blood.

Things aren't how they appear. Nobody is what they seem.

Find out more here—books2read.com/AbductedKILynn

Forever and All The Afters

He promised me forever.

Then he boarded a plane for a college a thousand miles away and never returned. A decade later there's a ring on my finger with a new promise from a new love.

Just as my life falls into place, pretty as the pages of a magazine, my world is knocked over. The moment he touches me everything around me begins to crack, exposing all the lies I've told myself.

Every glance reminds me. Every touch ignites.

Things aren't how they used to be.

Love isn't easy.

Find out more here—books2read.com/ForeverAndAllTheAfters

Welcome to the Cameo Hotel

I get what I want.

When I walked through the door of the Cameo Hotel I didn't expect such a beauty to be working the front desk.

The effect she has on me is intense, and I make her life a living hell because of it.

I love her spirit, her internal defiance when completing the most inane task I assign her. My two week stay has turned into unending, just to be near her.

She's under my every command if she wants to keep me happy.

There's one last thing I want.

Her.

Find out more here—
books2read.com/WelcomeToTheCameoHotel

Becoming Mrs. Lockwood

Every girl has dreams of meeting Prince Charming, or at least I know I did.

A fairy tale-like meeting of love at first site.

Real life and fairy tales are very different.

I'm just a small town Indiana girl that had a chance encounter with one of Hollywood's golden boys. You may think you know where this story goes—not even close.

Life is different. Marriage is hard. It's even worse when you're strangers.

Find out more here—books2read.com/BecomingMrsLockwood

Six

I had a one-night stand. It wasn't my first, but it would be my last.

A gun to the head.

A trained killer.

A deadly conspiracy.

Kidnapped and on the run, my life and death is in the hands of a sadist captor who happens to be my one-night stand. Armed with countless weapons, money, and new identities, the man I call Six drags me around the world.

The manhunt is on and Six is the next target. Can we find out who is killing off the Cleaners before they find us?

Two down, seven to go.

When it's all over he'll finish the job that dropped him into my life, and end it.

Stockholm Syndrome meets bucket list, and the question of what would you do to live before you died. The questions aren't always answered in black and white. Gray becomes the norm as my morals are tested.

Death is a tragedy, and I'll do anything to stay alive.

Are you ready for the last ride of your life? Six has a gun to your head—what would you do?

This isn't a love story.

It's a death story.

Find out more here—
books2read.com/Six-KILynn
Check out the Trailer—youtu.be/fzpON3PadIA

Breach Book 1

His body was sin, his cock was sin, and I was a sinner.

To keep myself safe I hide in the world and let life move around me.

My new partner, Nathan, isn't safe. Far from it.

The darkness coils around him, hidden by a shield created by a blinding smile. But those who live in shadows see past the façade we create.

Even in darkness, there is light. A spark that ignites, then explodes.

Every filthy word from his mouth, every possessive touch—I crave them, need them. Violent and passionate and everything I need to fill the void inside me, but one thing is missing.

He can never love me.

More than my heart is on the line, and I don't know if I'll survive our breach.

Find out more here—books2read.com/Breach

The Executive

Business is king, and I have an empire to topple.

Ivy is my new assistant and a threat to me. She's my undoing. If ever I was to believe in a cosmic connection, it was the moment I met her.

For years I've had one goal—revenge. As CEO, I have crafted a strategic plan for business, but never a life beyond.

With one touch from her, the veil is lifted. Things are different, and every moment I'm near her, my world begins to change.

A wall of propriety keeps me from her. I need her as my pawn in this war, beside me in battle. Sharing the secrets of my enemies, and her desires in my bed. Her body to claim as mine.

Getting what I want has consequences.

Collateral damage is real.

In the game of crushing kings of men, I never planned on my heart being a sacrifice.

Find out more here—books2read.com/TheExecutive

Cocksure
Co-written with Olivia Kelley
A life altering lie, ten years, and one wild night later, the game
has changed.

Niko

My life is great. I love my job, have awesome friends, and a great
family.

Women love me, even if they know it's just for a night.

I always thought love at first sight was bullshit. Then she came
storming into my life. She tore through my every rule, rocked my
world, and knocked me on my ass.

There's only one problem…she lied.+

Turns out my best friend's little sister isn't so little anymore.

Everly

I stole a night with my fantasy. Lied to him.

After ten years of not seeing each other, Niko doesn't even recognize me.

So I take what I want from him, what I need from him. Without
worry. Without consequence.

What I didn't count on was the lingering need for him.

Once the truth is out, the game changes. There are consequences.

I should have known nothing in my life is ever simple.

My brother is going to kill his best friend and I have nine months
to figure out what I want.

Find out more here—
books2read.com/Cocksure-Lynn-Kelley

Need Book 1

Co-written with N. Isabelle Blanco

I was Kira's from the first moment I saw her. Maybe it was love at first sight, but I was only ten.

She became my best friend.

My crush.

The girl I can't live without.

But I have to.

She was almost mine, but my father took away my chance.

Now she lives across the hall from me. Instead of the title of girlfriend, she's now my stepsister.

But that doesn't stop how I feel, how I want her. Thankfully, I'm off to college two hundred miles away, but even that doesn't help.

She's under my skin, all around me, and I watch her morph from a sexy teenager to an irresistible woman.

I can't take it anymore, I need her.

Is it possible to ever be happy without the one person you *need?*

"I'm Brayden, baby. The man you've been dreaming about your whole life. And I'm about to fucking show you why."

Part 1 of a 3 part series.

Find out more here—books2read.com/NeedSeries